The Battle for Andrea Maria

Holly Copella

ISBN-13: 978-0-9864416-0-8

To Crystal Rose and Avery Shannon
"In dreams, all things are possible."

ACKNOWLEDGMENTS

Copella Books
Cover Artist: diversepixel
SelfPubBookCovers.com/diversepixel
Printed by CreateSpace, An Amazon.com Company

PUBLISHER'S NOTE

Chapter One

$\mathcal{T}$he cruise ship, *Andrea Maria*, sailed along the calm, peaceful waters of the evening Caribbean Sea on her return voyage from Costa Rica to the United States. Although small in comparison to other luxury cruise ships, the power yacht was a well-appointed, ten-ton ship with six decks and every amenity offered by ships twice her size. Her capacity was a mere two hundred passengers with a crew of approximately one hundred and twenty-five. On one of the upper decks, an attractive woman in her early twenties with flowing, dark hair leaned against the railing and watched the ocean rushing past. She wore a slinky, black dress that revealed enough leg and cleavage to catch plenty of male attention. Jess Colten was enjoying her ocean voyage with a fashionably dressed man in his mid-twenties, Drake Stanton.

Drake was a tall, lanky man with more personality than actual good looks. They had been best friends since they were young children. They were such good friends that his parents took her in to keep her out of foster care after her parents died when she was sixteen. Drake had always believed he was looking out for Jess like a big brother, but Jess never had the heart to tell him she was the one looking out for him.

"I really hate the thought of returning home to our boring lives after this," Drake said as he casually leaned on the railing alongside Jess.

"You can say that because your suit still fits. If I gain one more pound, I'll pop out of my dress."

Drake eyed Jess with a pleased once over and grinned deviously. "The only parts of you popping out are the parts meant to be popping out."

"Friends don't ogle friend's cleavage," Jess said in a matter-of-fact tone with a smirk on her face.

"Then said friend shouldn't display said cleavage," he teased.

"Is it that time of month again?"

"Hey, I'm two rejections away from begging *you* to sleep with me."

Jess maintained her sense of humor despite her best friend's attempt at charm. "You're pathetic when you're horny." She straightened and lovingly clung to his arm. "I'm going to make it my mission to find you a nice, slutty girl tonight."

Drake grinned, patted her hand clutching his arm, and appeared playfully lustful as he guided her along the deck toward the nightclub.

"I love it when you sink to my level."

"What are friends for?"

"A casual hand job, if it's not asking too much," Drake replied with a smirk.

Jess playfully smacked his arm and pretended to be offended, but their friendship was stronger than any amount of sexual teasing he could throw at her. She knew him better than that.

†

*T*he ship's nightclub was large and swanky with a state of the art sound system, high-energy disc jockey, and a massive, modern bar with every imaginable bottle of alcohol on display. The massive bar nearly took up the entire back wall. Mirrors and strobe lights adorned the club. Despite the early hour, the club was slightly crowded with over fifty well-dressed men and women of varying ages who socialized and danced to the loud, modern music. Jess and Drake gained attention with their awe-inspiring dance moves. They looked as if they naturally belonged together and made quite the couple on the dance floor. Their dance moves easily gave the impression that they were more than just friends. Two attractive women in their mid to late twenties, Carla Rupert and Dana Langley, joined them on the dance floor and attempted to mimic their dance moves. The four danced together during the next song.

Once the song ended, the two women returned to their table. Jess nudged Drake and indicated the women while grinning. She was sure either one would be excellent overnight company for her friend.

Drake now lacked his earlier confidence and looked more like a lost puppy.

"I don't know. They're both a little out of my league, don't you think?"

"Don't start with that again," Jess said firmly. "You're an excellent catch."

Jess often accredited what few sexual conquests Drake had to her prodding him to go forth and procreate. The more she thought about it, the more she realized he hadn't successfully copulated with any woman without her pushing him in the right direction. Drake still appeared uncertain while looking at their table. Jess rolled her eyes, once again playing Drake's sex surrogate, and pulled him toward the two women at the nearby table.

"Would you mind if we join you?" Jess asked the two, attractive women.

"No, not at all," Dana replied and indicated the vacant seats.

Jess and Drake joined them at the small table. Carla was what most men would consider "hot". She had perfectly bleached blonde hair, a knock them dead body, and a flawless sense of fashion. Dana wasn't nearly the beauty Carla was, but she was attractive in her own right. She was slightly shorter than average with natural strawberry blonde hair. She didn't share the same flare for fashion as Carla, and that she sat alongside the blonde bombshell almost diminished her own attractiveness. Drake immediately began to fidget the moment they sat down at the table with the women.

"I'm Jess and this is my friend, Drake."

"I'm Dana, and this is Carla," she said with enthusiasm. "We just met on the cruise."

"Are you two professional dancers?" Carla asked mostly to Jess.

Jess appeared humored at the question but held back her laugh. "No, but Drake and I have been dancing together since Junior High."

There was a moment of silence. Jess slapped Drake's thigh under the table. Drake jumped and appeared surprised by the slap. He quickly took his cue, looked at Carla, and tried to act confident.

"I could show you some dance moves "

"You're not my type," Carla said flatly and with disinterest.

Jess stared at Carla with surprise at her callousness and became offended. She eyed Drake. Carla's devastating blow crushed him, and any confidence he pretended to have vanished. Dana appeared enthusiastic, leaned closer to him, and placed her hand on his lower arm.

"Would you show me those dance moves?" she asked with a warm smile.

Drake recovered from Carla's blow to his ego and returned with his own enthusiastic smile. "I'd love to."

Dana and Drake stood and approached the dance floor together. Jess strummed her fingers on the table and attempted not to loathe the woman across from her. Carla didn't even notice Jess's contempt for her. Carla appeared bored and disinterested while she looked around the crowded nightclub filled with passengers having a good time.

"Slim pickins on this cruise, huh?" Carla said without looking at Jess. "Dana's not exactly particular, but girls like us won't find any men worth our while around here."

Jess suddenly glared at Carla. She really wanted to hit this woman. Carla was too busy mocking the other passenger's wardrobe choices with a sweeping look of distaste to notice the ice-cold stare from Jess.

"And so many old ones," Carla continued. "This club is like the nursing home hot spot." Carla leaned on the table closer to Jess and indicated the bar with a disinterested nod. "You see that guy at the bar? He has to be in his forties or fifties."

Jess felt compelled to look at the bar to see what poor soul Carla was indicating. She looked at the non-impressive man in his mid-forties, Emry Hill, who wore a gray suit, colored vest, and glasses. Emry had a certain nerdy scientist appeal about him. He wasn't the most handsome man Jess had ever seen, but he was certainly far from homely.

"Can you believe he was actually hitting on me?" Carla said with distaste and wrinkled her nose at the mere thought.

"Imagine--" Jess hissed while her eyes pieced into Carla's profile.

"I know!" Carla squawked then indicated the handcrafted bracelet she wore. "He's, like, that's a nice bracelet. Can you believe it?"

Jess faked a look of horror. "The nerve--"

"As if *he'd* ever stand a chance with someone like me," Carla said in a snobby tone. "God, he's old enough to be my father."

Jess again thought about hitting her and wondered if she could actually get away with it. Doubtful. She wasn't that lucky. Jess once more eyed the quiet man sitting at the bar, smirked deviously to herself, and then looked back at Carla with all seriousness.

"Oh, my God! Do you know who that is, Carla?" Jess said while mimicking Carla's tone and dialect. "That's what's his name, the famous movie producer. He has, like, more money than God." Jess leaned closer to Carla, looked into her eyes, and appeared completely serious and possibly a little overly dramatic. "I heard he bought his last girlfriend a Ferrari for her birthday."

Carla suddenly appeared surprised and more than interested. "Are you serious?"

"I heard he's recently single too. I'll bet that's why he's alone. Are you sure you don't want him? I'd love a crack at a man with that much wealth and influence." Jess cocked her head and smiled. "I wouldn't mind having a Ferrari too. Why, I bet he could even get me part in one of his movies. That would be too cool."

Carla nearly bounced out of her seat with excitement and possible concern that Jess might steal him away.

"I saw him first," she said quickly while sizing Emry up from her position at the table.

"That *is* only fair." Jess hesitated then pretended to assess the situation while trying hard to keep a straight face. "You know, it's possible he might be offended from your earlier rejection. Why don't I lure him over here and you can have first shot at him, okay?"

Carla's eyes were wide with enthusiasm, and she nodded eagerly. Jess stood and approached the bar with a sly smile. She was pleased with herself and the stunt she was about to pull on Carla and her inflated ego. Jess sat down at the bar alongside Emry and partially turned on the barstool to face him. He didn't acknowledge her. Emry was by no means unattractive. He was just non-impressive. He was shorter than average, and his quiet demeanor gave him a sort of mousy appeal. On closer inspection, his clothes and haircut suggested he had expensive taste. She was convinced he even smelled expensive. The scent was actually quite pleasant. Jess casually leaned closer to him and attempted to hide her devious grin.

"We haven't met, but I believe we have a common friend," Jess informed him.

Emry didn't bother looking at her and stared straight ahead while sipping his scotch on the rocks. There was something strangely refined about him. Most women her age were attracted to the rocker type with tattoos, long hair, and a day's worth of stubble on their face. Not Jess. She preferred the clean-shaven, well-dressed, distinguished men. She loved them smart, but she was always more attracted to the men with a little edge to them. She somehow doubted this man had much of an edge to him.

"I'm aware of the company you keep," Emry informed her simply.

He casually indicated the large mirror behind the bar. Jess could see Carla primping through the mirror at the table behind them. Jess looked from the image in the mirror to Emry's profile. She wasn't sure if she was more surprised or concerned that he had been watching them.

"You should be a little more observant," she said lowly. "I came in with a dear friend who had his heart torn out at hello by that little prima donna. Simply put, I've got my bitch on."

Emry suddenly cast a surprised look at her, making eye contact for the first time, and hid his humored smile. He was obviously amused.

"You've got your bitch on?"

Jess flashed a smile and raised her brows lustfully in response. "I told her you were a famous movie producer, and now she wants to play nice."

"Do famous movie producers frequent these low-profile cruise ships?"

"Ironically, I run into famous movie producers everywhere I go," Jess teased with a smile. "And if you play along, I can practically guarantee she'll be begging you to take her to bed in less than an hour."

Emry stared at her a long moment with little emotion then casually returned to his drink and suddenly appeared disinterested.

"As much as I'd love to help you on your devious quest, I'm not the least bit interested in a girl like that."

Jess was a little surprised by his sudden lack of interest. Didn't all men want someone like Carla? She wondered if she had said something to offend him.

"I admire the whole gentleman thing you've got going," Jess said, "but there's nothing wrong with a little deviant behavior."

Emry suddenly glared her as if insulted by the comment.

"I assure you, I have nothing against a little deviant behavior, but that doesn't alter the fact that I'm not attracted to stuck-up little girls."

His candor surprised her. She was disappointed that he wouldn't play along. Maybe she had grown too accustomed to Drake's devious mind.

"Of course, if you come up with a plan B that doesn't require taking an interest, sexual or otherwise, in that one, I'm willing to hear you out."

Maybe she judged him too quickly. Jess considered his comment and tapped her fingers on the bar.

"Plan B, huh?" She sank into thought. Her sly grin soon returned. "I'm sure she'd be offended if she thought I stole you out from under her--metaphorically speaking. All you have to do is leave with me, and her imagination will do the rest." Jess gave him a teasing grin. "Although leaving together might compromise that whole gentleman thing you have going on."

Emry attempted to keep from laughing. "Either you're a real poor judge of character, or I've mellowed considerably with age. I don't think I've ever been accused of being a gentleman before." He then nodded toward Drake on the dance floor. "What about your friend?"

"Drake?"

Jess appeared surprised. She didn't think he had seen her with Drake, yet he easily identified him on the dance floor. She quickly brushed it off.

"I'm hoping he and Dana hit it off, in which case I'm demoted from wing man to third wheel, and my work here is done." Jess flashed a smile. "I'm sure he'll text me if he bombs, and I can meet with him later."

Emry appeared slightly bewildered and studied her with great interest. "Wing man, huh? You must be one hell of a friend."

"Don't let the dress fool you," Jess said. "I'm just one of the boys."

"Oh? Well, welcome to our team," Emry said then smiled slyly. "Now if you only play pool--"

"I play pool," Jess said then leaned closer to him on the bar, "and I'll kick your ass."

Emry grinned. "Now you're speaking my language."

Jess stood from her barstool and linked onto Emry's arm as he stood. He eyed her hand on his arm. It was hard to tell what was going through his mind.

"For show," Jess said. "I want to make sure she gets the wrong impression."

Emry raised a suggestive brow at the comment then took her hand in his and suavely kissed it without taking his eyes off hers. Jess was momentarily stunned by the exoticness of the sensual kiss. She immediately felt herself blush and hid her smile, although he must have seen it. Emry smiled charmingly and replaced her hand on his arm.

"How can you say you're not a gentleman?" Jess asked.

"I never said I couldn't pretend to be one."

Jess laughed and clung to his arm as they walked out of the nightclub together. Carla watched them leave with a stunned look on her face and her mouth hanging open.

Chapter Two

𝒯he elegant lounge was cozy and intimate with a piano, small bar, pool table, and a few sofas and chairs. A bored young bartender, Grant Peters, prepared a couple of drinks. Grant was a classically handsome man in his late twenties, who paid almost as much attention to his hair as Carla did hers. Grant looked toward the couple at the pool table. Jess and Emry played pool while having a good time razzing each other on every shot. Only one other couple occupied the nearly empty lounge. The young couple sat close and cuddled on a sofa toward the back. It was obvious they were a new couple by their seemingly intimate public displays of affection.

A man and woman in their early thirties entered the lounge and approached the bar. Grant appeared happy to see them. The elegantly dressed woman was the ship's nurse, Ella, and the man with her was her boyfriend, Phillip.

"So let's see it," Grant said with a broad grin on his face.

Ella proudly extended her left hand to him to reveal the exquisite diamond engagement ring. Grant took her hand and looked at the ring.

"That's stunning," Grant said. "Congratulations. I'm glad this creep finally made an honest woman out of you. I was ready to steal you away for myself if he didn't."

Ella giggled and clung to Phillip's arm. "My days of nursing sour stomachs on the high seas are over after this voyage. We're going to move to the Big Apple for some real fun."

"Real fun? You mean real crowds," Grant informed her. "Give me the open sea any day."

"You mean open season on single women at sea," Phillip said to Grant with a sly grin.

"Yeah, well, my reputation precedes me," Grant teased. "Living in the city, I'm just another nobody. At least on this ship, I'm somebody."

"We'd better get going," Ella said. "We don't want to be late for second seating at dinner."

As the happy couple left the lounge, Grant approached the pool table with Jess and Emry's drinks. He set them down on the nearby pub table and watched them play pool. Jess studied the pool table and contemplated her next shot. She glanced back at Emry and the bartender, who talked quietly. By the looks she was receiving, she was almost certain they were discussing her. That they stopped talking when she looked at them almost confirmed it.

"This place is dead," Jess said to Grant.

Jess only met Grant once during the voyage. Despite his outwardly good looks, he didn't impress her. He was likely that cruise ship bartender who "bagged babes" on every voyage. She would have staked her life on Grant's playboy status. Grant was the type of man she could read like an open book. Her attention again strayed to Emry. He was a closed book and the suspense was killing her.

"It's dinnertime," Grant said. "Tonight's highlight is the lobster bisque." He glanced from Jess to Emry. "Have you and your girlfriend been to dinner?"

There was an odd silence. Neither of them bothered to correct Grant's gaffe.

"I'm still struggling with my indiscretions at the all-you-can-eat sundae bar," Emry said cheerfully.

Jess cast a quick glance at Emry and hid her smile. She didn't mind if he wanted to give the wrong impression of their relationship, and she didn't intend to spoil his fun by correcting Grant either.

"I had a late lunch in Costa Rica," she replied

Jess leaned over the pool table to make her next shot. Her legs were spread comfortably apart, exposing one leg through the slit in her dress as she lined up her shot. Grant and Emry lustfully studied her sexy stance from behind. Grant was unable to control his grin and shook his head.

"That is one hell of a shot," Grant muttered just loud enough for Emry to hear.

Jess made the shot, sank the pool ball, and looked back at them. Both men quickly looked away and appeared innocent of any wrongdoing. Jess smirked at their attempted innocence and continued to line up her next shot. She had played pool with enough men back home to know when they were leering at her backside.

A little while later, Emry studied the pool balls for his next shot while Jess seductively leaned against the table in an attempt to distract him from winning yet another game. She studied his perceived shot.

"I know what you're thinking," Jess said with a devious smile, "and you're not going to make it."

Emry glanced at her, smiled slyly, and casually twirled the pool stick through his fingers with a certain style and grace. Jess watched him twirl the stick with more than a passing interest. He looked as if he was about to kick ass. Something about him strangely commanded her attention. Nerdy scientist aside, she was beginning to think he was somewhat sexy.

"You underestimate me, my dear," he said with a slight arrogance about him.

Emry leaned over the pool table and made the wildly impossible shot despite her seductive pose and obvious attempt to distract him. He won the game and grinned at her. Jess appeared almost stunned then smiled and shook her head while chuckling softly.

"You're some sort of mad genius."

"How kind of you to notice," he replied. "And for future reference, I'm not easily distracted, so you'll need to step up your game for *that*--" indicated her exposed leg, "--to work on me."

Jess eyed her exposed leg through the slit in her dress then looked back at him. "A pair of jeans and a tee shirt usually works on the good old boys back home," she said with a slightly humored smile. "Wearing this dress at the tavern would probably render them comatose."

Emry stared at her with a look that mystified her. His expressions were difficult to read. Did he want to jump her? Eat her brains? Or bore her with a lecture on quantum physics? Jess maintained her stare and smiled as she now sat seductively on the pool table. Trying to figure him out was turning into a game. She didn't know the rules, but it was exciting all the same. An excited crewmember hurried into the lounge and quickly approached Grant behind the bar. Emry and Jess watched the exchange between the two men from across the room. Emry approached her and began to rack the balls despite her legs near the ball return. Jess watched the exchange at the bar with great interest and was unaware of Emry's hand grazing her calf as he collected the pool balls.

"What do you suppose that's all about?" Jess asked with a curious look and a nod toward the bar.

Emry no longer paid attention to the exchange between the two men and removed the rack from the balls on the table. He casually retrieved his pool stick and prepared to play their next round.

"Something that's clearly none of our business."

"You're not curious?" Jess suddenly asked and looked at him with some surprise.

"Of course I'm curious, but there's no need to chase. Grant will come to us. He's like a gossiping old biddy in that respect."

The crewmember hurried from the lounge. No sooner had the man left when Grant quickly approached them with a concerned look on his face.

"A bunch of passengers are sick," Grant said to them. "They think it's food poisoning."

Jess and Emry appeared surprised.

"Is it serious?" Emry asked with noted concern.

"Serious enough. Sick passengers are to see the doc in the dining room. Everyone else should report to the ballroom. I have to close the bar."

Grant hurried back to the bar. His concern was evident. Emry suddenly appeared distracted as he looked at the couple on the sofa. He headed across the room toward them. His sudden departure surprised Jess, and she hurried after him. The young man and woman on the sofa were pale and sweated. Both gasped and heaved. Jess appeared alarmed and quickly shifted her attention to Emry. Emry stared at them with great interest and possible bewilderment.

"What's wrong with me?" the woman gasped as she clutched her stomach. "I suddenly feel so sick."

"We heard it might be food poisoning," Jess said gently and wasn't certain how she could help.

"I can't get up," the man said as he doubled over. "I'm really sick."

"When had you eaten?" Emry asked and studied their symptoms.

"An hour ago," the woman said faintly, "at first seating."

Jess attempted to move closer to them and reached out to help. Emry caught her wrist and stopped her while looking at the sick couple.

"You'd better wait here," Emry informed them. "Someone will be along to help you."

The couple appeared almost too weak to nod their response. Emry pulled Jess away by her hand and stopped her just short of the pool table. His look was serious.

13

"That's not food poisoning. It's arsenic poisoning," Emry said in a soft tone, so as not to alert the sick couple of his observation.

Jess appeared horrified and held back her gasp. "How do you mistakenly put arsenic--?"

"You don't."

Jess stared at Emry and his serious look. He then turned his attention to Grant, who frantically closed the bar, and called to him.

"Grant--"

Grant approached them and appeared even more tense then he had been a few minutes ago. He wasn't the sort of man you wanted to rely on in an emergency.

"We should go--" Grant began.

"You'll want to cancel that order," Emry informed him firmly.

Grant appeared surprised. Emry nodded toward the couple on the sofa. Jess and Grant looked across the room. The man and woman were slumped over each another. They were dead.

Chapter Three

*T*he massive kitchen extended on forever in never ending rows of counters, appliances, and cookware. Dirty dishes and food were scattered everywhere but there wasn't a single worker. Emry, Jess, and Grant slowly entered the kitchen armed with pool sticks. All three looked around the quiet kitchen with shared concern. They approached the dining room doors and slowly opened them. All three looked into the dining room. They appeared shocked and horrified. The large dining room once elegantly adorned with crystal, fine china, and flowered centerpieces was littered with nearly eighty dead men and woman either slumped over the tables or lying on the floor. Food and tableware lay on the floor with them. The stench of vomit was overpowering.

Jess stared helplessly at one dead couple in particular. Ella and Phillip were lying slumped together over their romantic table for two. Phillip's hand firmly clutched Ella's hand. Her beautiful diamond engagement ring was visibly noticeable and caught Jess's attention. The dead couple's image would be burned into Jess's mind a long time.

†

*J*ess sat on a cart and hugged her knees to her chest within the large, neatly kept linen closet. The closet was filled with table linens, cloth napkins, and white staff uniforms. She studied her two closet mates in silence. Emry leaned against the door with his hands casually in his pockets. He seemed unusually calm, but that was pretty much his normal state. He appeared deep in thought. Grant, on the other hand, paced the closet in a state near panic while frantically running his fingers through his hair. Jess was convinced Grant was close to losing it. He was starting to ramble.

"Were all those people poisoned?" Grant asked then appeared more terrified and looked from Jess to Emry. "My God, they were all poisoned!"

"Calm down and let me think," Emry said calmly without looking up.

Emry was definitely cool under extreme pressure. She couldn't imagine worse pressure than this. Jess wanted to think she was holding it together, but she knew that was only her outward appearance. Her concern for Drake was consuming her, and she felt she too was ready to erupt into something similar to Grant's state of mind. Emry's calm demeanor was the only thing keeping her from joining Grant.

"Think?" Grant said in a demanding tone and approached him with a concerned look. "Think about what?"

Emry appeared casual and glared at Grant. "About how screwed we are," he snapped. He returned to his thoughts but spoke aloud. "First seating was poisoned an hour ago but didn't show signs until now. Second seating was given a lethal dose that killed them almost instantly." He finally looked up at Jess and Grant. "They didn't want first seating turning up sick until it was too late to warn second seating."

"Who and why?" Jess asked from where she sat on her linen cart.

"My best guess would be drug smugglers," Emry said without hesitation. "The ship's probably already off course and heading for parts unknown. If I'm right, this nightmare is far from over."

Jess appeared concerned, lowered her legs, and was about ready to jump off her cart. She knew she was now one-step closer to joining Grant's hysterical condition.

"What do we do?"

Emry looked at her. "*We* do nothing," he said firmly. "You're going to stay here." He looked at Grant and straightened. "Cell phone service has been disabled. They've probably already taken out the radios and any other communication. If you can help me find some tools and get me to the ship's satellite, I can splice into it and get a distress call out."

"What about those people running around the ship killing everyone?" Grant asked.

"We'll need to proceed with extreme caution. Whoever did this is probably dressed in crew uniforms, and I suspect they're heavily armed. They're undoubtedly patrolling the ship and rounding up the strays."

"Passengers who weren't sick were told to report to the ballroom," Grant said while fidgeting.

Heavily armed? Rounding up strays? Jess suddenly lost control of her emotions and jumped off her linen cart with alarm and a terrified look.

"Drake is out there, Emry."

Emry glared at Jess with a scolding look. "He wouldn't want you running around the ship risking your life to find him. You're staying here." Emry turned to Grant with little emotion. "Let's go."

Jess and Grant protested to Emry simultaneously and spoke loudly over each another.

"You need me," Jess said. "I can help. I'm not just going to sit here--"

"You seriously expect me to run around this ship after what we've seen--" Grant said with hostility.

Emry glared at Grant with an annoyed look. "Unless you want to end up like the others, I expect you to give me the grand tour of the ship and help me secure the necessary tools that I need." He turned toward Jess and gave her an unimpressed once over. "And you--you're not exactly stealth in that dress and those heels. I can't do what I have to if I'm busy looking after you."

He thought she was helpless! Jess wasn't sure if she was more offended or annoyed. Jess suddenly kicked off her shoes and tore the slit in her dress up to her hip in one swift motion. She decided she was more annoyed. She startled both men with her sudden action and glared at Emry with limited patience.

"Don't assume it's you watching my back," she said with bitterness. "It might be me saving your ass."

Emry looked at the massive slit in her dress up to her hip, met her gaze, and appeared speechless.

✝

Emry, Jess, and Grant quietly hurried along the empty corridor with their pool sticks clutched in their hands while keeping watch for any signs of "would be" terrorists or drug runners. Grant jumped at every little sound and movement like a scared rabbit. The ship was eerily silent. Emry suddenly stopped them with a motion from his hand. Grant and Jess stopped and looked around with rising concern and then bewilderment. Jess wondered why he had stopped them. Emry listened to something. She attempted to hear whatever it was he thought he heard. She then heard it too. It sounded like a faint rat tat tat. Jess didn't know what the sound was, but it soon stopped and the ship was once again silent. Emry returned to his deep thoughts. She was starting to not like when he did that. They continued walking along the corridor for several minutes in silence.

The nightclub doors were suddenly before them. Jess stopped and stared at the closed doors. Her heart was in her throat. There was no sound, not even music coming from the club. Jess knew that was a bad sign. She fought the urge to run into the nightclub and look for Drake without consulting Emry first.

"Emry--"

Emry looked back at her. She indicated the closed nightclub doors. He stared at her a moment, and then reluctantly gave in. He approached the doors, hesitated a moment to smell the air, and then slowly pushed one of the doors open. Grant appeared completely strung out and ready to jump while clutching his pool stick. Emry looked into the nightclub. His look suddenly hardened, and he appeared disgusted but not terribly surprised. Jess and Grant looked past him and into the nightclub. The once crowded, lively nightclub was strewn with dead men and women covered in blood and riddled with bullets. The massacre was unlike anything Jess had seen before. The faint smell of gunfire lingered within the massive room. That must have been the sound they had heard. Jess and Grant stared with shared looks of horror and couldn't look away. Emry gently took Jess's hand and attempted to pull her away from the horrific scene.

"We need to go," Emry said softly.

Jess attempted to hold back her tears and resisted Emry pulling on her hand.

"They have no reason to come back here. I have to find him."

Emry stared at her with a surprised look that quickly turned more serious.

"You don't want to see that, Jess."

"Please, Emry--"

Jess and Emry stared into each other's eyes a long, silent moment. Emry groaned and shook his head with a defeated sigh.

"I'll need an hour to collect the necessary tools and hack into the satellite. Wait for us in the restroom and stay out of sight."

Jess nodded timidly. Grant appeared almost stunned by Emry's decision to allow her to stay and more so with Jess's wanting to stay.

"You're insane," Grant said to Jess.

Jess ignored Grant. Emry caressed her hand as he stared into her eyes. She could finally read his look. He cared what happened to her. Jess suddenly realized he had been right. He said he wouldn't be able to do what he had to if he was busy looking after her. If she was in trouble, he might die trying to save her and it would be her fault. Emry released her hand and left the club. Grant just looked at her, shook his head, and hurried after Emry. She stared at the nightclub door as it fell back into place. Jess finally turned toward the horrific sight within the room. She took a deep breath, slowly walked through the dead bodies, and fought back her tears. There were nearly fifty dead men and woman scattered throughout the nightclub. Judging by their positions on the floor, some tried to run when the shooting started. She couldn't imagine what those poor people had gone through before being gunned down. As a dying gesture, some held their loved ones on the floor while taking their last breath.

The image of one woman holding a man's blood soaked hand went through her. That could have been her and Drake. The thought sent a chill up her spine. There was blood everywhere with multiple bullet holes having riddled their bodies. Their once elegant dresses and expensive jackets were soaked with blood. Jess wandered through the dead bodies for several minutes, although it seemed longer, looking at their faces and their clothing while attempting to locate Drake. Emry was right; she didn't want to see this. She couldn't imagine what she would feel if she saw Drake with bullet holes in his body and that lifeless expression on his face. Some of the dead people had their eyes closed but most didn't. She almost felt as if they were watching her.

She heard the faint sound of voices from outside the club. Jess suddenly became alert then alarmed. She looked around as if uncertain what to do, cast her pool stick aside, and moved to the floor with the dead bodies. She remained motionless and stared at the dead woman just inches from her face. The dead woman stared back at her with blood covering her face and a bullet hole through her eye. The dead woman had light colored hair now tinged red with blood. For a brief moment, Jess thought it could be Dana. The starboard doors opened and two men with automatic weapons appeared in the nightclub. They wore crew uniforms just as Emry had predicted. The taller of the two men in a steward's uniform, Donnie, looked at the bodies as they walked through the nightclub. He shook his head and appeared disgusted.

"What a waste of perfectly good female flesh," Donnie said callously. "Could have saved a couple for the voyage to Mexico."

The shorter of the two men, who was wearing a waiter's uniform, Mitch, glared at Donnie and appeared annoyed by the suggestion.

"You're a sick bastard, you know that?"

"All I'm saying, if we're going to just kill them anyway--" Donnie said but was cut short.

"Can you not talk to me?"

They left the club through the same set of doors as Emry and Grant. Jess slowly moved to her feet, reclaimed her pool stick, and quietly continued through the bullet-riddled field of bodies. She then noticed the blood on her hands, held back her sobs, and hurried into the women's restroom just a few feet away. Jess entered the women's restroom and looked under the elegant, closed stall doors. She then approached the sink and washed the blood from her hands. She scrubbed her hands and held back her frightened sobs. She saw a stall door slowly opening through the mirror. Jess grabbed her pool stick, turned, and swung without a second thought. Carla screamed and ducked back inside the stall. Jess stopped mid-swing and appeared stunned.

"Carla?"

"Jess, thank God!"

Carla jumped out of the stall and hugged Jess without warning. She returned the quick embrace then pulled away to meet her gaze.

"What happened?"

"I don't know," Carla said and rubbed her chilled arms. "I was only in here a minute or so when I heard what sounded like gunshots and screaming. I hid in one of the stalls. Next thing I knew, crewmen burst in and dragged out the other women. I heard them screaming as they drug them out and then more gunshots--"

Carla fell silent, stared blankly, and appeared shaken. She had obviously been through hell and was still attempting to make sense of it. Jess just stared at her in silence and waited for her to continue.

Her voice was soft. "Then the screaming stopped." She snapped out of her trance like state and stared at Jess. "I couldn't move. I was terrified. When I didn't hear anything, I finally got up enough courage to look out the bathroom door. It was horrible. I can't believe they're all dead--shot like that."

"Those men poisoned most of the passengers and hijacked the ship," Jess said. "I'm with some guys who are trying to send a distress call. They said to wait for them here. They're coming back for us."

Carla continued to cling to her bare arms and leaned against the sink. What she had witnessed obviously still traumatized her. Jess hesitated, took a deep, nervous breath, and stared at Carla a moment in silence.

Jess didn't want to ask, but she had to know. "Did you see Drake? What happened to him?"

"I don't know. He left with Dana long before the shooting started."

Jess wasn't sure if she was encouraged by that or not. She cast her back against the bathroom wall, shut her eyes, and groaned softly.

"Please, Drake, be okay," Jess muttered softly.

Chapter Four

Grant followed Emry along one of the lower deck corridors. Both carried their pool sticks and continued cautiously. They heard the faint sounds of gunfire from somewhere close by. Emry quickly scanned the corridor and opened the nearby storage closet door. He gestured Grant toward the closet and both men slipped inside. Emry remained by the closet door and listened to the sound of continuous gunfire. Grant looked around the large storage closet filled with extra chairs, dining carts, and other items possibly used for parties held in the ballroom. He stared at the unusually placed, loaded flat cart covered with a tablecloth.

"That's a lot of gunfire," Emry said softly to Grant while listening by the closet door. "That's definitely not a good sign."

Grant studied the covered flat cart a moment longer. A small amount of blood soaked through the sheet, and a small pool of blood was collecting on the floor just beneath the cart. Grant stared the cart and appeared alarmed. He reached for the tablecloth, hesitated, and then pulled it back. Nearly ten crewmembers, mostly waiters, lay piled on the cart in their blood soaked uniforms. Grant suddenly gasped and dropped the tablecloth. Emry quickly turned and looked at the sight of dead crewmembers carelessly tossed on the flat cart. Almost all of them had their throats slit.

"These men have been dead several hours," Emry said. "My guess is they were killed before dinner and our friends out there took their shift to help distribute the poisoned lobster bisque."

Grant stared at the dead crewmembers with horror and couldn't look away.

"I know some of them," Grant said softly. He suddenly looked at Emry and appeared surprised. "How do you know it was the lobster bisque that was poisoned?"

"Nearly all the dead people within the dining room had the lobster bisque setting on the table before them. The poison was fast acting, so it had to be in the bisque." Emry glanced back at the door with a concerned look. "We need to find out where those shots came from."

"Sounded like they came from--" Grant suddenly hesitated and stared at Emry with a concerned look on his face. "--the ballroom!"

✝

Emry and Grant slowly entered the ballroom with their pool sticks raised and ready for a fight. The stench of gunfire lingered heavily in the air. Both men stopped and stared at the scene before them. At least sixty dead men and women lay along the back wall, which was now riddled with bullet holes and blood. The mass execution was worse than they found in the nightclub. The passengers and crew who had obediently reported to the ballroom had undoubtedly been forced along the wall and were executed in firing squad fashion. Most were shot multiple times in the front, indicating they had little chance to run. Emry glanced over the piles of bullet casings lying on the floor nearly twenty feet away from the bodies. He pushed the casings with his foot and appeared to study them.

"These casings are from assault rifles," Emry said to Grant.

Grant held his stomach and appeared sickened at the sight before them. With that many people shot that many times, the blood surrounding them had collected into an enormous pool that appeared to spread across half the room.

"Judging by the shell casing piles spaced out along the floor, I'm guessing there was at least five shooters." Emry shook his head with disgust. "Poor bastards never stood a chance."

"Can we go?" Grant asked softly and was no longer able to look.

Emry approached a dead man in uniform and checked his pockets. He was the ship's purser. Grant watched Emry checking the man's pockets and appeared both surprised and sickened at the same time.

"What are you doing?"

"It's the ship's purser." Emry removed a card key from the dead purser's pocket. He flashed the card key to Grant. "This is access to every door on the ship. He has no use for it, but we might." Emry stuck the card in his jacket pocket and straightened. "We're going to need something a little more intimidating than pool sticks if we're going to survive this cruise."

"We should find a quiet little hiding spot and wait for this to blow over or until the Coast Guard comes to rescue us," Grant said firmly.

"We won't survive long enough for them to find us. These men are organized and coordinated. They knew when and how to hit us. I doubt they intend for this ship to stay afloat long enough for any rescue to find us on their own. Our only chance is to get out that distress call. We're the only ones who can save our asses."

"If you're thinking about being a hero, Emry, you should know you're going to end up a dead one."

"Being a hero is furthest from my mind, Grant." Emry then turned and headed toward the ballroom doors with Grant quickly following. "The last thing I want or need is any sort of media attention. I'm a bit of a recluse, and I'd like to live long enough to keep it that way."

Grant gave Emry a strange look then quickly followed him from the ballroom.

†

An hour had passed since Emry and Grant had left. Jess and Carla stood outside of the women's restroom within the nightclub. Carla paced the area and tried to avoid looking at the bodies, which proved difficult. Jess occupied herself by attempting to twirl her pool stick the way Emry had when they played pool. She was having little success with it. The port nightclub door opened. Both women appeared alarmed and quietly darted into the bathroom. Jess motioned Carla into one of the stalls then ducked behind the entrance door with her pool stick firmly clutched in her hands. Jess held her breath and appeared tense with her eyes fixated on the door. Faint male voices were heard beyond the bathroom door. She knew neither of the voices belonged to Emry.

"Do you think there are more of them?" came Mitch's familiar voice.

"Maybe one or two here and there," Donnie replied. "Nothing we can't handle."

"What do you suppose he was doing all the way up there by the satellite dish?" Mitch asked.

Jess suddenly became alarmed. Were they talking about Emry? Did something happen to him?

24

"Who knows," Donnie said. "It doesn't matter anymore. He was taken care of."

Jess held back her gasp.

"You check that way," Donnie said as his voice trailed off. "I'll check this way."

Jess remained immobile alongside the bathroom door and listened to the faint sound of the men walking around the nightclub. The sound faded and there was silence. She felt relieved and confident that they had continued on their way. She shut her eyes and relaxed. The bathroom door moved slightly. Jess was suddenly alarmed and horrified as the door slowly opened. Mitch entered with his assault rifle grasped firmly in his hands and approached the stalls. He caught a glimpse of Jess out of the corner of his eye and spun toward her. Jess swung the pool stick and knocked the rifle from his hand then immediately swung again and struck him in the head. He quickly dropped to the floor. His assault rifle clattered loudly as it struck the floor near him. It was too much noise! Jess lunged for the assault rifle.

Donnie suddenly appeared in the doorway and fired at Jess. One bullet whizzed past her head and ricocheted off the wall. The second shot grazed her arm. Jess cried out, dropped the pool stick, and hit the stall door. The stall door flew open to reveal Carla crouched on the toilet seat. Carla stared at Jess with a look of horror. Jess met Carla's horrified stare then slowly looked back at the man with the assault rifle and moved just far enough away from the stall door that it shut, keeping Carla hidden. She clutched her bleeding arm and looked at Donnie with the assault rifle aimed at her. She waited for him to pull the trigger. He lowered the rifle, looked at his partner on the floor, and gently nudged him with his foot. The injured Mitch groaned while clutching his head and slowly moved to his feet.

Donnie motioned Jess toward the door with his weapon. "Move it."

She slowly approached the door and headed from the bathroom. If Carla remained silent, maybe they wouldn't find her. Jess walked out of the bathroom with Donnie behind her and his weapon aimed at her back. Mitch followed them with his own rifle limp in his arm as he held his bleeding head. She had gotten him good. A thousand thoughts ran through Jess's head as she waited for the man to shoot her. She finally decided she wanted to see it coming and bravely turned to face him. She wasn't sure why, but Donnie seemed unwilling to pull the trigger.

"Make your sweep," Donnie said to his partner. "I'll secure this one in a cabin."

His lustful grin at Jess revealed his intentions. Jess then remembered his earlier conversation with Mitch. She was suddenly aware of her current situation, and she liked it less than she had just two minutes ago.

"Just shoot her," Mitch said and appeared disgusted. "There's no reason to prolong it."

"Let me worry about entertaining our female prisoners," Donnie said in response.

"Sick bastard," Mitch scoffed.

Mitch headed toward the starboard doors with disgust and passed through them. Jess held her bleeding arm and stared at the man with the lustful grin and his weapon aimed at her. He motioned her toward the starboard doors.

"Let's go," Donnie said firmly.

Jess took a moment to assess her situation. There was no way she was going to let this man touch her. She was going to make sure he had no choice but to kill her first. Jess watched him again motion with the assault rifle and contemplated her plan of attack.

"Move it, bitch."

Jess knew she stood a better chance of survival making her move while passing through the doorway. The close quarters would work to her advantage, and she had to make her attack count. Jess felt a rush of adrenaline in anticipation of her last stand. She took a deep breath and turned toward the starboard doors. Emry stood casually in the starboard doorway before them with an assault rifle in his hands. Donnie saw him and appeared surprised or possibly stunned.

"Good evening--" Emry said in an almost pleasant tone with a strange smirk on his face.

Donnie suddenly aimed his rifle. Emry fired a single shot into the man's head. Jess cried out with surprise as Donnie's head appeared to explode from where he stood almost alongside her. He immediately dropped to the floor. Jess was paralyzed with fear as she watched the man's blood rapidly spill out across the floor toward her bare feet. She could do little more than stare.

"I'll be terribly disappointed if you don't take that weapon," Emry said bluntly.

Jess snapped out of her trance to Emry's familiar voice, appeared relieved, and quickly grabbed the discarded rifle. Emry made a quick assessment of her bleeding arm from several feet away. Jess hurried to the bathroom door, opened it, and peered inside.

"Carla--"

Carla uncertainly stepped out of the bathroom and looked from Jess to Emry. Her expression suddenly dropped into something resembling a sneer.

"Oh, God. Not him." Carla looked at Jess. "This is your promise of salvation?"

"I haven't promised you anything, pumpkin," Emry retorted lowly. "Consider yourself lucky I'm letting you tag along."

Emry turned and headed for the starboard doors. Jess glared at Carla with an annoyed look. Even when faced with life and death, Carla was superficial and petty. Carla frowned and realized she had just pissed off Jess. For some odd reason, it mattered to Carla. Both followed Emry through the starboard doors. They entered the corridor behind Emry. Grant nervously paced the hallway and stared blankly at the floor. Mitch lay dead in an unnatural position on the floor not far from the nightclub doors. Jess appeared surprised and stared at the dead man as well.

"What happened to him?" Jess asked.

Emry shrugged with little emotion. "He didn't want to share his toys. Let's get you to the infirmary and fix that arm."

Emry walked past the dead man as if he wasn't even there. Grant glared at Jess and hurried after her as she followed Emry.

"He broke the guy's neck without even flinching," Grant said softly and with concern.

Carla appeared surprised and looked at the dead man as she passed his lifeless body.

"I'm telling you, he's crazy," Grant said softly.

"I'll take crazy as long as he's on our side," Jess replied simply.

"We need to get away from that lunatic as soon as possible and find a safe place to hide."

"If he's right there won't be any safe place to hide," Jess replied. "This entire ship will end up on the ocean floor."

"And you believe him?"

"He's been right so far."

Grant looked at Carla. "You look like you have an ounce of common sense. Don't you think we should find someplace to hide?"

Carla glared at him and appeared offended by his comment. "Right now, I'm going to follow the guy with the gun."

Jess realized Grant was right about one thing. Carla did have an ounce of common sense.

Chapter Five

*J*ess sat on the infirmary exam table and clutched the edges while Emry cleaned the deep bullet graze on her arm. Jess cringed from the powerful sting of the antiseptic that almost hurt worse than the actual shot. She attempted to conceal the pain to avoid his "I told you so" that she felt was sure to follow. Emry slid his chair toward the cabinet and routed through one of the drawers. Jess watched as he removed a small bottle and a syringe. She suddenly cringed while eyeing the syringe.

"What's that for?"

"A local numbing solution," he said simply. "You're going to need stitches."

Jess was about to question him. He glanced at her above the bottle as he drew the solution into the needle. She somehow knew he was just waiting for her to protest, so he could rub it in. Jess turned her head and looked away. Emry rolled his chair back to her on the exam table and injected the needle into her arm near the wound. That the needle prick caused her to flinch almost embarrassed her. Carla sat nearby on the counter and appeared sickened while watching Emry stitch Jess's wound. Although Jess only felt a slight tugging on her skin, Carla reacted with a grimace at each stitch. The look on Carla's face was enough to make Jess queasy. Grant paced near the partially opened door, looked at them several times, and maintained his concern for their situation.

"I don't like this," Grant said softly. "What if they find us here?"

Emry stitched Jess's wound with great care and focus. He showed little interest to acknowledge Grant and even less with his response.

"Then I suggest you shoot them."

"Did you get the distress call out?" Jess asked while putting up a brave front.

"They shot out the satellite," Grant grumbled.

"The call went through," Emry replied.

Emry remained calm and stayed focus on his minor surgery. He would make a convincing doctor.

Grant turned and glared at Emry. "You don't know that."

"You're a very negative man, Grant," Emry casually informed him without looking.

Grant returned to his pacing.

A few minutes later, Emry taped a dressing to Jess's stitched wound. He appeared satisfied with his work, stood from his chair, and hovered over her with his hands on the exam table on either side of her. His face was unusually close to hers. Jess was certain "I told you so" was sure to follow by the look in his eyes. As she stared back at him that close to her, she suddenly didn't care. She realized she was just happy to see him. Emry smiled warmly.

"Are you a little less John Wayne now that you've been shot?"

Jess hid her smile of embarrassment and attempted to retain some of her dignity.

"If you believe help is coming, I'm willing to nurse my wounds with you."

"That's a smart girl," Emry said cheerfully and quickly kissed her forehead. He then straightened and looked at the others. "You three can hole up in one of the nearby cabins. You should be safe if you remain quiet."

Jess appeared surprised by his remark. "What about you? What do you intend to do?"

Emry casually picked up the assault rifle and offered a strangely devious grin. "I'm going to bag my limit of bad guys."

He cocked the rifle, causing Carla to jump then hold her chest. Jess couldn't bear the thought of him running around the ship without backup.

"Not without me," Jess said firmly. "There are two rifles. You need someone to cover your back."

Emry gave her a look that nearly silenced her. "I'm flexible enough to cover my own back. You're sitting this one out."

Jess suddenly felt offended and possibly betrayed by his matter-of-fact look. She glared back at him and no longer cared what he thought.

"When you say those things, do you actually hear yourself? Because all I hear is blah, blah, blah, blah, blah."

Emry appeared surprised by her harsh tone and stared at her a moment while unusually silent. She feared his wrath that was sure to follow.

"You know, you're kind of scary," Emry said. A strange smile crossed his face. "I'm a little turned on."

Jess was uncertain what to make of his comment and maintained her stern look despite her obvious bewilderment. Emry handed her the assault rifle, which surprised her. She realized she knew nothing about this man, but she knew she loved him.

†

Emry and his assault rifle led the way along the stateroom corridor on deck three. Carla and Grant followed with a shared look of fright and dread. Jess brought up the rear with the second assault rifle securely in her hands. With her torn, dirty dress, mussed hair, bloodstained legs, and wrapped arm, the assault rifle gave her the appearance of some deadly woman with whom no one would dare mess. She carried off the illusion brilliantly to keep Emry from finding out how scared she really was. She had to be strong for him and help keep him alive.

As they passed a large amount of blood streaked along the floor, Jess felt her body twitch at the sight. Emry motioned for them to stop. All three stopped and looked around with concern. Jess stared at the blood streak a moment longer. She wasn't sure she wanted to know what happened to the body. Emry peered down the nearby stairwell then looked at the cabin door alongside it. Cabin #302. Emry removed the key card from his pocket and slid it through the reader. Jess wondered where he found that. The door hummed and unlocked. Emry opened the cabin door. Drake suddenly lunged through the open door and swung at him with a towel bar clutched in his hands. Emry swiftly kicked Drake in the chest and dropped him to the floor. Jess gasped with surprise and leaped to Drake's side. She gently patted his face with concern.

"Drake!"

Drake groaned softly, looked at Jess, and attempted a tiny smile. "Jess? Making new friends?" he asked then immediately groaned while he gingerly rubbed his chest.

†

*M*oments later, Emry stood by the open door just inside Dana's cabin with his assault rifle and maintained his watch on the corridor. Jess, Drake, Carla, and Dana appeared happy to see one another and chatted quickly and softly. Grant made himself comfortable on the bed.

"When we heard shooting in the hallway, we looked through the peek hole and saw crewmen randomly shooting passengers," Drake said to Jess. "We didn't know what was happening, but we decided it was best to stay locked in the cabin."

"That was my idea," Dana said. "He wanted to go out looking for you, but I wouldn't let him. Don't blame him. It's my fault he didn't come for you. I was scared."

"It's okay, Dana. No one's blaming you." Drake looked back at Jess. "I had no idea where you'd gotten too, and my cell phone stopped working, so I couldn't even contact you to see if you were okay. I just hoped you had found someplace safe to hide."

"You don't want to know *where* I looked for you," Jess said with a slightly sickened feeling.

"Do you really think they're all dead?" Dana asked with a terrified look.

"With all the bodies we found around the ship, I'd say everyone's pretty much dead," Grant said from his relaxed position on the bed.

He received several cold stares from the other three over his callous remark. Emry looked back at them and interrupted their reunion.

"This is a good place for you to stay until help arrives," Emry said.

"Help?" Drake suddenly asked with surprise. "What help? Just before the television signal went out, we heard they couldn't locate the ship. They have no idea where we are or where to start looking for us."

"They don't even know what happened onboard," Dana said while insecurely rubbing her arms.

"If they remove their cargo, they'll probably sink the ship before a rescue locates us," Emry said. "If we want to prevent that, we'll need to take out the ship's engines to buy the rescue some time to find us."

"You're crazy," Grant said in protest and suddenly bolted upright from his position on the bed. "You said they'd be manning the bridge."

"But not necessarily the engine room. Once she's left floundering, it'll be easier for the Coast Guard to find us. If their friends arrive before the Coast Guard, we're pretty much screwed."

Grant suddenly became rigid and glared at Emry. "Oh, no! I did my part. I'm not going out there again. I'm a bartender not a commando. Find someone else to take on your suicide missions."

"I'll take out the engines," Drake said. "My uncle used to give me tours of the freighters he'd be repairing. I think I can figure it out."

Jess gave Drake a stunned look. What was he trying to prove?

"You're in," Emry said to Drake. "I need to have a look around the cargo hold. I want to see just how far up the creek we really are."

"I'm going with you," Jess said.

Emry gave her that look she had already grown to fear. She emotionally prepared for another argument.

"I doubt you'd listen if I said no." Emry then looked at Grant. "You stay here with Dana and Carla."

Grant returned to a reclined position on the bed and relaxed. "That's more like it."

"We'll find you a weapon on the way," Emry said to Drake as he walked out the door.

Drake appeared a little surprised and possibly curious as he followed them from the cabin.

"Where do you intend to find another weapon?"

Chapter Six

*T*he sound of a man's neck breaking echoed through the silence. A terrorist in a crewmember's uniform fell lifelessly to the lounge floor with a thud. Emry casually picked up the discarded assault rifle and handed it to Drake. Drake and Jess stared at the dead man with shared horror. Drake was suddenly pale as he uncertainly accepted the rifle. Jess noted the unaffected look on Emry's face to the life he had just claimed. There was no remorse or emotion. It came a little too easy to him.

"We'll know when you've disabled the engines," Emry casually said to Drake. "If you need us, we'll be in the cargo hold."

"The cargo hold is massive. How will I find you down there?"

Emry shrugged with little emotion. "Just follow the gunfire."

Drake suddenly appeared uncertain about his role. Jess noted the concerned look on Drake's face and was frightened for him. She wasn't going to be there to look after him. How would he survive without her? She quickly hugged Drake and held back her concerned sniff.

"Don't play hero, okay?" she whispered softly in his ear while clinging to him.

Drake returned the embrace and laughed nervously. "Come on, Jess. You know me better than that," he said softly then pulled away from her and smiled reassuringly. "Don't go turning all girly on me now. It doesn't suit you. We're going to be fine."

Jess kissed Drake quickly on the lips. Drake choked up slightly then quickly turned and hurried from the lounge to avoid showing weakness in front of her. Drake wasn't a hero, and he certainly wasn't brave. She stared at the empty doorway and wondered if she would ever see him again. The thought scared her.

"He'll be fine," Emry said simply as if reading her thoughts.

Jess looked back at him but didn't comment. She wanted to know how he could be so sure. She wanted further reassurance that he couldn't possibly provide.

"It's a short trip to the engine room, and they'll be far too busy guarding their cargo and manning the bridge to be looking for anymore stragglers."

She didn't know how he did it, but somehow he managed to provide that reassurance--and she believed him.

†

The cargo hold was a massive maze of rows and rows of secured, strapped crates and various other cargo, some stacked over six feet high in the vast compartments. Emry and Jess darted behind a row of crates with their assault rifles. They peered between the crates and looked at a group of five men, who were guarding three crates twenty yards across the hold from them.

"I count five men," Jess said softly.

Emry remained close to her with his back to the crates and his assault rifle securely against his chest. He again looked through the opening. It was obvious that he had extensive military training. He looked a little too at home with the assault rifle clutched in his hands. As she now studied him, she wondered how she had ever mistaken him for a quiet, timid man.

"That leaves two on the bridge and four patrolling the ship," he casually informed her.

Jess stared at him with a puzzled look on her face. He appeared so confident of himself, but she couldn't understand why.

"What makes you so sure?"

Emry kept his eye on the men across the hold. "Simple mathematics. Maximum capacity for the ship is three hundred and twenty-five. One hundred and twenty-five are crewmembers. We found fifty percent of the crew shot in the ballroom and another twenty-five percent dead in the dining room. Grant and I found another ten in a storage closet, so that leaves about fifteen percent posing as crewmen--or approximately twenty bad guys. Nine are dead, five are down here, and at least two will secure the bridge. That leaves four patrolling the ship." Emry gave her a quick look with little emotion and raised his brows cleverly. "You can double check my math, but I'm rarely ever wrong."

Jess stared at Emry with her mouth hanging open and a bewildered expression of amazement or possible fright on her face.

"Who are you?" she suddenly demanded to know.

"A substitute teacher."

"Bullshit--"

Emry flashed a sly grin. Jess hid her smile and rolled her eyes. She couldn't help but think that he was too cute for words.

†

The massive engine room was a mechanical marvel with modern machinery, some in frighteningly close quarters. Drake stood by the control panel of what would be the nerve center of the ship's engines. He set his assault rifle down and pondered a moment while he eyed the switches, buttons, and gizmos. He pulled a few levers then pushed a few switches. The loud whirling of the engines silenced. Drake appeared satisfied with himself and grinned proudly.

"Piece of cake--"

Drake turned and reached for his discarded assault rifle. A man appeared out of nowhere and swung a large wrench for Drake's head. Drake cried out and dove from the weapon's path. The wrench struck a console with a deafening, metallic clang and sparked. His attacker, Conner Blake, wore a once expensive suit now covered in blood and dirt. He pulled back for another swing. Drake appeared horrified and held his hands up defensively.

"Whoa! Whoa! We're on the same side!" Drake cried out with fright.

Conner stopped mid-swing and looked at the assault rifle near them. He glared at Drake with a slightly psychotic look in his eyes.

"No! You're one of them!" Conner shouted with limited patience and coiled back with the wrench for a second swing at Drake's head.

"No! No!" Drake cried out in panic while frantically waving his arms. "There's this creepy guy who killed some of them and took their weapons. He told me to stop the ship's engines so the rescue could find us."

Conner slowly lowered his wrench with the return of hope and trust in his eyes. "There's a rescue?" he asked. His rush of adrenaline appeared to fade.

Drake slowly and uncertainly lowered his arms with a relieved look. "Trust me--I just want to go home."

Conner's tall frame sagged with relief and exhaustion as he uncertainly set down the wrench. Conner was a decent looking man beyond the dirt, grease, and bloodstains on his clothing, hands, and face. He was possibly in his thirties, but the wear and tear of the night and lack of sleep had aged him rapidly. His dark hair was dirty and gray with dust from the engine room, indicating he had probably been hiding down there shortly after it all began.

"I'm sorry about--you know," Conner said softly while indicating the massive wrench. "It's just--my girlfriend got really sick after dinner. I went to find help, but they just kept herding me to the ballroom. I'd heard the doctor was in the dining room with other sick passengers, so I slipped out when they weren't looking. I was about to cut through the casino, when I heard gunshots coming from the dining room. I mean real gunshots. The kind you only hear in war movies. That's when I found the bodies--"

Drake stared at the look on Conner's weary face. Conner sank against the control panel and stared off a moment in silence. It was a long night for all of them. It appeared as if he had been through more than his share of terror since the nightmare began.

"I went back to the cyber café for my girl, but she was already dead. I didn't know what to do. I heard more gunfire and people screaming in the corridors. I panicked and came down here to hide." Conner held his head in his trembling hands and attempted to control his need to sob. "I didn't try to help anyone. I just *hid*."

"I hear you, man," Drake said gently. "I hid too. Self-preservation is a natural instinct, but we can't hide anymore. Our lives depend on us, and my friend is out there fighting this battle to save us. She needs me to look after her. I'm all she has."

Conner sniffed and straightened with renewed confidence. "What can I do to help?"

36

Chapter Seven

*J*ess and Emry maintained their position behind the crates while they spied on the five, armed men guarding their merchandise. The faint sounds of the engines ceased and the cargo hold no longer vibrated. Jess and Emry became alert and looked at each another with shared grins. Drake had succeeded in his mission, which also meant he was probably still alive. The five men guarding the crates looked around and appeared concerned at the silent engines. Emry kept a watchful eye on the five men then looked at Jess.

"I'm moving to higher ground." Emry pointed up with his assault rifle. "When I draw their fire, you shoot." Emry was about to scale some crates when he looked starboard. His expression suddenly dropped. "Oh--"

"What?"

Emry slowly sank alongside her and frowned. "Two more to our rear. I don't like our position. We're boxed in."

Jess appeared alarmed and stared at him. "What should we do?"

Emry appeared deep in thought while tapping his fingers on his assault rifle barrel. He finally looked at her with little enthusiasm.

"I'm thinking of two scenarios, but neither has a very happy ending."

"Then come up with a third," Jess quickly said with a look of horror on her face.

Emry contemplated their situation and indicated the crate before them. "You should fit beneath this crate. I'll hold them off as long as I can. If you're quiet, I'm confident they won't find you."

"Emry, no," Jess protested softly.

His eyes met hers. As she stared at him with a look of horror, he offered a tiny, strange smile.

"Don't worry about me, Jess. I'm pretty much dead no matter who finds me."

Jess stared at him and appeared momentarily bewildered. She didn't want him to die. She wanted this man in her life, but she couldn't think of any way to stop him. Jess threw her arms around his neck and held onto him. Emry uncertainly returned the embrace.

"Please, Emry, don't do this," Jess whispered softly while clinging to him. "You'll think of something. You're an evil genius, remember?"

Jess suddenly realized she was becoming hysterical and feared the tears welling up in her eyes. She slowly pulled back to meet his gaze. As she stared into his eyes, she knew she had to say something useful and intelligent that would help save him. Only one thought came to mind. Jess suddenly kissed him passionately on the mouth. Emry appeared slightly surprised but wasted little time eagerly returning the kiss with warmth and added aggression. Jess was suddenly aware of the salty taste of her tears invading their kiss. She hoped Emry hadn't noticed. She didn't want him to know she was crying. She wanted him to think she was brave. His hand gently brushed the tears from her face as his kiss turned more warm and loving.

A few minutes had passed. The five men continued to guard the three crates while the other two patrolled the rear cargo hold. Soft, female moans of pleasure echoed through the hold and alerted both groups of men. Four of the five men who were guarding the crates followed the sounds. Both men patrolling the back followed the sounds as well.

Jess could be heard as she softly moaned. "Oh, oh, God--yes!"

The two men from behind closed in on a cluster of crates, which seemed to be the source of the moans. They exchanged devious grins. The sound of moaning ceased. The four other men joined them and attempted to locate which crate the sound had been coming from. They stopped before one of the crates, studied it, and then kicked it.

"Typical men--" Jess said from behind them.

All six men turned toward Jess, who casually leaned behind a nearby crate.

"--don't let a lady finish."

An assault rifle cocked behind them. The armed men turned with their rifles aimed. Emry stood behind a crate and fired a

38

controlled burst of gunfire at them. All six men were struck with multiple shots, without getting off a single round, and fell to the floor. Jess made a face and cringed. The remaining man across the cargo hold heard the gunfire and aimed his weapon at them. Jess appeared alarmed and fired her assault rifle past Emry at the distant man. As the rifle unexpectedly fired multiple rounds, the powerful thrust threw her backwards, causing her rifle to shoot upward into the air as she fell against a crate behind her.

Emry shielded himself from the wild, random burst of gunshots. Jess gasped, straightened, and looked at Emry with concern for his life. Emry felt himself for bullet holes and appeared stunned to be alive. He looked behind him at the man by the crate twenty yards away. There was blood on the crate, and the man lay dead on the floor. Emry glared at Jess behind her crate, casually stepped over one of the dead men, and shook his head with a frown as he approached her.

"I was impressed until three seconds ago," he said flatly.

Emry snatched the assault rifle from her and scolded her with his look. Jess frowned and climbed onto the crate. Emry placed his hands on her waist and assisted her down. As she landed, Emry appeared reluctant to release her. He pulled her into his arms and smiled warmly.

"But since you didn't shoot me, I'll forgive you this time."

Jess smiled with relief and subconsciously ran her hands along his chest. Emry lowered his mouth to hers and was about to kiss her. Jess felt her heart race with anticipation as his lips brushed past hers.

"Emry!" Drake called from across the hold.

Emry hesitated, groaned, and pulled away from Jess as Drake and Conner hurried toward them. Jess had mixed feelings on whether she was happy to see Drake at that particular moment. Drake and Conner looked at the six dead men with shared surprise. Drake glanced back at Emry with a serious look and shook his head.

"You're scary, man."

"There should only be four left," Emry said while fiddling with Jess's rifle.

"Four?" Drake asked. "How do you--"

"Don't ask," Jess said with a groan. "He'll just end up telling you."

Emry collected the assault rifles from the dead men and handed one to Conner and a second one to Drake. Both men accepted the weapons.

"Go back to the cabin with the others and secure the area," Emry said firmly to Drake. "Jess and I are storming the bridge."

Drake appeared surprised and seemed concerned for their safety. "I want to storm the bridge," Drake whined.

Jess suddenly realized Drake wasn't concerned. He was feeling left out!

Emry gave him a matter-of-fact, fatherly glare. "You can storm the bridge next time." Emry reluctantly returned Jess's assault rifle to her and gave her a stern glare. "You're on semi-automatic from here on out." Emry then looked at Drake, indicated the six dead men, and appeared completely serious. "Will you look at the mess she made? Never piss off a woman--"

Emry walked away while carrying his assault rifle and a second one slung over his shoulder. Drake stared at the dead bodies and then looked at Jess with surprise. Jess hid her smile and shrugged innocently. She had to admit, Drake's look was priceless.

Chapter Eight

*T*he once elegant bridge was strewn with blood spatters and the bodies of several crewmembers. The captain lay dead not far from the helm with several bullet holes in his back and his starched white uniform was now soaked with blood. Two men in waiter's uniforms, Brahm and Lester, manned the bridge and carelessly stood over the dead captain with no remorse. Another man in a crewmember's uniform, Hobbs, hurried onto the bridge and stepped over the bodies to join them. He seemed concerned.

"They're dead," Hobbs quickly said to Brahm.

"Who's dead?"

"All of our men."

Brahm suddenly realized the impact of what Hobbs had said and became angry and threatening.

"Go to the engine room and get this floating cemetery running," Brahm ordered. "We can't have a search party finding us before we unload the cargo."

Hobbs nodded and hurried from the bridge. Brahm immediately turned toward Lester with an angered look on his face.

"What the hell is happening here? Did the ship add extra security that I don't know about? This was your department, Lester."

"Whoever killed our men doesn't work for the shipping lane," Lester said defensively. "He has to be acting on his own."

Brahm's foul temper became evident as he glared at Lester. "That makes it even worse. I want him found before he can do anymore damage."

"We'll take care of him, Brahm. Don't worry."

"I am worried," Brahm said with hostility in his eyes. "Do you know what the boss will do to us if something *unforeseen* happens to that cargo?"

"I have a pretty good idea--" Lester muttered. He was about to turn and leave.

"And, Lester--"

He turned and looked back at Brahm.

"Before you kill him, find out what he was doing with that satellite dish we'd shot out. Find out what he knows, and I want to know who he is."

"Sorry, I'm fresh out of business cards," Emry said from behind.

Brahm and Lester turned and attempted to aim their handguns at Emry, who had silently appeared on the bridge behind them. Emry had his assault rifle aimed at them and wore a devious grin.

"Trust me, you really don't want to do that," Emry casually informed them.

Emry's devious, twisted grin reassured them they didn't want to do it either. Brahm and Lester frowned and dropped their weapons. Jess entered the bridge with her own assault rifle aimed at them. Emry expressed playful delight at Jess's presence.

"Ah, my lovely assistant, Consuela," he said charmingly. "Please kick your weapons to her."

Both men appeared disgusted and kicked their guns toward Jess. She eyed Emry with her own humored smile as she collected their weapons.

"Consuela?" Jess admired Emry's playful mood.

Emry seductively raised his brows and retained his boyish grin. "It flows. Con-sue-la," he teased.

Jess smiled at his charm and placed one of the guns down the cleavage of her dress. Emry strained to look without taking his eyes from the men and tried to hide his lustful smile. Brahm and Lester also eyed the weapon down her cleavage. Emry glared his disapproval at both.

"Don't do that," Emry said lowly.

Jess slung the assault rifle over her shoulder and aimed the second gun at them. Emry casually approached the nearby controls while Jess covered them.

"I suppose your friends are on their way to pick up their cargo. Please, don't feel obligated to answer that. That was rhetorical. Unfortunately for you gentlemen, Consuela and I have other plans. When they see the ship's distress flares, they'll realize something went wrong and leave you as a sacrifice."

Hobbs suddenly appeared behind Jess and placed his gun to her head. Jess gasped with surprise. Emry turned with his rifle aimed and tensed at the gun Hobbs held to Jess's head. Emry showed little emotion, almost as if it was just a minor annoyance and nothing to worry him.

"Move away from that switch and drop your weapon," Hobbs said lowly with a frozen expression, "or I scatter Consuela's brains across the bridge."

Jess remained motionless to the gun against her temple and stared at Emry. She knew the seriousness of their situation and that she was dead either way. There was no reason to take Emry down with her.

"Shoot him," Jess whispered softly to Emry.

Emry kept his rifle aimed and was in a standoff with Hobbs. He didn't react to her words even though she knew he heard her. Neither man moved. Emry stared at the gun at Jess's head, frowned with disgust, and tossed his rifle aside. She suddenly felt defeated and alarmed. Had she just killed Emry? Hobbs removed Jess's gun from her hand and the rifle from her shoulder. He then moved the gun away from her head. Hobbs, while standing behind her, hadn't seen the gun handle sticking out of her cleavage. Brahm mocked Emry with a smile as he approached Jess.

"You should have listened to your girlfriend," Brahm remarked.

Brahm looked at the gun down the front of Jess's dress and grinned lustfully.

Emry glared at Brahm and appeared wildly unpredictable. "You don't want to do that," he warned.

Brahm maintained his lustful grin and reached for the gun handle sticking out of Jess's cleavage. Emry suddenly spun into a backwards roundhouse kick, struck Brahm in the head, and knocked him forcibly into Hobbs behind Jess. Emry turned back in the opposite direction and kicked Lester in the chest. Lester was thrown backwards and across the dead captain's body. Jess stared with a shocked look at Emry's sudden explosion of skilled physical violence. Emry threw himself to the floor, snatched his discarded assault rifle, and sat up prepared to fire. Brahm and Hobbs grabbed the other discarded rifle and bolted from the bridge. They narrowly avoided several shots as they ran. Emry lunged for the console and threw the switch for the distress flares. Red flares discharged from the ship and jetted brilliantly into the night sky. Jess grabbed the handgun from the floor and aimed it at Lester, despite his unconscious condition.

"Stay here," Emry ordered then ran from the bridge after the two men.

Emry hurried down the outer steps only moments behind Brahm and Hobbs. Brahm turned and fired at him. Emry leaped over the stairs railing, rolled across deck, and sat up firing. Brahm and Hobbs dove for cover from the barrage of bullets. Emry rolled behind a support beam to the anticipated return fire. They fired feverishly in his direction. Emry waited a moment then fired back at them. His rifle fired once then, to his surprise, clicked empty.

"Ah, hell--"

Brahm and Hobbs remained hidden a moment, realized Emry was out of ammo, and hurried toward the stairs. They jumped into the opening with their weapons aimed. Emry was gone. They uncertainly looked around for him. Emry dropped down on top of Hobbs with his legs around his neck and flipped him as he rode him to the deck. Brahm fired at Emry as he rolled off Hobbs and accidentally shot Hobbs in the leg. Hobbs cried out in agony. Emry catapulted across Hobbs' back, using him as a springboard, leaped through the air, and kicked Brahm in the chest with both feet and amazing force. Brahm struck the railing and his rifle flew overboard. Hobbs aimed his gun at Emry. A bullet suddenly ricocheted near Hobbs' head. Hobbs retreated around the nearby corner. Emry looked at Jess, who stood on the steps with her gun aimed.

"What took you so long?" he demanded to know in all seriousness.

Jess appeared surprised while staring at him. "But you told me to--"

Brahm lunged for Emry. Emry kicked him in the abdomen. As he doubled over, Emry rammed his elbow into his back. Brahm gasped and collapsed to the deck. Jess hurried down the steps to join him. Emry signaled to the corner where Hobbs had retreated. Brahm slowly pulled himself to the railing and clutched a nearby life ring. Emry indicated for Jess to give him her gun. A shot fired behind Jess. She saw the bullet and blood erupt from her right shoulder before she even felt the painful sting from the shot. The gun flew from her hand and across the deck as the force of the shot threw her against Emry. He caught her and, for the first time, appeared alarmed as he stared into her eyes. He looked behind her at Lester, who stood on the steps with his handgun aimed at them.

Jess clutched her bleeding shoulder and stared at the blood between her fingers. She was momentarily stunned or possibly going into shock. Emry hastily removed her hand, looked at the wound, and then replaced her hand to the wound.

He forced her to look into his eyes and whispered softly, "You're okay, I promise. Just stay calm. I need you to trust me."

"I trust you," Jess whispered softly while cringing with pain.

"Hobbs!" Lester called out.

Lester walked down the remaining steps from the bridge. Hobbs slowly appeared from around the corner then relaxed and straightened. Brahm loosened his grip on the life ring near the railing and appeared annoyed.

"Kill them both."

Lester and Hobbs aimed their weapons. Emry suddenly tackled Jess to the deck as both guns fired. He rolled off her with the gun from her cleavage and shot Hobbs as he fired at them. The sound of an assault rifle repeatedly firing echoed loudly. Lester's body jerked and jolted as several shots entered his body. Drake stood on the steps while staring over his assault rifle and watched Lester collapse. Emry sprang to his feet and turned toward Brahm, who leaped for the discarded gun. Emry pulled the trigger. The gun clicked empty. Drake attempted to fire but his rifle jammed. Emry suddenly leaped for Brahm as he fired his weapon. Emry took a shot to the shoulder, but it didn't stop him from taking Brahm and the life ring with him over the railing into the dark water below. Jess and Drake ran for the railing with horrified looks on their faces.

"Emry!" Jess screamed as she attempted to climb over the railing after him despite her wounded shoulder.

Drake grabbed her around the waist and pulled her back. She fought against Drake's hold and attempted to reach the railing.

"Emry!"

Jess continued to scream while fighting Drake's arms around her. Drake held onto her waist in silence and refused to release her. Jess began to sob softly and clung to him. The life ring floated in the water alongside the motionless ship. Neither man surfaced.

✝

*T*wo days had passed. The *Andrea Maria* remained motionless within the calm waters as the warm afternoon sun beat down on her. The six survivors were sedately reclined within lounge chairs on the bridge deck with several empty bottles of alcohol surrounding them. There had been small hope that others had survived and were hiding throughout the ordeal, but an announcement over the intercom despondently revealed no one else was alive. Jess appeared distant while clinging to the life ring she had fished out of the water. She had said very little after Emry had gone overboard. Drake had crudely patched the gunshot wound on her shoulder. Since the bullet had gone straight through, the best he could do was keep the wound clean and dry. Her emotional state concerned him more than her physical injuries.

The remaining four were more than likely drunk. The general mood among them was solemn and quiet. No one ventured inside much. The stench of decaying bodies was already overwhelming even in the corridors where there hadn't been any dead passengers. The air-conditioning had shut down with the engines, allowing the ship's interior to heat up greatly, which accelerated the decaying process. Meals consisted of anything canned and were eaten on deck. Pillows and blankets piled on a vacant lounge chair indicated they were sleeping on deck as well. Carla played with her unkempt hair, appeared depressed over her appearance, and sighed softly as she looked at the others with little enthusiasm.

"I need a shower. Would someone come with me to my cabin?" she asked softly.

No one even looked at Carla let alone responded. There was no enthusiasm to venture inside except for the occasional bathroom break. Carla frowned and returned to playing with her hair. Grant, who was obviously drunk, picked up an empty bottle of whiskey, turned it over, and frowned.

"We're out of whiskey."

"We'll get a couple of bottles on our next trip to the kitchen for more rations," Drake said softly and with little interest. "I need to get fresh bandages for Jess's shoulder anyway."

"My shoulder is fine," Jess said soft but firm.

"Your shoulder is not fine. Let me give you another shot of morphine."

Jess glared at Drake with a "touch me and die" look on her weary, pale face. Drake frowned and looked away so she wouldn't see the tears in his eyes. The sound of a helicopter in the near distance broke through the silence. All six suddenly sat up straight and looked around for the familiar and welcomed sight. Grant leaped up from his chair and ran to the bridge above them. The ship's horn sounded loudly, startling the remaining five on deck. They continued to scan the empty sky. A U.S. Navy helicopter appeared in the distance and rapidly approached. Dana, Carla, Drake, and Conner sprang up from their seats and waved their arms at the approaching helicopter. Jess didn't bother moving from her chair. There was a mixture of relief and shock among them. They couldn't believe the nightmare was finally over.

Chapter Nine

*O*ne month had passed since the six survivors were rescued from the *Andrea Maria*. The talk show studio, "Gabbing with Wendy", was filled with energy as they sat on the studio stage with their energetic host, Wendy. The six survivors were neatly dressed and looked their best for their television interview with Wendy, a perky and attractive African-American woman in her early thirties. The audience applauded after they returned from break.

"For those of you at home just tuning in, we're here live in the studio with the six survivors of the cruise ship, *Andrea Maria*," Wendy said to the television camera as it rolled past her. She looked at the six guests. "Aside from the book, I heard there might be a movie deal in the works. Is there any truth to the rumors?"

Carla appeared to soak in the attention and had the expensive wardrobe and hairstyle to match. She had apparently rebounded nicely after her ordeal and was enjoying her fifteen minutes of fame.

"We've been approached by several movie studios for the rights to our story," Carla said to Wendy then flashed a sexy smile for the camera.

Wendy turned on her chair toward Grant, Conner, and Drake with a more than interested grin at them. "Everyone has their eyes on you three--the heroes in this tragic story. Is it true the three of you took down nearly twenty armed drug cartel hit men?"

Drake was uncomfortable with the fabricated story being told and lacked enthusiasm for the spotlight, but he willingly played along.

"We're not heroes. We were just trying to survive a nightmare, Wendy."

"Drake is being modest," Grant suddenly interrupted and appeared even more interested in the attention than Carla had. "We had the women to think about, which is why we risked our lives to disable the ship and overthrow the men controlling the bridge."

Wendy nodded her head with interest and awe. "I know I'm not alone. Everyone wants to know what happened on the bridge deck dubbed "the battle for *Andrea Maria*"," Wendy said while she studied the six.

"We knew we had to launch the flares to scare off their approaching friends. There was no telling how many armed men we would have faced if they got to us first." Grant gave his best heroic pose. "So Drake, Conner, and I stormed the bridge and took out the last of the armed men. If you want to know the details, you'll have to buy the book."

"The book, *The Battle for Andrea Maria*, should be available in stores in a few months," Wendy cheerfully informed the viewing audience.

Jess sat silently alongside Drake and appeared distant and disinterested with the interview. She was hoping that if she remained quiet, she wouldn't be forced to participate. Wendy finally looked at Jess and appeared curious at her continued silence.

"Jess, we haven't heard from you yet. What was your role in this? Tell us your story."

Jess appeared tense and shifted in her seat while she avoided looking at the camera. She didn't want to be there. Jess clearly didn't want to be anywhere. All eyes in the audience were on her, which didn't help.

"Dana, Carla, and I remained hidden in one of the cabins during the bridge battle," Jess said softly. "I don't really have a story."

Wendy appeared unconvinced and continued to study her. "In the original reports, you narrowly missed the nightclub shooting after leaving with a gentleman, and I'd heard you were in the lounge with him when all hell broke loose. As a matter-of-fact, I believe you had been shot prior to joining Carla and Dana. Tell us what happened."

Jess remained uncomfortable, subconsciously rubbed her right shoulder that appeared to throb in response, and again shifted in her chair.

"I was playing pool with--" Jess was nearly down to tears at the mere thought. She sniffed, attempted to compose herself, and continued, "--with a very wonderful man."

Jess wiped the tears from her eyes and tried to hold it back. Drake offered a timid smile and handed Jess a tissue. She dabbed her eyes and warmly touched his arm. Drake gently caressed her hand on his arm.

"What happened to him?" Wendy asked softly with great sensitivity.

"He, uh, he died saving my life." Jess suddenly broke down and cried softly. "And I never knew anything about him except he was a schoolteacher."

Wendy appeared almost down to tears herself and dabbed the corners of her eyes as well. Her sensitivity to her guests was part of the reason her show was so popular.

"We are so sorry for your loss, Jess," Wendy said softly then looked at the camera and attempted to compose herself. "We will return with more stories from the survivors of the *Andrea Maria* after our break."

†

*F*our weeks later, the six survivors sat in another talk show studio, "Gaining Perspective". Grant and Carla did most of the talking and grandstanded Conner and Dana, who appeared annoyed with them. The tension among the four was becoming more noticeable with each passing day. The tension on stage was nothing compared to their frequent outbursts and catfights backstage. Drake put on a good show in front of the camera, as he settled into his new role of hero, but he kept close watch on Jess, who retained her distant appearance throughout the show. Jess was not herself, and it didn't seem as if she was coming back anytime soon. Physically she had healed, but her emotional wounds were much deeper.

Jess's thoughts often transported her back onboard the *Andrea Maria*. Some days she would be playing pool with Emry, and other times, she would be staring helplessly at the dead woman with a bullet through her eye lying across from her on the nightclub floor. Drake gently nudged Jess. She snapped out of her trance and realized she was sitting on stage before a studio audience. It took her a few seconds to remember where she was and how she got there. She appeared uncomfortable and looked at the show's host, Mort.

"I'm sorry, could you repeat the question?" Jess asked gently.

Mort smiled knowingly. In their short time of touring, this was already becoming Jess's trademark catchphrase. Talk show hosts and reporters knew Jess was never really among them and relied on Drake to bring her back to reality.

†

𝒪t was nine weeks later, and the survivors were touring in another city. Fans lined up outside the studio for the talk show "What's New". The crowd of fans clung to various magazines, which all featured the six survivors on the covers. Grant and Carla were plastered front and center on every magazine cover and appeared to be the main draw. As the six arrived, fans waiting for autographs and photos swarmed them. Jess appeared unenthusiastic but signed the magazines thrust in front of her by overzealous fans. Despite her dispassion for the spotlight, the fans still gravitated toward her. Jess didn't know how much more of the attention she could handle. She suddenly felt weak and had trouble focusing. Reporters shouted questions, cameras flashed, and the fans continued to wave magazines while cheering for them. Jess appeared overwhelmed, turned toward Drake several feet away from her, and clutched her head.

"Drake--"

He didn't hear her weak cry. Drake was extremely polite to his fans and smiled cheerfully while signing everything they put in front of him and even posed for pictures with them. Jess looked at the swarm of fans surrounding her while holding her head. The crowd began to spin. A man with a press badge and baseball cap took her hand, placed his arm securely around her waist, and pulled her through the crowd toward a security guard posted at the studio door. Jess didn't even remember walking with the reporter, who nearly held her up, let alone how she got to the door. The security guard spoke to the reporter, but his voice sounded garbled and unrecognizable to Jess.

"Take her inside," the reporter with a Russian accent told the security guard.

The security guard took Jess from the reporter. She leaned heavily on him as he helped her through the back door and away from the crowd. Jess no longer knew where she was. She clung to the security guard to keep from falling down. Drake looked around and realized Jess was gone. He saw the security guard hurrying Jess into the studio and frantically pushed through the crowd toward the building.

"Jess!"

Chapter Ten

*J*ess stood alone on the bridge deck of the *Andrea Maria* in her dirty, black dress and looked around with bewilderment. Where was everyone? A chilling nighttime breeze blew past her. Jess rubbed her bare arms, gasped painfully, and pulled her bloodied hand away from the gunshot wound on her shoulder. She stared at the torn, bleeding wound with horror. Jess quickly turned toward the railing and looked into the dark waters below.

"Emry!"

There was no response. The life ring gently lapped on the water alongside the motionless ship. Jess turned and ran along the deck in her bare feet covered in blood. She threw open a door and immediately stopped. She stood in the doorway to the empty lounge. Everything was so quiet. The distinct sound of billiard balls clinking broke the silence. Jess looked at the pool table. Emry straightened with his pool stick in his hand, looked at her, and smiled. Jess stared at him. He was alive! Somehow, he had survived being shot and falling overboard. Jess hurried toward him, threw her arms around his neck, and clung to him.

She sobbed softly into his neck. "Oh, Emry, I missed you so much!"

His arms tightened around her as he held her against him. For a moment, she felt complete bliss. The world was as it should be.

"Why did you do it, Jess?" he asked in a low, demanding tone as she clung to him. "You lied about what happened on the bridge. You sold out my memory."

Jess was overwhelmed with guilt, clutched his jacket, and sobbed harder. "I didn't mean to, Emry," she sobbed. "Drake and I checked the passenger list, but you weren't on it. You didn't exist. We didn't know what to do. I didn't want the attention without you. I'm sorry we listened to Grant and did it his way!"

His jacket was wet in her hand. His entire body now felt cold and damp while pressed against her. Jess uncertainly pulled back and looked at him. His body was badly decomposed and saturated with seawater. Emry stared at her with anger in his dead eyes.

"You're going to pay for what you stole from me. All of you will pay."

Emry clutched her throat and pushed her back against the pool table. She fought his hand but couldn't force herself to harm him.

"Emry, please, don't--"

Jess suddenly woke with a gasp. She looked around the quiet, unfamiliar room. She lay on the leather sofa within the elegant, studio lounge. Drake sat on the edge of the sofa alongside her and gently patted her hand. He smiled warmly and was relieved she was finally awake. Jess slowly sat up on the sofa and looked around with disorientation.

"What happened?"

"I think you forgot to eat again this morning," Drake said gently even though it was evident the stress was adding to her depression. "I'm going to get you tea and one of those muffins from the buffet table over there. You just stay here and take it easy, okay? I'll be right back."

Jess uncertainly nodded and ran trembling fingers through her hair. She sniffed softly as Drake poured her a cup of tea from the table across the room.

"He was here," Jess said softly.

Drake approached with a cup of tea and a muffin. He set them on the coffee table before her and sat on the sofa alongside her.

"Who?"

"Emry. I heard his voice. He spoke to me," she said softly. A tiny smile crossed her face as a tear rolled down her cheek. "Did you see him?"

Drake placed his arm around her shoulder and held her to his side. He was worried that Jess was starting to lose her sanity.

"I'm sorry, Jess. He's not coming back. We had no business changing the story like that. I've been having nightmares about him too. It's guilt over what we took away from his memory."

The lounge door opened and startled Drake. He released Jess and quickly wiped the tears from his face. He handed her the muffin, stood, and headed for the coffeepot as Dana and Carla entered the lounge. They were arguing as usual. Drake carried his cup of coffee to a nearby chair and collapsed into it. He watched Jess pick at her muffin. Drake didn't like her weight loss or her ashen complexion. She rarely ate and never smiled anymore.

"Oh, go to hell," Dana said hotly while avoiding Carla as she stormed across the room.

"If what few fans you have could hear you now," Carla said while following her across the room. "Not quite the angel they think you are. Maybe you should mention your sexual romp with Drake in your next interview. Might make you seem less boring to the viewers."

Drake listened to Carla's comment and rolled his eyes. Jess sat on the sofa holding her cup of tea while staring blankly at the tiny tealeaves on the bottom of the cup. Drake finally looked back at Jess while slumped in his chair near her with his fist to his temple. Carla and Dana moved to the corner to continue their argument, as was their usual warm up before every public appearance. Grant and Conner entered the lounge just moments after Carla and Dana. Both were laughing and joking around like old friends. At least they were getting along better in recent weeks.

"Did you see the one with the thong?" Conner asked with cheap grin on his face.

"I'm definitely getting some phone numbers today," Grant said with a chuckle.

Grant approached the bar, poured a glass of whiskey despite the morning hour, and then looked at Jess on the sofa huddled over her cup of tea. He approached and sat on the coffee table before her. She barely looked at him and that arrogant face she had come to hate. He talked to her as if she was a child. He looked at her as if she was a child. Emry would never have allowed him to treat her this way. She started to wonder why she allowed it.

"What's with you?" Grant asked. "We're famous. You should be enjoying yourself."

"Leave her alone, Grant," Drake muttered and appeared even less tolerant today.

Drake tried, she thought. Why wasn't she trying? Why was she allowing him to talk to her like this? She felt as if she was screaming and no one was listening to her. She had been in a fog since Emry went overboard. She initially blamed the gunshot wound and then the dreaded morphine Drake injected into her, causing her to have little memory and horrible hallucinations during the two days that followed. It was now four months later, and she still wasn't right.

Jess suddenly realized Grant was still sitting before her and had been talking the entire time. She didn't even know what he had said.

"Those people out there want to hear from us, Jess, all of us. That's what they're paying us for," Grant told her firmly. "They want to hear your story."

Jess finally heard what he was saying and glared at him. She wanted to punch him in his arrogant face. She wanted to tell him how much she hated him. Her anger continued to build inside her. Emry wouldn't have allowed this. He would have put Grant in his place as he did so many times onboard. Jess's look suddenly turned cold and hateful. The fog she was in had finally lifted.

"My story?" she scoffed with a slightly unsettling laugh. "That's a good one."

Grant appeared uncomfortable by her comment and knew exactly what she meant by it. The way she suddenly came to life possibly startled him more.

"Don't start with that. We all agreed to do it this way. He never wanted any credit and neither did you. It's too late to change the story now."

Jess suddenly lurched forward, tossing her teacup carelessly onto the table near him, startling him. The anger was evident in her eyes. It was a look only Drake had seen before.

"I know that, Grant," Jess hissed lowly, "but you're prancing around like some sort of rock star! You can play it up to the media, but don't pull that shit with me. I was there. I *know* what happened!"

Carla and Dana suddenly fell silent and were now staring at Jess and her sudden outburst. Drake was also surprised. She had been in a state of grief and silence so long; they forgot with whom they were dealing and what she had done to ensure their survival.

"Okay," Grant said defensively. "You're stressed, I get it." He moved closer and attempted a more soothing tone. "They love you, Jess. They love your *Romeo and Juliet* tragic love story."

"No, Grant, you don't get it," Jess snapped with the fire still in her eyes. "I don't want to be the *Romeo and Juliet* of the *Andrea Maria*, and I don't want the fame!"

It was as if she spoke some foreign language Grant couldn't comprehend. Grant stared at her with a surprised look on his face.

"How can you not want the fame?"

Dana casually folded her arms over her chest and glared at him from across the room. Dana never started the fights, but she enjoyed adding fuel to the fire.

"I think she's trying to say that some of us are enjoying their fame a little more than others."

Carla suddenly glared at Dana with irritation. "Hey, it's not my fault I'm the hot one of the party," Carla said boldly and gave her a snobby, quick once over. "A makeover wouldn't hurt you."

"Oh, give it a rest!" Dana suddenly shouted as she turned.

They were now in each other's faces and the shouting match had begun. The war between them was about to erupt.

"Look out," Grant said with a humored smile. "The catfight is about to begin."

Conner quickly moved into the center of the lounge and attempted to smooth things over. Being peacekeeper seemed to be his full-time job these days.

"Okay, okay! Everybody just needs to relax," Conner said gently. "We've been on every talk show and magazine cover for four months straight. There has been a lot of pressure on all of us. Maybe we should cancel next week's appearances and just take it easy. Soak up a little sun. Get a little shit-faced. Have a little fun."

"Are you insane?" Carla said hotly. "If we leave the spotlight, we may never get it back."

"I'm with Carla," Grant said firmly and moved away from Jess while shaking the spilled tea from his hand. "I've been getting movie offers. I'm not giving this up. We agreed to tour for six months--all of us together." Grant glared at Jess. "That's the deal."

Drake suddenly came to life with his own hostility, glared at Grant, and sat up straight in his chair.

"Or what, Grant? You'll tell on us? Be my guest." Drake jumped to his feet and flung his arms around wildly as he often did when his adrenaline rose. "Go on, tell everyone all you did was whine and cower while Jess covered the back of the real hero."

"You're just pissed because I'm getting offers and you're not."

"No, I'm pissed because my best friend is under a lot of stress and the rest of you only care about who's offering what and for how much. We're not heroes. We're survivors. The real hero died saving our asses!"

Everyone now stared at Drake, including Jess. No one, apart from Jess, had ever heard Drake explode. Drake looked at Jess with little emotion. She was suddenly very proud of her friend.

"Come on, Jess. We're going home."

Jess jumped to her feet and approached Drake without question or protest. Drake took her hand and pulled her from the lounge behind him. The others stared after them with shared looks of shock.

Chapter Eleven

Seven weeks had passed since the talk show tours abruptly ended. The small, charming farm town of Luxington was the prime example of quintessential America. It boasted itself as the friendliest town in America. People greeted one another as they passed, women talked over white, picket fences, and kids chased after the ice cream truck. There was a plaque boldly displayed in the center of town, which read, "Hometown of *Andrea Maria* heroes, Drake Stanton and Jess Colten". Within the police station, the bullpen was more of a collection of neatly dressed country boys and girls then a police force. They had little more to do than drink coffee and eat doughnuts between writing out parking tickets to tractors and helping farmers catch escaped cattle.

In a quaint corner office, the charming county sheriff, Sheriff Stone, sat behind his desk with his cowboy boots propped on the desktop. He was a handsome man in his early thirties with more charm then any one man should have. If his flowing, golden-brown hair begging to be rumpled didn't charm a person, his brilliant smile and dazzling blue eyes would certainly do the trick. Despite his popularity, good looks, and charm, Sheriff Stone wasn't nearly as innocent as he pretended to be. His reputation was well-established among the good folks in town. Everyone knew his reputation and few wanted to get on his bad side. Sheriff Stone held the phone to his ear while throwing darts at the dartboard. He showed little enthusiasm for the caller on the other end.

"I know it's a nuisance, Mrs. Feldman," Sheriff Stone said pleasantly, "but if your husband wants to go fishing tomorrow, there's really nothing from a legal standpoint--" The phone clicked. Sheriff

Stone smirked charmingly to no one in particular. "Have a nice day," he said to the dead line and hung up the phone.

He threw another dart at the board and hit dead center. All the darts were grouped close to center. He obviously had too much time on his hands to perfect his game.

"Becky!"

"Yes, Sheriff?" came the female voice from somewhere beyond the office.

"Screen all future calls from Mrs. Feldman!"

"Yes, Sheriff," Becky replied.

Jess appeared in the open doorway and tapped on the open door. She finally looked more like her old self and not as if she had been put through several months of touring through hell. Sheriff Stone looked at Jess, grinned, and quickly sprang to his feet.

"Good morning, Jess," Stone said cheerfully and with a little too much enthusiasm. "Come in. Have a seat. Can I get you some coffee? Better yet, why don't we head over to the diner--"

Jess gave him an unimpressed glare but maintained a tiny smile. She wasn't taken in by his charm or his boyish good looks.

"Cut the crap and stop kissing my ass."

She approached his desk and flopped into the seat before it. Jess was definitely back to her old self. Stone shrugged casually, not the least bit surprised by her attitude, and collapsed back into his own chair.

"Get your own damned coffee then." His charming smile quickly returned as he studied her. "What can I do for you today-- that doesn't involve expunging your name from the town square plaque?"

Jess frowned with displeasure to his beating her to the punch. "Sheriff--"

"Acht," Stone lectured and pointed a dart at her. "What did I tell you about that?"

Jess rolled her eyes and groaned lowly. "*Mayor* Stone," she said reluctantly, "I don't want my name splattered all over town like I'm some sort of celebrity."

"Sorry, Jess, you are some sort of celebrity. Our little town has three claims to fame. You, Drake, and "Anna's Homemade Pies, Jams, and Scented Soaps"."

"Come on, Sheriff--Mayor." Jess caught her fumble.

Sheriff Stone had been impossible to live with since he won the election and became mayor of Luxington. The fact that he was the only candidate didn't deter his ego from inflating any, and the only perk to the non-paying position of mayor was free coffee at the diner.

"I survived a nightmare. Stop punishing me."

"I'm sorry if you're unhappy with your celebrity status, but there's nothing as Mayor, or Sheriff, that I can do about that. It's only been six months. It'll wear off." Stone playfully spun the dart in his hand, as if attempting to impress her. "You know how this town is. Tomorrow it'll be something else. I should know. I'm usually the prime target for gossip around here." He flashed a grin and suggestively raised his brows. "You know that." He was a little too proud of his tarnished reputation.

"Yes, I'm familiar with your reputation."

"You want my advice?"

He looked at her as if waiting for her to say that she did. She hated listening to Sheriff Stone's "prehistoric caveman" advice. He was extremely old-fashioned for a man his age. Some women in town found it refreshing and endearing. Jess found it annoying.

"Get married and have half a dozen kids. Once you're off the market, things will quiet down." Stone leaned forward in his chair, played with the dart in his hand, and grinned charmingly. "So how about Friday night?"

"You're really not helping."

Sheriff Stone had taken a romantic interest in Jess since she graduated high school, but he had stepped up his "wooing" since the *Andrea Maria* tragedy. In fact, she had a lot potential suitors since her survival tale and tragic love story came out. She would cringe every time she received fan mail addressed to "Juliet". It seemed there was an endless supply of "Romeos" wanting to whisk her away. She wished that would wear off as well.

"Most people would love to be in your shoes. Money, fame, and youth are quite the combination. You should take advantage of it like the others. Drake started dating that actress from the city. Never would've landed someone like her otherwise. That Grant guy is filming his first lead role this summer, and I caught Carla in *Playboy*--"

Stone suddenly cleared his throat, appeared slightly embarrassed, and smiled timidly. His good old boy, country cop reputation certainly didn't allow him to admit he'd ever even looked at a girly magazine. Jess figured his mother would probably chase him around the house with a yardstick if she had ever heard him admit that he had.

"Aside from dating the sheriff slash mayor of Luxington," he teased with a grin, "there must be some dream that this tragedy could bring you."

Jess stood with little enthusiasm and frowned. "Thanks anyway, Sheriff."

"What happened to Mayor?" Stone asked with disappointment. "Are you done with him?"

"Yeah, between us, he's a bit of a prick," Jess said and flashed a teasing smile.

"Oh, now that's cold," Stone teased.

She had called him worse plenty of times but never meant anything by it. Jess turned and gave a tiny wave as she left his office. Stone's eyes strayed to her backside and admired the view as she walked away.

"What about Friday night?" Stone suddenly called after her with a grin on his face.

†

*I*t was late evening. The wealthy city neighborhood was lined with several expensive homes, each with tall gates and immaculately landscaped lawns. Grant's home was no exception. He had made a fortune off the cruise line and his story. The others had done well themselves, but Grant milked his fame for every cent it was worth. Grant's red Ferrari pulled up to the elegant home along the cobblestone, circular driveway. Grant jumped out of the car, gave it an admiring glance, picked off a speck of dust, and hurried into the mansion. Grant entered the massive, marble foyer, locked the door behind him, and turned toward the state of art alarm system. The alarm was pulled away from the wall. He appeared concerned and looked around the dimly lit hallway. Everything was quiet. The quietness disturbed him most. Grant hurried to the foyer closet and removed a baseball bat. He cautiously walked along the hall while clinging to the bat and paused before the open study door.

The study lights came on to reveal Grant holding his baseball bat in the open doorway. As he stared into the study, his expression dropped. Items were scattered everywhere within the ransacked study. All of the desk drawers were pulled from the desk, papers were thrown everywhere, pictures were pulled from the walls, and books were carelessly tossed from their shelves. He appeared annoyed, shook his head with disgust, and removed his cell phone as he approached the desk.

"911--what's your emergency?" a woman's voice was heard on the other end.

Grant was about to speak when he suddenly stopped and stared at the desk with more concern than annoyance. The *Andrea Maria* movie script lay open on the desk with a knife stuck through one of the pages. The page read, "EXT. BRIDGE DECK". Grant suddenly appeared alarmed and looked around the room.

Chapter Twelve

It was two days later. Jess's elegant plantation style home sat on an immaculately landscaped lawn nestled on a large parcel of land. The estate included a large horse barn, several fenced pastures, and horses grazing on the lush grass by moonlight. Between her settlement with the cruise line and what she had been paid for her tragic love story, she had done well for herself. It was nearly one o'clock in the morning. Jess sat on the old porch swing in her tank top and sleep shorts with her legs curled up beneath her and a cup of hot tea in her hand. Her tank top clearly revealed both of her scars. The one on her arm that Emry stitched had healed nicely. The exit wound scar on her right, front shoulder was unsightly from several days of improper healing prior to professional treatment. She stared out across her farm and the outline of grazing horses while smiling with a look of contentment. The peaceful farm was exactly what she needed to pull her life together after the tragedy.

The crisp, fall night was perfect for sitting on the porch, especially since Jess couldn't sleep *again*. She had many sleepless nights, and when she did sleep, she had nightmares about the *Andrea Maria* and Emry's death. Some nights she saved him from falling overboard, but most nights, he just plummeted into a dark, watery grave. Despite her new, quiet life, not a day went by that she didn't think about Emry. It seemed almost insane that a man she knew less than eight hours could affect her life so deeply.

Jess's black and white, Tobiano paint horse stood near the fence and watched her on the porch. The horse snickered at her. He was probably wondering if it was feeding time. She smiled and shook her head. Out of the corner of her eye, she swore she saw something move past the third-story, barn loft window. Jess stared at the third-story window a moment longer, appeared curious, and moved off her porch swing. She set her tea down and picked up a military sword propped against the wall near the swing. She slipped into her sandals and walked toward the barn. Her horse again snickered at her. Jess slowly entered the barn and turned on the interior lights. The massive barn consisted of a wide, concrete aisle, eight elegant box stalls on each side, a tack room on the right, and a wash block on the left. Jess walked along the aisle toward the stairs in the back leading to the second floor loft. Headlights suddenly moved past the open barn door and the sound of a car was heard on the gravel driveway. Jess suddenly became concerned to her late night visitor and quickly headed from the barn.

Sheriff Stone's police blazer pulled up to the house. Jess walked out of the barn and saw Stone getting out of his vehicle. She was dismayed to see him here this late. He never stopped by her place at such a late hour. Sheriff Stone looked at the barn, noticed her, and approached as she headed toward him and the house. Jess was suddenly conscious of her worn, revealing tank top with no bra and her sleep shorts that were thin and floppy. Stone immediately noticed her casual sleep attire as well and stared a moment longer than he should have as she approached him. He noticed the sword she carried with her then became concerned.

"Is everything okay?" Stone asked.

"Yes, Sheriff, everything is fine. What brings you out here at this hour?"

"Just making rounds. I didn't expect you to be up so late," he announced.

"Just my usual cruise ship nightmares."

Jess wasn't buying his story about just making rounds. His usual rounds consisted of parking in his speed trap on Morgan Hill and sleeping until a call came in. Luxington was a boring town at night. Most residence didn't even lock their doors. His expression suggested there was more of a reason for his visit.

"What *really* brings you out here at this hour, Sheriff?" she again asked.

Jess could feel Stone's eyes on her thin tank top that undoubtedly revealed her nipples poking through. It was the only reason she could think for him to stare as he had. She insecurely placed her arm across her chest to cover herself.

Stone appeared tense after being caught staring and gently cleared his throat. "Someone broke into Drake's house tonight."

Jess appeared alarmed and allowed her arm to fall down to her side. Stone's eyes immediately strayed back to her tank top.

"Drake wasn't supposed to be home tonight," Jess said with surprise. "He told me he was staying in the city with Ivy at her place."

Jess felt his gaze upon her chest. She snapped her fingers to get his focus back on business. He snapped out of his perverse trance and met her gaze.

"He wasn't home when it happened. His silent alarm went off, and we were called. His study was trashed, but nothing seemed to be missing far as we can tell. I was worried about you alone out here and thought I'd check on you."

"I suppose I should start locking my doors at night, huh?" Jess muttered.

Stone glared his disapproval and slowly shook his head. "Yeah, maybe you ought to. You should probably invest in a shotgun too, because that dull wall ornament ain't cutting through paper."

Jess eyed the sword she held and frowned. He was right, of course. She had developed a slight fear of guns after being shot. Some days she could almost feel the sting of the bullet ripping through her shoulder.

"Now if you don't mind, I'm gonna have a look around out here," Stone said firmly then turned official on her. "I'd consider it a personal favor if you made sure your doors and windows were locked."

"Yes, Sheriff," Jess said with a tiny, embarrassed smile. "And thank you."

Sheriff Stone's charming smile once more returned. "Anytime, Jess."

✝

It was three o'clock in the morning. Jess's master bedroom was elegantly decorated with hand-carved furniture boasting a large, canopy bed and a huge, stone fireplace. Double glass doors led to the second floor balcony. The outside lights and moonlight provided natural lighting within the large bedroom. Jess slept restlessly beneath the covers. It was obvious she was having another nightmare. A faint thump sounded from somewhere downstairs. Jess slowly woke but was not sure why. She stirred slightly and nuzzled her pillow. Another thump was more clearly heard from downstairs. Jess opened her eyes, appearing alarmed, and quickly sat up in bed. She listened a moment and appeared curious.

Jess walked down the wide, elegant staircase in a short, satin robe with the sword clutched in her right hand and her cell phone in the other. She avoided calling Sheriff Stone, since she wasn't exactly sure what she had heard. Maybe some animal had gotten into the house. She didn't need Sheriff Stone storming into her house with his guns a blazing over some stray cat. She paused at the bottom of the stairs and strained to see down the dimly lit hallway.

A commotion was heard further down the grand hallway followed by a loud crash. It sounded as if it came from the study. It certainly wasn't a stray cat making that sound. Jess fumbled with her cell phone and again looked down the hall. An intruder suddenly appeared and knocked her to the floor as he ran for the door. Her sword and cell phone slid across the hall. Jess moved to her knees and reached for the sword as the intruder ran out the front door. The sword was suddenly kicked away by another man who now stood over her. Jess gasped with alarm, spun on her backside, and swept his legs out from under him. The man crashed to the floor. Jess moved to her knees and attempted to reach for the sword. The man tackled her to the floor and landed on top of her. Jess swiftly kicked him in the groin. He groaned and fell off her.

Jess jumped on him and tried to punch him. He caught her wrist, flipped her to the floor, and was again on top of her. He pinned her wrists down and was only inches from her face. Jess fought and thrashed against him from her compromising position beneath him. He finally subdued her enough to keep her from thrashing. She breathed heavily beneath the man, gathered her strength, and plotted her next move.

"You are scary sexy, Consuela," Emry said softly from his position on top of her.

Jess stopped struggling and looked at the man's face in the dim lighting only inches from hers. It felt as if her heart stopped.

"Emry?" Jess suddenly gasped.

Her heart began racing in her chest as she stared, unable to speak, at the man on top of her. In the dim lighting, it looked as if it could be him. She was sure she was awake and this wasn't just another one of her dreams, but it didn't seem possible. She'd spent the last six months convincing herself he was dead.

"I know you're probably mad about the whole dead thing, but please don't kick me in my sensitive area again. I might take it personally."

Emry slowly released Jess's wrists and moved off her and onto his knees alongside her. Jess slowly sat up, stared at him through the dim lighting, and uncertainly moved to her knees before him.

"I know you probably hate me--"

Jess couldn't believe he was here. She couldn't believe he was alive! Her heart was pounding and her thoughts were racing. For a moment, she was unable to move and could only stare. Jess suddenly threw her arms around Emry's neck and kissed him passionately while nearly knocking him to the floor. Emry appeared surprised but returned the passionate kiss without hesitation. Jess attempted to undress him without even thinking about it. Emry suddenly broke off the kiss and stopped her from slipping him out of his jacket.

"I didn't come here to seduce you."

"I believe I'm seducing you," she said teasingly.

Jess again kissed him with a passion and aggression she had never experienced before--at least not from her end. Emry briefly returned the kiss as she melted against him and again tried to undress him. Emry groaned softly and once more stopped her. Jess remained ready to pounce and refused to release him as her hands firmly caressed his body. He attempted to pry her gently off him, but she was lustfully persistent. He finally stopped her hands from traveling his body and gave her a serious look.

"There can never be anything between us, Jess. It has to be that way."

Jess stared at him with some surprise. She couldn't believe what he was telling her. Why did it have to be that way? She uncertainly released him and slid away while staring at him.

✝

A few minutes later, Jess sat at the island counter within the large, no-frills modern kitchen and studied Emry as he leaned on the opposite side. She still couldn't believe she was looking at him, and he was standing in her kitchen. Despite his tense and withdrawn appearance, he looked good to her. She had to keep from pouncing on him. She wanted to pounce on him. He needed a good pouncing, this she was positive.

"After I'd heard about the break-in at Grant's house, I needed to make sure you were safe. I had to be certain what happened to Grant wasn't related to the attack on the ship. After stopping that man from trashing your study and hearing about the break-in at Drake's house tonight, I'm even more concerned it's connected somehow."

Emry avoided looking at her despite her conscious effort to leave her robe open. Unlike with Sheriff Stone, she wanted Emry to look.

She wanted him to be turned on, but he wasn't playing along. Then something he said suddenly sank in.

Jess appeared bewildered. "You didn't just arrive, did you?"

"No, I've been hanging out in your barn loft for the last couple of days."

That's what she had seen in the loft window. Was he watching her on those sleepless nights while she sat on the porch? A realization began setting in.

"You never intended to tell me you were here, did you? If it hadn't been for that man breaking into my home, I never would have known you were here."

Emry stared blankly at the counter and didn't respond. Who was this man? Jess was no longer sure. He looked like Emry, but it couldn't be him.

Jess frowned and nodded. "I see." She avoided looking at him. Her mind was racing in a thousand different directions.

"I followed the media craze surrounding the *Andrea Maria* and your account of what happened between us." Emry finally looked at her. "You turned a Greek tragedy into a romantic illusion. We survived a night of hell together. That's not a love story, Jess. You don't even know me. You have no idea who I am."

She looked up and met his gaze. She was starting to believe he might be right. "So tell me who you are."

She needed him to tell her something. Her urge to pounce on him was diminishing and her hostility was growing rapidly. It was as if he was going out of his way to make her hate him. She paused to consider. Was he?

"The people who want me dead make those on the *Andrea Maria* look like choirboys. If they found me here, they wouldn't hesitate to hurt you to get to me. Trust me, that's more than you need to know."

"So that's it?" Her rage continued to grow, and her look became unpredictable. "You're leaving and there's nothing I can do about it?"

"I'll stick around for a few days in case that intruder comes back, but then I have to go." He hesitated and gave her a serious look. "You need to forget about me and get on with your life."

She stared at him for a long, uncomfortable moment then looked away and appeared defeated. She frowned and slowly nodded.

"You're absolutely right," she said gently.

Jess suddenly bolted up from her chair, which flew to the floor with a loud crash, and glared at Emry with rage in her eyes.

"Get out! Get out of my house and out of my life! I can take care of myself! And if you ever set foot in my home again, I'll shoot you myself!"

Emry remained silent and stared at her while showing little emotion to her outburst.

"That's a good girl," Emry said gently with a tiny, sad smile.

Chapter Thirteen

$\mathcal{I}$t was six months later and nearly a year since the tragic events onboard the *Andrea Maria*. Two horses were tied to the old-style hitching post outside Jess's barn. One was the tall paint gelding, and the other was a stocky, Dun gelding. Jess was almost finished saddling the two horses when a brand-new, black Mustang convertible pulled up to the house. Jess and both horses looked at the sports car. Drake got out of the car and suavely approached. He was dressed in an expensive, fashionable suit with a million dollar smile and sunglasses to match. He removed his expensive sunglasses as he stopped near her and the horses.

"Am I early or are you late?" Drake asked with humor and enthusiasm.

"Both." Jess eyed his fancy attire with a sly smirk on her face. "Are you actually riding like that?"

Drake eyed his expensive wardrobe, gave his best male model pose, and spun for her while flashing a charming smile. He seemed to have more than his share of self-confidence since their rescue.

"You like?"

Jess casually leaned on the horse's rump and gave him an approving once over.

"You look very handsome, but not practical for horseback riding. You look like an Italian mobster."

"Damn, I was going for British spy." Drake grinned. "Don't worry. I have a change of clothes in my bag. It'll only take me a minute to change. I wanted to pop in and say g'day to Jeeves anyway."

"Please don't call him that, Drake," Jess said with disapproval. "Ridley is my house manager. Show him the proper respect he deserves. I'd be very upset if he found an excuse to leave."

"House manager? Translation--butler. Ergo--Jeeves," Drake teased with enthusiasm.

"If he spits in your iced tea, don't cry to me," she said casually and patted the stocky horse's rump.

Drake's grin suddenly faded to a look of surprise. "He spits in my iced tea? But he's so--so proper." He flashed a teasing smile and laughed. "Okay, I won't call him Jeeves, but if he's wearing an apron and holding a feather duster, all bets are off."

Drake walked back to his car, removed an overnight bag, and headed into the house. Jess sighed, moved to the horse's head, and playfully petted its nose.

"And that's what happens when Drake gets laid too much," she said to the horse.

The horse snickered softly as if agreeing.

✝

*J*ess and Drake rode along the well-groomed trail in the woods. It was a perfect day for an afternoon ride. The woods were peaceful with only the sound of the leather saddles breaking the silence. Drake tied the reins around the saddle horn and leaned back onto the horse's rump with his hands clasped over his abdomen. The stocky gelding was as calm and mellow as any horse could be. Drake looked up at the clear sky above the treetops and sighed.

"Now this is the life," Drake said to Jess. "Total freedom."

"If I had known sleeping with an actress would make you this mellow, I would have gotten you one years ago."

Jess hid her humored smile as she glanced back at him. Drake sat up straight but didn't bother untying the reins from around the saddle horn. He appeared preoccupied and deep in thought.

"I sometimes wake in the middle of the night with a horrible feeling that this is all going to end," Drake said in a serious tone. His playful smile quickly returned and he shrugged. "Then I roll over, make love to my hot girlfriend, and go back to sleep."

Jess shook her head with a groan and kept her smile hidden. She didn't want to encourage him anymore than she already had. He was already a handful.

"Fame and fortune hasn't changed you any. You're still a dirty pervert."

"Yes, but I went from sex monthly to sex daily. I've been flying high since I met Ivy six months ago." His look once again turned serious. "The guys at the tavern said I'd never get someone like Ivy before the *Andrea Maria*. Do you think that's true?"

Despite all of his perceived self-confidence, Drake still sought reassurance. The fame and fortune *hadn't* changed him at all. He was still the self-conscious little boy he had always been, and Jess loved him just the way he was.

"They're just jealous, Drake. You may not have met Ivy before your fame, but that doesn't mean she wouldn't have found you attractive."

"You always know what to say, Jess."

Drake felt better. Jess was always his balance, which was why they remained best friends for so long.

"I'm starving. How about some lunch? My treat," Jess said cheerfully.

Drake suddenly glared at her on the trail ahead of him with a concerned look on his face. "You're not thinking about lunch at the tavern?"

"Yep."

"Crossing Victor Raymour's property?" Drake asked with noted concern.

"It's the fastest route."

It was obvious she had an ulterior motive for the sudden decision and choice of lunch spots. Drake appeared tense and not particularly pleased about cutting across Victor Raymour's property.

"Why do you hate me?"

Jess turned her horse onto the neatly groomed trail on the right. A "no trespassing" sign was clearly visible on a tree. The sign had a perceived bullet hole through it. Drake stared at the sign with a grimace as he passed and appeared almost sickened. Victor Raymour's mansion was visible beyond the woods. It was nestled on a well-groomed parcel of land with decorative stonewalls meant to keep out people. Victor was a very wealthy man. He was a very wealthy man who didn't appreciate anyone on or near his property. Rumors around town made Victor out to be some mobster, but Jess doubted it. He didn't dress well enough, in her opinion. As Drake and Jess rode along the trail in the woods, Drake looked around with increasing tension. Jess appeared unusually calm and relaxed. The sound of a four-wheeler cut through the silence and sent fear through Drake.

"Oh, that can't be good," Drake muttered while he nervously looked around.

As they rounded the curve in the trail, a well-dressed, ruggedly handsome man with dark hair sat casually sideways on the four-wheeler. Jess and Drake stopped their horses. Brody Kroft was handsome but intimidating. His build was somewhat impressive, although more athletic than muscular. His quiet, cold disposition sent fear through Drake but provoked Jess to taunt him. Drake nervously chewed his finger and waited for what would happen next. Jess smiled at the intimidating man and showed little concern to his harsh, cold stare.

"Well, good afternoon, Brody," Jess said almost too pleasantly.

Brody offered no response or emotion. He instead pointed to a sign near him on a tree, which read, "no trespassing". He then indicated the sign below it, which read, "trespassers will be shot". Jess appeared ready for the confrontation and removed her jacket to reveal her white tank top, which read, "town celebrity". The gunshot scarring on her shoulder was visibly noticeable. Drake stared at the printing on her tank top with concern as his mouth fell open.

"Oh, boy--" Drake muttered.

Jess turned her horse and revealed more writing on the back of the tank top. The bullet entrance wound scar was much smaller. The words on the back of her tank top read, "kiss my ass, Brody". She turned her horse in his direction and smirked. She was pleased with herself. Brody and Jess glared at each another in a long, nerve-racking silence. Jess loved the challenge that was Brody. He was fun to taunt. In her mind, they were playing a game, and she intended to win. Every day he didn't kill her was probably considered a win. Drake couldn't take any more of the chilling staring contest between them.

"This might be a good time to mention Sheriff Stone's unhealthy attraction for Jess and his slightly tarnished reputation," Drake suddenly said in an attempt to keep them from being shot.

Jess still didn't move or look away from Brody. Brody suddenly frowned, turned forward on the four-wheeler, and drove away. Drake was finally able to breathe. He glared at Jess with limited patience.

"Seriously? You had a tee shirt printed special just to piss off Brody? He's going to do a lot more than spit in your iced tea."

†

The local tavern sat in the middle of nowhere on some back, unmarked dirt road. It was a single story building with a dirt parking lot and an old hitching post along the far end of the building. Neon signs from decades past were the only indication that this was a bar and not someone's hunting cabin. There were several pick-up trucks parked out front despite the early afternoon hour. The two horses were tied to the post. The inside of the tavern was even more rustic than the outside. It was truly nostalgic with an old, western style bar, hardwood dance floor, raised stage for local country bands, and pool tables in the back. Country music played on the old-fashioned jukebox with old, vinyl records. Jess and Drake played pool at one of the tables in the back. Drake spent most of his time leaning on his pool stick while Jess dominated the table as usual.

"Like it or not, you're going to be part of rumors and gossip among those in our renowned, little hick town," Drake said to her. "You're available, even slightly forbidden, which just increases the attraction."

Jess glared at him as she lined up her next shot and muttered, "You're as bad as Sheriff Stone." She made her shot and sank the ball.

"Half the men in town want to *do you*, Jess," he said while grinning. He was always pleased with his sexual references when they involved her. "I'm just saying if you were seeing someone, there would be a lot fewer guys around town sporting wood for you."

Jess gave him a look. Drake had a flair for crudeness and always found new ways to get her going. He grinned and raised his brows lustfully. Jess rolled her eyes then leaned over the pool table to make her next shot. Brody and another man, Victor Raymour, entered the pool area. Victor was a decent looking man in his late thirties. His good looks were attributed more to his perceived wealth and expensive clothing then his actual physical appearance. He lacked impressiveness when standing alongside Brody. Although they were the same height, Brody had more stature and less arrogance than Victor had, if that was possible. Jess eyed them and made her shot. The cue ball jumped the table and propelled for Brody's crotch. Brody caught the ball and glared at her as she straightened with a slightly mocking smile.

"Oops," Jess teased.

Brody played with the cue ball in his hand as he approached Jess and the table. His look was unpredictable and cold. Jess didn't back down and maintained her smirk.

"Brody, play nice," Victor muttered a warning.

Brody handed her the ball and walked away. Jess carelessly tossed the ball over her shoulder to Drake without looking. Drake fumbled to catch the cue ball and nearly dropped it. Jess casually looked at Victor and attempted sincerity, although she failed miserably.

"Sorry about cutting across your property this afternoon. But if you'd like to press charges, I'm sure Sheriff Stone would love an excuse to get me in his jail cell."

Victor was a hard man to read, although not nearly in the same league as Brody. Victor was the ultimate agenda man, and his motives needed to be questioned even when he simply smiled or said hello.

"We certainly wouldn't want to do him any favors," Victor said with a tiny, humored smile.

She wondered if he was up to something.

"I'd like to end this little war between us, Jess. You're my neighbor, so I think it's only proper that I give you permission to ride across my property. Besides, Brody's been enjoying himself a little too much lately, and it's starting to make me nervous."

Now she was positive he was up to something.

"That's a very nice gesture, Victor. I'm willing to call a truce."

Jess knew better than to trust this man, but she was working on her own agenda.

"Then it's settled. We're good, right?" Victor asked with a pleased smile.

"Yeah, sure. We're good. And if you ever want to discover your inner cowboy, I'd love to take you out riding some time. I have plenty of novice friendly horses."

Drake eyed Jess suspiciously. Jess caught his look but chose to ignore it.

"Me on a horse?" Victor said with a laugh. "I think I'm too much of a city boy for that."

Jess offered a knowing smile. "Relax, the McClellan "ball breaker" saddle went out with the Cavalry."

It was a common theory among men with limited horse sense that their ability to reproduce would be stunted if they rode horses. That simply wasn't true. Although Drake was living proof that it was possible while riding bareback on a horse with high withers. Jess always felt bad about that sudden stop she purposely made that time with Drake. He didn't walk right for days. Victor looked at her as if she had read his thoughts. He suddenly smiled and laughed.

"Maybe I'll take you up on that offer."

Chapter Fourteen

$\mathcal{I}$t was late afternoon when Jess and Drake returned from their lengthy ride. After unsaddling and brushing their horses, they released them into the pasture with the others. Jess closed the stock gate behind them and walked with Drake toward her house and his sports car. The house appeared unusually quiet for late afternoon. They either didn't notice or simply didn't care.

"Are you staying for dinner?" Jess asked as they neared his car.

"Nah, give Jeeves my most sincere apologies," he said in an overly dramatic tone.

Jess rolled her eyes.

"I'm going to run home quick and shower before heading back to the city to meet Ivy."

They stopped by his car as Drake patted down his pockets for the keys. He suddenly appeared worried when he didn't find them.

"I could have sworn--"

Jess picked his keys up off the ground and dangled them before him. He made a face, snatched them from her, and groaned softly.

"I knew love was blind, but I didn't know it was clumsy and forgetful too," Jess teased.

Although she enjoyed teasing him, Jess was happy Drake found someone special. He had never been in love before, and it was clear he was in love with Ivy. She envied their relationship.

"That's really strange, because I would have sworn I'd left them in my other pants when I changed. I wonder how they got on the ground."

"You must have dropped them when you got your bag from the car."

"No, I had them in my hand when I went inside to change," Drake insisted. "I remember, because you sometimes lock the door when we go out riding, you know, so no one steals Ridley, and I had your house key ready just in case."

It wasn't the first time Drake had lost his keys. He was always putting them down and forgetting them. Although he remained deep in thought over it, Jess felt it best to change the subject.

"It's your six month anniversary, isn't it? Are you and Ivy going out somewhere special tonight?"

"No, our anniversary was two weeks ago. We spent the weekend in bed," Drake said while suggestively raising his brows. "Ivy's performing in her play tonight, and I want to be there to support her."

"You really are crazy for her. How many times have you seen that play?"

"Umm, tonight will make thirteen," Drake said then grimaced. "That's unlucky. Why don't you and Ridley drive into the city and join me?"

"I've already seen the play three times. And, honestly, it's not good enough to warrant sitting through it a fourth time."

"Tell me about it," Drake muttered. "Some of the musical numbers get stuck in my head and repeat themselves in my sleep. It's always the bad songs." He then appeared enthusiastic. "Ridley's never seen it. I know Ivy would love to get his opinion, being he's all artsy and stuff. Why don't you persuade him to come?"

"Good luck in getting Ridley out of the house. I'm sometimes amazed when he leaves to shop for groceries. I ran into him on the street in town once and couldn't believe how strange it was seeing him there. It was almost like an Elvis sighting."

Drake laughed then kissed her quickly on the lips. "Give Jeeves a "smack me bum" from me," he said as he opened his car door.

"Give him your own "smack me bum", if you dare."

Drake laughed while getting into his car, gave her a wave, and drove away. Jess shook her head with a smile and headed onto the large porch. She hesitated by the front door. It was partially open. Jess appeared curious only a moment then entered and shut the door behind her.

"Ridley, I'm home!"

There was no response. Jess didn't appear to notice. She walked along the spotless grand hallway then suddenly stopped. She looked down at the dirty riding boots she wore and appeared alarmed.

"Oh, crap--"

Jess quickly hurried on her tiptoes back to the foyer. She removed her boots, placed them neatly on a mat in the foyer that read, "barn boots here", and then padded along the hallway in her stocking feet. Ridley was opposed to barn boots in the house and made his feelings about horse manure known. To say he was a clean freak was an understatement. There were fresh flower arrangements on several hall tables, which added certain elegance to the grandeur of the hallway. The carved, wooden banister and hardwood floors shined from hours of painstaking buffing. There was no doubt Ridley did his job well. She knew she couldn't live without him. Her house was in total chaos before he came along and whipped it into shape with his good housekeeping skills and elegant touches.

"Ridley?"

There was still no response, but Jess didn't seem particularly concerned. Ridley was often engrossed in some book he always had in front of him. She entered the study and approached the large, carved antique desk. The study was breathtaking with its antique furnishings, hardwood floors, and *Andrea Maria* tribute décor. The two pool sticks from the lounge hung proudly on the wall in an "X" below the life ring with *Andrea Maria* boldly stamped on it. It was the same life ring that went overboard with Emry; the same one Jess clung to and cried on for two days before their rescue. Framed magazines and newspaper articles about her, Drake, and the survivors were proudly displayed on the walls.

Jess approached the large desk and picked up the day's mail sitting on the corner. She rifled through the stack with disinterest. Thankfully, Ridley enjoyed managing her finances. His keen business sense and wise investments had maximized her returns in a very short time. He was possibly the smartest man she had ever met. As Jess shuffled through the mail, Emry appeared in the study doorway behind her. He had a look of hostility on his stern face. Jess was unaware of his presence as he approached her from behind.

"I'm very disappointed in you," Emry said in a low and chilling tone.

Jess suddenly turned with a gasp and stared at Emry with a startled look on her face. There was a moment of eerie silence. The exchange between them was tense. Emry sharply raised his brow and held up a letter.

"Dear Ms. Colten, we hope you will reconsider and attend the *Andrea Maria* anniversary cruise this weekend. Your presence blah,

blah, blah--" Emry glared at her with a disapproving look. "You're going on that cruise, and you're attending the movie premiere."

"No, Ridley, I'm not," she said with irritation and tossed the mail down on the desk. "The movie is a true story based on a lie." She spoke in a mocking tone, "The role of Emry Hill will now be played by Grant Peters." Jess glared at Emry and folded her arms stubbornly across her chest. "I'm tired of Grant pretending he's you."

"I didn't do it for the glory. Let Grant have his fun. Although it really should have been you receiving the hero worship and fame."

"Fuck the fame," Jess muttered and cast herself against the desk with disgust.

"Hey--"

Emry disapproved of her language and it showed in his expression. He often told her he didn't approve when she "talked like a sailor".

"Sorry," she said softly and straightened. "I just hate that you were erased from it. No one ever knew what you did that night, and it hurts."

Emry moved closer to her and tossed the letter on the desk. He looked into her eyes with all seriousness and offered a gentle smile.

"I have to stay off the radar, you know that. Besides, I have everything I want. You gave me a home to live in, a job to feel useful, and a better life than I've had in years. Stop worrying about what Grant took away from me. I just wish you hadn't given up your role. I'd love to see you on more of those magazine covers."

Jess frowned. "Your room creeps me out."

Emry appeared humored by her lack of enthusiasm for the room's tribute to the *Andrea Maria*.

"This is ours even if that night does have significantly different meanings to both of us," Emry said with a compassionate smile.

Jess offered a sly grin. "You mean your Romeo to my Juliet versus my Watson to your Holmes?"

"We were great together, weren't we?"

"You were great. I just had your back."

Emry took Jess's hand while smiling charmingly and gently caressed it. "Don't downplay your role, my dear. You saved my ass on several occasions."

"I don't know about several--"

"After I'd finished my drink in the nightclub, I was going to have dinner at second seating. I heard the lobster bisque was to die for." Emry hesitated then grimaced. "Oh, that came out wrong."

"You were? You never mentioned that before."

"It seemed unimportant at the time. Fortunately for me, the prospect of playing pool with an attractive young lady took precedence."

There was an awkward silence and possible tension as they stared into each other's eyes. Jess was certain she was sending strong, sexual signals, but she couldn't help it. She knew he was reading her loud and clear and would soon make his usual, hasty retreat when confronted with her lingering desires. Emry tensed, patted her hand, and released it.

"I'd better check on dinner."

He quickly turned and left the study as if on cue. Jess groaned softly, ran her fingers through her hair, and followed him. He was infuriating to say the least.

Jess followed Emry into the spotless kitchen, which was more attractive than it had been six months earlier and contained nostalgic décor as well. It was obvious Emry had a knack for decorating, which explained the house's sudden transformation into something more stylish. Emry headed for the main counter and an opened bottle of wine while Jess sat at the island counter with less enthusiasm.

"Did you happen to see my feather duster?" Emry asked as he poured two glasses of wine. "I've been looking for it all week."

Jess eyed his profile and played innocent. "Uh, no, I haven't seen it."

Of course she had seen it! She had also carefully hid it where he would never find it. There was no way in hell she was going to allow Drake the satisfaction of seeing Emry holding that feather duster. Emry handed her a glass of wine while standing on the other side of the island counter with his own filled glass. She accepted the glass and eyed it with skepticism.

"What am I drinking tonight?"

"2007 Tenuta dell'Ornellaia Masseto," he casually informed her. "A rare and exclusive 'Cru'." Emry suddenly hesitated and stared at the bewildered look on her face. It was obvious she hadn't understood a word he said. "It's very expensive. You sip it."

Jess raised her brow with a curious look. "I shudder to think what your definition of expensive is."

She sipped the wine and made a face. Emry glared his disapproval. She hid her smile. He was always trying to share his appreciation for fine wine with her. She continued to try because she knew it meant a lot to him, but she still didn't understand it. A hardbound book, written in a foreign language, lay on the counter.

Jess eyed the book, picked it up, and appeared intrigued by the foreign writing on the cover.

"What are you reading?"

"It's *Das Boot*. The German version. It's about war."

Jess hid her humor and smiled at him. "Oh, really? That's strange, because I'm pretty sure I recognize Agatha Christie as the author."

Emry hid his embarrassment and snatched the book from her. "Okay. It's *Death on the Nile*. Don't tell Drake I'm reading murder novels. He's already on my last nerve, and I'd really hate hitting him."

Jess snorted a laugh. "I can't believe you'd read books in foreign languages just so Drake won't know what you're reading. There's something freakishly devious about you." She suddenly eyed him and appeared curious. "How many languages *do* you speak?"

"Fluently? Because I can curse like a sailor in every known language," he said with great pride.

"Fluently," Jess said with a soft laugh.

"Six."

"Six?"

"Yes, just six. English, Spanish, French, German, Russian, and Mandarin."

"What? Not Korean?" she teased.

"What I know in Korean isn't considered polite, and I'd be extremely uncomfortable translating it in mixed company."

"When did I become mixed company?"

"I'm guessing you were born that way."

Jess considered his comment then shrugged it off as she often did. She leaned on the counter across from him and smiled deviously.

"Come on, who were you a spy for?"

Emry glanced at her and appeared offended but not nearly offended enough. "I resent the insinuation, my dear."

His inability to look at her spoke volumes. He couldn't look her in the eyes when she was on to him. She still knew nothing about his past, but he was continually dropping his guard around her and letting little things slip. She knew he had been in nearly every known country, particularly the hardcore ones, and used military references on many occasions. Dangerous men were hunting him, so it was obvious he had to be some sort of military spy.

"It's just us. Who am I going to tell? You're not Emry Hill, and you're certainly no substitute schoolteacher. I know just about everything there is to know about you, yet I know absolutely nothing."

Emry finally looked at her with his arrogance once more returning. "That translates into "you know all you need to know", my dear."

Jess lost enthusiasm for the conversation. As usual, she was getting nowhere.

"You give me a headache," she muttered and changed the subject in order to maintain her sanity. "We're having dinner guests tomorrow night."

"Drake hardly qualifies as a guest. He has a million dollar estate less than a mile away, yet he's always over here messing up my kitchen."

Jess gave him a strange look and slowly shook her head. "My God, Drake's right. I have domesticated you." Her mood again lightened. "He's bringing Ivy with him. She's looking forward to your martinis."

Emry suddenly appeared humored and raised his brows suggestively. "Midweek drunk fest?" he teased. "Haven't had one of those in a while. What's the occasion?"

Jess shrugged with little interest. "Victor Raymour wants to go out riding tomorrow afternoon."

"Victor Raymour?" Emry appeared surprised and studied her. "So now he wants to get in your pants, huh?"

Jess suddenly eyed him and appeared surprised by his usage of the sexual reference. It would seem Emry had been spending too much time around Drake. They were starting to sound a lot alike.

"Not you too? Drake seems to think every man in town wants to bang me."

"Drake's a pretty reliable authority when it comes to whoring around," Emry said bluntly then frowned. "And, incidentally, that term is number three on my "most offensive sexual reference" list."

"Oh, really? What was that comment you made the other night?" Jess pretended to consider then smiled deviously. "That's right; it was number *one* on your little list, wasn't it?"

Emry frowned and avoided looking at her. "That was a private conversation between me and Drake. It was not intended for mixed company."

"There's that mixed company again," Jess muttered. "I find it very interesting that supposedly every guy in town wants to get in my pants *except* you."

Emry glared at her and was not amused. Jess wondered if she had pushed it too far that time. She smiled innocently and sipped her wine. She again made a face. The mood once again lightened.

"Is Victor bringing his attack dog?" Emry asked with a curious look.

"Never leaves home without him. I'm considering putting him on Girthy Gertrude. Her trot is so choppy; he won't walk right for a week."

"Yes, I remember her from the last time you took me out riding. Ironically, I never rode again."

Jess appeared embarrassed and smiled timidly. "I didn't do that intentionally. She barely broke out of a walk when I rode her in the riding ring."

"Admit it; it was an all-out assault on my sensitive areas."

"I would never dream of hurting your sensitive areas," Jess said simply. "You know how I feel about your sensitive areas."

Emry brushed off the conversation and refilled his wine glass. "Would you be terribly offended if I did some homework on Victor?"

"I'd be offended if you didn't--007," Jess said with a smirk.

Emry suddenly appeared annoyed, placed his hands firmly on the counter, and glared at her. "Seriously, Jess?" he demanded. "Do I look British to you?"

Chapter Fifteen

The condominium complex was an assortment of beautifully crafted, two-story homes within the gated community. The homes were a status symbol of wealth and influence in the rural area not far from the city. It was nearly two in the morning and the entire complex was mostly dark apart from elegant street lamps lining the winding lanes. A newer sports car pulled up to one of the darkened condominiums. Conner got out of the car, hurried to the passenger side, and opened the door for a ravishing woman in a revealing dress and daringly high, stiletto heels. Tina was a voluptuous, blonde-haired woman in her mid-twenties that he had found either at a trendy nightclub or at an expensive escort service. His boyish grin toward her was a good indicator that he had proudly picked her up at little to no cost. He placed his arm around her and escorted her into the home.

Conner and Tina stepped out of the small, private elevator into the second floor hallway. Tina marveled at the impressiveness of his expensive home and the elevator. Conner marveled at the impressiveness of her cleavage and double "D" breasts.

"I never knew, like, anyone with an elevator in their home before," Tina said in a slightly squeaky voice and a tone of diminished intelligence. "You must be, like, rich or something."

It was obvious how he could pick up the raving beauty, and even more obvious that he didn't bring her home for stimulating conversation. Conner kept his arm securely around her while he held her close and guided her toward the master bedroom at the far end of the hall.

"You seriously never heard of the *Andrea Maria?*" he asked with a grin.

"Is that, like, some religious song?"

The wideness of her eyes indicated that no one was home inside that pretty head of hers. Conner wasn't in the least put off by her limited knowledge about his celebrity status--or her limited knowledge about much of anything. It actually seemed to be working to his advantage.

"I think that's "Ava Maria"," he teased. "They made a movie about my story. It comes out next month. I'm flying out to Hollywood for the premiere."

"You mean, like, red carpet premiere?"

She appeared ready to bubble over with enthusiasm at the thought of it all.

"Movie stars--after parties," he said. "It's going to be wild."

They stopped before his bedroom doorway. Tina threw her arms around his neck and smiled lustfully.

"You want wild? I'll give you wild," she purred and kissed him passionately.

Conner immediately clung to her and returned the aggressive kiss as they clumsily stumbled into his dimly lit bedroom without releasing each another or breaking off the kiss. They shed off most of their clothing on their way across the room, leaving just their undergarments as they fell on the bed with Conner on top. Tina suddenly broke off the kiss and cried out with surprise.

"Oh, God! Your waterbed is leaking!"

"Waterbed?"

Conner jumped off Tina and turned on the bedside light. Tina was propped on her elbows while on her back and looked at the scantily dressed, dead woman in the bed alongside her. Tina bounded off the bed with blood on her hands, the back of her lacy panties, and her legs. She screamed hysterically. Conner stared in horror at the young, dead woman with the gaping slit in her throat and enormous amounts of fresh blood covering her and the bed. He then noticed the blood covering his hands as well

"Oh, my God!" Tina screamed while grabbing her dress from the floor. "Who is she?"

"Some girl I, uh, met the other night." Conner fumbled with his cell phone, which was now smeared with blood from his hands. "The maid must have let her in."

"I am so out of here--"

Tina quickly slipped into her dress on her way to the bedroom door and hurried out. Conner held the cell phone to his ear and looked after Tina as she ran from the room as fast as her stiletto heels would carry her. He suddenly appeared alarmed.

"Tina--no!" Conner ran after her in his boxer shorts with the phone to his ear. "It might not be safe!"

Conner entered the second floor hallway with his cell phone still to his ear and looked down the hall. The emergency call appeared to ring endlessly. The elevator was already descending to the first floor. He hurried along the hallway toward the staircase not far from the master bedroom. Conner rushed down the main stairs and headed toward the now opened front door while talking to the emergency operator on his cell phone. It would appear Tina had run outside. He looked around the hallway with concern.

"I don't know," Conner said into the phone then called to the open door. "Tina, wait up!" He returned to his conversation with the emergency operator. "My date just ran out the door. I need to go after her. Can you get someone here right away?"

Conner suddenly paused by the partially opened elevator door. A woman's stiletto shoe kept the elevator doors from closing. Conner hesitated and uncertainly opened the elevator. Tina lay on the floor in a bloody heap with her throat slit and a pool of blood quickly surrounding her head and soaking into her blonde hair. The elevator walls were streaked and spattered with blood. Conner appeared horrified, and the fear paralyzed him.

"The killer's still here!" he suddenly shouted into the phone as he nervously looked around the dimly lit hallway. He heard police sirens in the near distance. "I hear the sirens," he said into the phone with panic in his voice. He then listened to the emergency operator on the other end. "Yes, I'll wait outside."

Conner disconnected the call and hurried for the open front door. A man dressed in black and wearing a mask suddenly appeared from one of the darkened rooms and tackled Conner to the floor. As they struck the floor with the killer on top of him, the cell phone flew from his hand. Conner struggled to push his attacker off him then punched the man twice in the face. The killer punched him back, grabbed his throat, and revealed a hunting knife. As the knife thrust downward, Conner clutched the man's wrist with the knife and attempted to keep it from striking him. The police sirens grew louder. Conner's confidence grew with the increasing wailing of the sirens. He just had to hold him off a few minutes longer. Any minute now, the police would charge through the open door with their guns blazing and save the day. The killer pushed his full weight onto the hand clutching Conner's throat. Conner suddenly gasped while attempting to breathe and loosen the pressure on his throat. Any minute now, the police would rescue him.

The killer pulled sharply back with the knife, yanking his wrist free from Conner's grip, and thrust the knife downward into his throat. Conner's body convulsed as blood pulsated from his neck. Blood seeped out of his mouth as he attempted one last scream. His eyes fixated on the dark figure towering over him then became motionless. The killer moved off Conner, removed a copy of the movie script from his jacket, and tossed it into the rapidly collecting pool of blood. As the police sirens were almost upon the house, the killer casually turned and headed for the back door. Conner's open, lifeless eyes appeared to stare after him.

Chapter Sixteen

*O*t was late in the afternoon on the following day. The sun was shining and a gentle breeze was blowing. Five horse and riders rode along the worn trail in the lush field at a leisurely canter. Jess led the group on her black and white gelding, while Drake brought up the rear on his stocky, Dun gelding. His girlfriend, Ivy, rode alongside him on a small but plump, golden chestnut Haflinger that lazily kept up with Drake's horse. Ivy's beauty was evident even while casually dressed in a pair of old jeans and an oversized sweatshirt with her hair carelessly tossed into a ponytail. Drake was in love with the young theater actress, which was more than obvious by the way he kept his eyes on her and maintained his lustful boyish grin while he did so. Ivy, on the other hand, kept her attention focused on the scenic beauty as it rushed past her while she rode the smooth canter. She was enjoying the ride and the freedom it offered so far from the city. She was always reluctant to return home.

Victor and Brody remained in the center of the group as a safety measure, since Victor was a first time rider. Brody was at ease and comfortable on his horse at the faster gait. It was obvious by his confidence and his free hand resting by his side that he rode before. Victor clung to the saddle horn and maintained a permanent grin to his enjoyment with the ride, but he obviously lacked riding skills and confidence as he bounced in and out of the saddle.

†

*L*ater that afternoon, the weary riders had returned to Jess's house and sat on the porch while Emery served his famous martinis.

Although its origin remained a mystery, somehow word got out around town that Jess's house manager made the most amazing martinis. She credited his overnight popularity to the gossiping of a handful of lonely, older women who had recently discovered Emry was a bachelor. The town lacked single men over forty but was brimming with single women over sixty. Emry joined the group on the porch with his own martini and sat in his usual spot close to the house door. Jess always occupied the spot on the railing across from him. She claimed preference to that spot so she could freely talk facing company and still admire the landscaped beauty of her property. In actuality, she preferred facing *Emry*, because she enjoyed admiring *him*.

Brody was suspiciously missing from the porch. He expressed his distaste for martinis and went inside to fix a drink from the game room bar. He had been gone some time although no one seemed to notice his absence. Victor, who was already feeling stiff from the lengthy ride, was cheerful and more relaxed than he had been. He was also on his third martini, which may have contributed to his pleasant mood and chattiness.

"I have to thank you, Jess," Victor said while sipping his martini. "I never thought I'd enjoy horseback riding. Although I'm pretty sure I'm going to regret that decision in the morning."

There was a round of knowing chuckles.

"The horseback riding was fun," Ivy said cheerfully, "but the martinis are the star attraction." Ivy raised her glass to Emry. "Cheers to Ridley."

Emry offered a pleased smile and raised his glass in response. Emry turned his attention to Victor, slipped into his best, non-threatening persona, and began his subtle interrogation.

"So, Victor, what is it you do for a living? I hear you're some Wall Street mogul."

Victor chuckled drunkenly. "Hardly. You can stop fishing; I'm not into organized crime. This town is desperate for gossip."

Victor and Emry laughed. Both knew that to be true. Jess finally noticed Brody's absence from the group. She stood from her seat on the porch railing, set her martini down on the table near Emry, and headed into the house. Emry casually watched her enter the house with a curious look but appeared to resist the urge to follow or question her hasty departure. His interrogation of Victor was just getting started.

Jess walked along the grand hallway, stopped before the open study door, and peered inside. Brody stood in the study with a glass of brandy in his hand and scanned over the framed articles on the walls. Jess entered and paused behind him. She appeared curious by his obvious interest in one particular newspaper article. She didn't like him in her house let alone in Emry's "trophy" room.

"Find anything interesting?"

Despite not having seen or heard her enter, he wasn't the least bit startled by her appearance behind him. He casually indicated the framed article on the wall and glanced at her with great interest.

"In this interview, it says you were in the lounge with Emry Hill, the man who died saving your life, when all hell broke loose that night."

Hearing Emry's name mentioned aloud in connection with his death sounded almost creepy to her. It was hard to hear about the death of Emry Hill when he was sitting on her porch sipping martinis.

"That's a bit of a sore subject, Brody."

Her comment didn't even register with him as he paid closer attention to the article.

"According to this, you said the gunman entered the lounge with an assault rifle and opened fire on the two of you," he continued.

Brody turned and moved alongside her and fixed his attention on the imaginary gunman. She didn't know what he was up to or where he was going with this conversation, but she was uncomfortable with his analysis and his closeness to her.

"That's when Emry stepped in front of you and took the brunt of the gunfire except the one that got you in the shoulder."

Maybe it was just the martinis talking, but Jess was irritated and lacked patience. She folded her arms across her chest and glared at him.

"Yes. Your point?"

Brody suddenly turned toward Jess. He made a gun with his hand, shot at her, and indicated her right shoulder. She flinched slightly while clutching her shoulder as if she had felt the imaginary shot. Her shoulder seemed to throb in response.

"Right shoulder, assault rifle, thirty feet away," Brody stated the facts. "Thirty feet?" He made a face and shook his head. "Obviously, that bullet didn't hit you directly or it would have torn off your shoulder at that close range. Did it pass through Emry and then hit you?"

"Yeah, I suppose it did," Jess said simply.

"That would make more sense. Although when you so kindly showed me your scar yesterday, it was from a 9mm pistol with the exit wound in the front." Brody studied her and appeared puzzled. "If you were standing behind Emry while facing the shooter, how were you shot from behind?"

Jess tried to keep her surprise at his comment from showing. How had he figured that out from one quick glance at her scar?

"It all happened very fast. Maybe I turned. I really don't--"

"Yes, maybe you turned, but that still doesn't explain how an assault rifle left a 9mm bullet wound," Brody said with cleverly raised brows and a smile that mocked her. He was playing with her and wanted to watch her squirm. "And what about the second gunshot wound?"

Jess could feel her body twitch with concern and possible hostility. She wanted to lash out at him, but she knew that wasn't in her best interest.

"Excuse me?"

"In all the interviews, you supposedly ran from the lounge and hid with Carla and Dana in her cabin. That scar on your arm looks like a bullet graze. When were you shot in the arm?" He was no longer asking. He was accusing! "Someone onboard stitched your arm. I can't help but wonder why you never mentioned that in any of your interviews."

How was he coming up with this? Jess maintained her calm stare, but her mind raced for an answer that wouldn't make him suspicious.

"I ran into the ship's nurse. She stitched it before she was killed," she replied and almost immediately realized she had messed up.

It was a known fact the ship's nurse died in the dining room at second seating from the massive dose of poison placed in the lobster bisque. Tragically, her boyfriend had joined her on that particular cruise and had proposed to her in Costa Rica at some romantic rain forest location. It was a well-reported, tragic love story that circulated the papers for weeks. The image of them in the dining room lying dead together still haunted Jess's nightmares.

"No, she was poisoned, which means she died before you were shot," Brody said as he dug deeper for information. "Whoever stitched your arm didn't fix your shoulder, telling me you were shot in the shoulder long after being shot in the arm. They didn't happen at the same time or in the same location on the ship. Your story doesn't add up."

Jess realized she liked Brody better when he didn't talk. Her concern quickly turned to hostility that she could no longer control.

"You want details, buy the fucking book!"

Her outburst didn't faze him or even break his train of thought. "What I can't figure out is why you would lie about when you were shot and where it happened."

Brody stared at her a long moment in silence. He was reading her expression and possibly her thoughts. Brody tilted his head with a curious look as if some divine inspiration suddenly came to him. Jess didn't like his expression. It made her nervous.

"Unless you didn't hide--" He suddenly grinned while staring at her. "You ran with the boys, didn't you? Of course you did. You were on deck with Drake during the battle for *Andrea Maria*. That makes sense. He was your friend. You never would have left him." He chuckled and shook his head with surprise and a bold grin on his once serious face. "Wow, that's really huge."

Jess suddenly tensed and felt cornered. How did he do that? She needed to stop him before he told the world that she had actually been on deck.

"I've tried very hard to forget about that night, Brody. If word got out I was on deck during the battle for *Andrea Maria*, I'd never have any peace."

She was proud of herself. There wasn't a single lie in that entire statement.

"You've got that right," Brody said with a chuckle. "The media hounds would be all over you." He moved closer to her, gently touched her arm, and offered one of his more sincere smiles. "Relax. Your secret is safe with me."

Jess wasn't sure she liked him touching her, not even innocently. His more sinister smile quickly returned as if on cue.

"And one of these evenings, you can tell me what really happened onboard the ship that night. Maybe you'll be able to clear up some other discrepancies that I've uncovered with your stories."

Something in his eyes frightened her. She suddenly felt as if he knew everything about that night and about Emry. Brody walked past her and headed out of the room. Jess cursed softly under her breath and followed him.

Brody walked onto the porch and took Jess's spot on the railing. Jess reclaimed her drink on the table by the martini pitcher near Emry. She drank the entire contents from her martini glass and immediately refilled it. Emry and Drake were the only ones who found that odd. Emry cast a strange look at her. She knew that look. He was trying to figure out if she was okay. Jess offered a tiny smile in response that she hoped would put his mind at ease. She didn't need Emry pulling her aside to grill her about her sudden mood change. Brody was cleverer than she gave him credit, and she didn't need him figuring out Ridley was actually Emry. Jess intended to protect Emry's identity at all costs. She would never allow someone like Brody to be the reason Emry had to leave.

†

*L*ater that evening, Jess was alone in the game room playing pool. She had too much to drink already and wanted to avoid the scene on the porch, particularly any further confrontations with Brody. Jess leaned over the pool table to make her next shot, grazed the cue ball, and sent it spinning wildly for destinations unknown. She frowned and straightened with disgust.

"That's a first," Emry said from across the room.

Jess looked at the game room doorway. Emry stood in the doorway and watched her. He often prowled around the house with a cat-like sneakiness. She was sure it was a spillover from his past life as a spy--or whatever it was that he didn't discuss.

"Is everything okay?"

"Yes, why do you ask?"

Emry shrugged. "Maybe because you were going to the bathroom and never returned. I was worried you passed out somewhere."

"I got sidetracked."

"That was two hours ago," he said bluntly. There was a moment of silence. When she didn't elaborate, Emry continued, "Drake ordered pizza. It should be here soon. Are you joining us?"

Jess frowned and appeared distant. "I'd rather not deal with Brody right now."

Emry's look hardened at her comment. He quickly approached her by the pool table.

"Why? Did something happen that I should know about? I knew you were upset when you came back on the porch. What did he do?" Emry's tone was chilling.

"He didn't do anything, not really. He was just asking a lot of questions about what happened onboard the *Andrea Maria*. He went into this whole *Sherlock Holmes* routine and somehow figured out I'd been on deck that night."

Emry's aggression quickly diminished. "Let him fish. There's no proof--"

"I admitted I was."

Emry groaned softly.

"I didn't know what to say. He surprised me. I felt cornered. Trying to lie to him was almost as bad as trying to lie to you."

"It's okay, Jess," Emry said gently. "So he knows you were on deck. What's the worst that can happen? You become a little more popular." Emry grinned with delight. "Don't worry; there's plenty of room on the study wall for more framed articles."

"Real funny, Ridley."

Emry smiled and chuckled softly. Jess studied him a moment, appeared slightly curious, and then grinned with a realization.

"Are you *drunk*?"

"No, I'm happily buzzed," he replied cheerfully and removed the pool stick from her hand. He set it down on the pool table then suavely extended his hand to her. "Would you care to dance?"

Jess attempted to contain her pleased grin and placed her hand into his. "I'd love to."

Emry spun her into his arms and began to waltz with her. A few steps into their dance to the silent song, Emry gracefully dipped her backwards and grinned playfully. She was dizzy with ecstasy and tried hard not to giggle in her drunken state. He pulled her back up and into his arms, holding her daringly close. As he stared deep into her eyes, their dancing ceased. Jess stared back with anticipation. The last time he looked at her like that, they were in the cargo hold and he was about to kiss her right before Drake--

"Ridley!" Drake called from the hallway. "The pizza's here!"

That was exactly how she remembered it the last time too! As if on cue, Emry released Jess and moved away from her. He hid his mildly drunken smile.

"We should join the others," Emry said gently.

"Only if you promise we'll finish our dance later."

Emry smiled timidly in response and extended his hand toward the door, indicating for her to lead the way. That wasn't an answer. Jess smiled despite her disappointment and reluctantly walked past him. She was going to need a few more drinks in order to forget that dance. Jess then considered something she hadn't before. Maybe Emry needed a few more drinks.

Chapter Seventeen

$\mathcal{L}$ater that night, Emry helped Jess stumble across her bedroom while she laughed drunkenly and clung to him. Emry was in a particularly good mood and enjoyed her giddy, drunken state. Despite his sober appearance, it was evident he was intoxicated as well.

"Okay, last stop," he said cheerfully. "I'm going to turn down your bed. Try not to fall over."

Emry released Jess, waited for her to regain her balance, and then turned to pull down the covers on her bed. Jess carelessly began undressing for bed and removed her shirt to reveal her lacy bra. Emry turned, appeared surprised to see her partially undressed, and stared silently at her through the dim lighting. She finally realized he was standing there and hid her embarrassment. She casually turned her back to him and continued removing her bra. Emry stared a moment longer then looked away but appeared deep in thought about what he had witnessed. Jess slipped into her tank top and sleep shorts then turned toward him, still in her giddy mood, and placed her arms around his neck to keep from falling. His arms subconsciously slipped around her waist to support her. She laughed and looked into his eyes. Emry stared at her with an oddly serious look. Her giddy mood suddenly vanished. She stared back in silence. She still loved him. Nothing had changed. She had avoided coming on too strong, because she feared he would leave. She was always afraid something would make him leave, but tonight she wanted him no matter what the cost.

She gently ran her hands along his chest while staring into his eyes and carefully considered her next move. Even drunk, she knew better then to seduce him physically. The penalty was steep and usually involved a lengthy lecture. He continued to stare back at her with his odd expression and kept his arms securely around her. Something about the way he looked at her seemed different, almost lustful. As she warmly caressed his chest, she considered allowing her hand to stray further down. When her fingers touched his abdomen, he tensed. She immediately came to her senses, resisted groping him, and switched gears.

"Don't go," she begged softly.

There was a long, silent moment as they stared into each other's eyes. Emry suddenly pulled her against him and kissed her passionately and aggressively. It was then she realized how drunk he really was. Jess returned the kiss and attempted to keep pace with his rising passion. She had never before known him to be this way. He was sexually aggressive, and she was the object of his desire. Emry aggressively took her with him to the bed, pulled her leg up to his hip, and easily maneuvered himself between her legs. She groaned as he pressed against her while firmly running his hands along her body. Her head was spinning with ecstasy and too much alcohol. As she attempted to return his aggressive kiss, she hoped she wouldn't pass out. His left hand slipped under her shirt in the back, while his right hand slid down her shorts and along her buttocks in a clumsy attempt to part her hastily from her shorts.

She writhed beneath him as he continued to firmly press against her. He removed his mouth from hers and kissed her neck while his hands still worked on shedding her shorts. Jess clung to Emry and groaned softly while enjoying his hands firmly caressing her body. She knew he wanted her, and he was finally admitting it by his aggressive, sexual advances. He returned his mouth to hers without slowing his passion. Drake and Ivy were heard talking and giggling in the hallway as they drunkenly headed to their room. Emry suddenly tensed and broke off the kiss. Jess feared his preoccupation with the couple entering the room next door and attempted to return his focus on seducing her.

"It's okay," Jess whispered reassuringly and warmly kissed his neck. "They won't hear anything."

Emry quickly moved off her and nearly fell while standing. He clutched the nightstand for support then held his head. He appeared disoriented while possibly trying to make sense of his actions. Jess groaned softly while shutting her eyes. She realized reality had returned to him--the reality that kept him from humping her like a mutt in heat. She couldn't pretend she wasn't disappointed. Her head was spinning and her body was still aching for him.

"I'm so sorry, Jess. I shouldn't have." He avoided looking at her and tried to maintain his balance. "Please forgive me."

Emry stumbled from the room and gently shut the door behind him. Jess stared at the canopy above the bed and frowned. One of these days, she promised herself she would give up on him. The sounds of Ivy and Drake engaging in wild, uninhibited sex echoed through the walls from next door. Jess suddenly groaned with disgust. Even drunk, they would be at it all night.

✝

Later that night, Jess's house was mostly dark and quiet in the peaceful night setting. The vapor light from the barn lit just enough of the area to make out the house and the surrounding property. Drake's sports car remained parked out front, although Victor's car was gone. Jess slept peacefully in bed while curled on her side beneath the covers in her sleep shorts and tank top. The sounds of crickets and the occasional horse were heard beyond the open window. A gentle breeze blew through the window, causing the sheer curtains to flutter. A floorboard creaked from within the house. Jess remained soundly asleep and completely undisturbed possibly due to all the martinis.

In the second floor hallway, an intruder dressed completely in black silently crept toward Jess's bedroom. He quietly pushed open the door to the nearly dark room. The open window lent just enough light to reveal the outline of the massive bed. He quietly entered the room and approached the bed, now clutching a hunting knife in his gloved hand. He paused before the bed, raised the knife, and was about to plunge it downward when something made him hesitate. He uncertainly pulled back the covers to reveal a rumpled, empty bed. Despite his black mask, his bewilderment was evident. A floorboard creaked within the room behind him. The intruder appeared alerted and quickly turned with the knife prepared to strike.

✝

It was early the next morning, still hours before sunrise. Jess remained sleeping peacefully while curled on her side. There was movement on the bed alongside her. She stirred and slowly woke to an arm firmly around her waist from behind. She appeared bewildered and uncertainly turned her head. Emry nestled snugly

95

against her from behind and appeared to be asleep. She didn't want to risk waking him in fear he would pull away. She thought about how great his body felt pressed against hers. Had he been humping her? Is that what woke her? He must have been alerted to her movement and woke but didn't bother opening his eyes.

"It's early," he muttered softly. "Go back to sleep."

Jess felt confused by her current sleeping arrangements. She remembered something happening, but she was certain he walked out. Her head remained filled with martinis and details were hazy at best. Maybe she missed something--something rather important.

"Did something happen that I should know about?"

"You crawled into my bed with me and passed out," he muttered with his eyes still closed. "I didn't see any harm, so I let you stay."

Jess gave it some thought, realized she was, in fact, in his room, and then turned toward him. She moved into his arms and wearily nuzzled him. He smelled shower fresh and of that expensive soap he paid too much for. She was actually glad he bought it, because she loved the way he smelled. Emry was more receptive than usual and held her securely against his chest. He appeared unusually pleased with her closeness.

"I don't know why you came down here last night, but I'm glad you did," he said softly in a weary tone. "I really needed to hold you."

Jess suddenly became fully awake and very alert but tried to act casual. She wanted to remain in his arms, even if just respectfully, but she couldn't pretend he hadn't made that comment.

"You know you have unrestricted access to everything in this house--including me."

She knew she shouldn't have said that. He didn't like when she offered herself to him. Emry's arms tensed around her and he groaned his disapproval.

"I really wish you wouldn't say those things," he said softly.

Jess frowned even though he couldn't see it and buried her face into his chest. It wasn't right that he smelled so good. She resisted the urge to caress his chest more than she already had. She would have to be satisfied with him just holding her for now.

Chapter Eighteen

It was a little after six o'clock in the morning. Jess slept with Emry once again snuggled against her from behind. A sudden, urgent knocking came at the bedroom door. Jess and Emry jumped apart at the sound and shot up in bed as the door flew open. Jess held her pounding chest and pounding head while hunched over partially beneath the covers. Emry had his hand halfway to the gun that he kept hidden and strapped to the back of the headboard. Drake appeared in the doorway in a whirlwind of excitement.

"Ridley! You've got to come--" Drake saw them and was rendered speechless.

Emry held off removing the hidden gun when he saw it was just Drake, but it was never a good idea to startle Emry. Emry saw Drake's shocked expression to Jess in bed alongside him and immediately appeared tense and possibly embarrassed by how it looked. Drake stared at them a moment longer and slowly shook his head.

"Oh, hell no--"

Drake quickly waved it off to the bigger news and appeared ready to jump out of his skin. His hands were wildly gesturing as if in an epileptic fit. He always got that way when he became overly stimulated.

"You've got to see this before Sheriff Stone gets there. Hurry!"

†

Jess's blazer pulled out of her driveway and drove only fifty yards down the back, country road. She pulled up to an abandoned car near the cornfield. Jess, Emry, and Drake got out of the blazer and looked at the abandoned car. Drake frantically pointed at the cornfield beyond the scarecrow. He appeared unable to speak. The look on his face was close to horrified.

"I don't see it," Jess said.

"The scarecrow," Drake said while practically dancing around with anxiety.

Jess and Emry looked at the scarecrow that was unusually dressed in black. The intruder from Jess's bedroom hung from the platform, his arms outstretched and tied by his wrists, with a straw hat on his head. He had been sliced open from sternum to groin and his body completely hollowed out. His innards lay in a bloody pile on the ground several feet below him. A flock of crows picked at the gruesome heap of innards. Jess and Emry appeared horrified at the sight. Drake was barely able to stand still to the vile image.

"I saw it when I was driving Ivy home. She was so freaked; she wouldn't even get out of my car at your place."

A siren wailed in the near distance. Sheriff Stone's police blazer flew along the road and skidded into a wild turn before them. The blazer barely even stopped when Stone jumped out of the cruiser. Stone slowly approached, looked at the dead man, and appeared shocked then immediately sickened by the grisly sight.

"Son-of-a-bitch!"

†

Later that morning, Sheriff Stone sat sedately on the porch railing in Jess's usual spot with his head against the support beam. Jess watched him from where she now sat on the railing a couple of feet away. Drake held Ivy on the opposite end of the porch and attempted to console her. She clung to him and cried, but at least she wasn't nearly as hysterical. Emry appeared from the house and handed Stone a cup of coffee. Sheriff Stone gratefully accepted it with two hands to conceal his shaking hands. It was obvious the country sheriff had never seen anything like it before. Emry then approached Ivy and Drake and offered Ivy a colorful drink in a glass tumbler.

"What is it?" Ivy asked as she wiped the tears from her face with a trembling hand.

"A special cocktail to settle your nerves," Emry said simply. "I got the recipe from an enchanting old lady in New Orleans."

Ivy uncertainly accepted the drink and sipped it. She appeared to like it and drank some more. Drake suspiciously eyed Emry and leaned closer to him.

"Enchanting old lady?" Drake asked softly.

"Voodoo priestess," Emry muttered without making direct eye contact.

Drake stared at Emry with a concerned look on his face then looked at Ivy as she drank the colorful concoction. It was apparently very good. Emry joined Jess and Sheriff Stone on the other end of the porch.

"He wasn't from around here," Stone said with a frown and some reluctance while sipping his coffee. "The car was reported stolen from the city."

Stone appeared preoccupied with more than the grisly sight in the cornfield. Emry was the first to notice the sheriff's mood.

"Is there something you're not telling us, Sheriff?" Emry asked with a curious look.

Stone suddenly groaned, shut his eyes, and returned his head to the support beam.

"Conner Blake was murdered the night before last. They found a copy of the *Andrea Maria* movie script next to his body." He hesitated then drew a sharp breath. "We found a copy of the same script in the dead man's car--along with a magazine photo of Jess."

Drake suddenly took Ivy by the hand and pulled her toward Sheriff Stone with a concerned look on his face. Ivy clung to her drink and barely noticed Drake's mood.

"Someone murdered Conner, and you think he was coming after Jess?" Drake asked hotly.

It was obvious Sheriff Stone was concerned that he was in over his head and reacted appropriately with frustration and irritation.

"I ain't no damned psychic," he snapped then made an effort to control his rising temper. "The detective on Conner's case is coming out to have a look at our boy." He looked at Drake and suddenly appeared curious about something. "Were you and Ivy here last night?"

Ivy suddenly giggled. Drake gave her a strange look. She grinned and sipped her drink.

"Yes, we were drinking until midnight."

Stone eyed Emry with raised brows. "Martinis?"

"Yes, Sheriff," Emry replied.

"I hear they're pretty famous." Stone returned his focus to the investigation. "Our guy was strung up between midnight and three according to Charlie."

"Charlie?" Jess asked with surprise. "The mortician?"

"He ain't much, but he's the best we've got until the city coroner gets a hold of him." Stone's patience was now limited. He regained his composure and returned his attention to Emry. "The kitchen lock was tampered with. Your room is right down the hall, Ridley. Did you hear anything last night?"

"No, Sheriff. I had quite a bit to drink myself."

"What time did you turn in?" Stone asked.

"It was a little after midnight."

Jess listened to the exchange with great interest and concern. Was Sheriff Stone fishing? She suddenly made a bold decision.

"He wasn't alone, Sheriff," Jess said.

Stone and Emry looked at Jess with shared surprise. Even Ivy, who had been engrossed in her drink, reacted to her words.

Emry suddenly fidgeted and scolded Jess with a look. "Jess--"

Jess ignored him and stared Stone in the eyes with her head proudly raised. "After Drake and Ivy went to bed a little after midnight, I left my room and went down to Ridley's. I had a little too much to drink and wanted the company. I woke around two, and we talked until nearly three."

Emry frowned and looked away. Jess knew she was going to pay for that with another one of Emry's long-winded lectures on protecting her reputation--or was it his reputation he was protecting?

"Drake woke us after he called you," Jess continued.

"Well, that explains a lot," Stone said lowly under his breath.

"When she says "talked", she means we actually talked," Emry scoffed. "Nothing happened."

Victor's Bentley pulled up to the house and abruptly stopped. Victor sprang from the passenger side and hurried onto the porch. Brody got out of the driver's side and followed with less urgency. Victor hurried up to Jess and placed his hands on her shoulders with a concerned look in his eyes.

"Are you okay?"

His actions were startling to Jess and surprising to the others. When did he suddenly become an interested party? Stone stood from the railing and glared at Victor with annoyance at the interruption.

"How the hell did you hear about this already?" Stone demanded to know.

Victor gave Stone a quick look with little reaction. "Charlie told us out on the road."

"That damned gossiping old fart," Stone muttered with annoyance.

Jess appeared uncomfortable with his closeness and took a step back from Victor's hands on her arms.

"We're fine. If that guy was here, he never made it into the house."

"Brody and I are going to stick by your side the rest of the day," Victor said firmly.

Jess wasn't sure how she felt about that. She wasn't exactly comfortable around either of them. Sheriff Stone appeared offended and placed his coffee cup down on the porch table with a little more force than necessary, spilling coffee on the glass top.

"Thanks, but I've got that covered, Victor," Stone snapped hotly.

Sheriff Stone's tarnished reputation was about ready to surface. It was never wise to piss off the good sheriff, although Drake enjoyed his front row seat. Emry magically produced a napkin and wiped up the spilled coffee without missing a beat.

"That was a professional hit. No offense, Sheriff, but this is beyond your limited capabilities," Victor said in an arrogant tone.

"Limited capabilities?"

Stone took a quick step toward Victor. Brody stepped in front of Stone, although he remained non-confrontational. Obviously, Brody wanted no part of an irate country sheriff either.

Stone proceeded to shout past Brody as if he wasn't even there. "I don't know who the hell you think you are, but you'd better get your city boy ass off this porch and out of my face before I arrest you for interfering with a police investigation!"

And there was the real Sheriff Stone. Victor took a step closer to Stone in a threatening manner. Brody attempted to keep Victor from moving too close.

"You just try it and I'll have my lawyers up your ass so fast--"

"I ain't afraid of your big, fancy lawyers in their expensive suits. I'll lock them up right alongside you--" He cast a glare at Brody through narrow eyes. "--and that ill-conceived pet of yours."

Brody sneered at Stone but didn't add to the shouting match. That he was avoiding the conflict seemed odd. Drake watched with some secret pleasure as the sheriff and Victor went at it over top of Brody, who almost appeared to be playing peacekeeper. Ivy sedately drank the colorful drink and appeared oblivious of everything unfolding before her. Emry observed the display with a disapproving shake of his head, took Jess by the hand, and pulled her into the house behind him.

Chapter Nineteen

*J*ess followed Emry around the kitchen later that afternoon while he prepared dinner and once again tried to convince him to go out to the tavern with her and Drake. In six months, she had yet to be successful with that. Emry turned several times and nearly collided with Jess, who remained directly behind him with every step.

"Please come out with us tonight," Jess pleaded to him with an innocent look in her eyes. "You saw what happened today on the porch. I thought Sheriff Stone and Victor were going to cross swords. And you know Drake's no help whatsoever. He gets some sort of perverse pleasure watching Sheriff Stone explode on people. I need you there."

Emry turned and again nearly collided with her. He groaned, swiftly picked her up, and placed her on the counter. He then casually proceeded past her.

"You know how strongly I feel about public appearances, Jess. And now that you started the rumor about us sleeping together, those gossiping busybodies will no longer think I'm gay. They'll be at our doorstep in their Sunday wigs and finest support hose attempting to win my affections with homemade pies."

Emry turned toward the main counter and seasoned his pot roast in the roasting pan. Jess remained seated on the counter and watched him prepare dinner.

"It's not my fault women over sixty find you sexy," she said with a teasing smile. "You're the one with the charming disposition and expensive taste in clothes. Maybe if you didn't smell so damned good--"

Emry leaned against the main counter with his back to her and exhaled deeply. It was obvious he had been holding back and could stay silent no longer.

"Why did you feel the need to tell Sheriff Stone you were in my room in the first place?" He finally turned toward her, raised his brow sharply, and appeared offended. "Did you think I needed an alibi?"

"No, of course not. That guy was gutted," she said simply then flashed a teasing smile. "Everyone knows you're more of the neck breaking type."

Emry glared sternly at her. "That's not funny."

"I'm serious, Ridley," Jess begged. "I'd feel better if you were there. You're my self-appointed protector. I need you there tonight."

Emry approached Jess, placed his hands on either side of her on the counter, and looked into her eyes only inches from his with all seriousness. She knew he was going to lecture her. He always hovered over her when he intended to lecture her. His lectures were tedious and boring, but she loved the way he hovered.

"It's not my protection you want. You want me to thwart off possible suitors." He raised his brows with arrogance. "You want my advice? Put on your big girl panties and pick one already. I vote for Sheriff Stone. His butchering of the English language amuses me."

Jess placed her arms around Emry's neck and moved her face closer to his with a playfully lustful smile.

"Drake thinks you'd make a good wife someday."

"How about someone a decade or two younger and maybe a little less *controversial?*" Emry said without appearing the least bit intimidated by her closeness or that lustful smile of hers. "Maybe someone who can actually tell you his real name without fear of being shot."

"But we're great together."

Emry hesitated, placed his arms around her waist, and held her as he smiled warmly. He was obviously up to something, but Jess just loved when he played along. The temptation to pounce on him was hard to resist.

"Yes, you're like the daughter I've always wanted."

His comment stung her pretty good, but she refused to let it show. She instead smiled and affectionately caressed his chest.

"Until you've had too many martinis then it's "shock and awe" on my ass," she said lustfully and suggestively raised her brows.

Emry stared at her teasing smile and immediately frowned at the comment. She stung him back.

"You said you didn't remember what happened last night in your room."

"That's partly true. I don't remember *how* you got on top of me, but I definitely remember you being the aggressor." Jess smiled lustfully with her mouth close to his. "You're so sexy when you're aggressive."

Emry immediately tensed and stared into her eyes. His gaze slowly strayed to her mouth. For a moment, she was almost positive he was going to kiss her. Jess remained still with anticipation. It would be easy for her to initiate the kiss with how close her mouth was to his, but she was playing by his rules. If he broke his rules, he couldn't blame her when something happened. Emry groaned and quickly pulled away. He turned toward the main counter and began applying even more seasoning to the pot roast.

"I have dinner to make, and you have a table to set," he quickly informed her.

Jess jumped off the counter with a groan. "Tease--"

Emry kept his back to her and avoided looking at her as he continued to season the meat.

"I think if you gave Sheriff Stone a chance, you'd realize you like him."

Jess sighed deeply. "I'd rather live with the fantasy that you may one day want me." She stared at his turned back then appeared to reconsider. "Or at least have you get drunk enough that you forget your manners."

She wondered just how much seasoning he would put on the pot roast before he noticed it was too much. Emry stopped working with his back to her. There was a long silence. He turned toward her with a serious look.

"I don't know if you've noticed, but things have been very tense around here lately."

"That's probably because you're always trying to fix me up with Sheriff Stone."

"That's not the problem, and you know it. One of the conditions of my living here was our relationship remained platonic."

Jess rolled her eyes, cast her back to the island counter, and folded her arms across her chest. She always dreaded that lecture.

"I wish you wouldn't roll your eyes at me," Emry said firmly.

"It's my only recourse to your "platonic relationship" lecture."

Jess almost immediately regretted saying that aloud. Now he would lecture even longer. Maybe he really was a schoolteacher. Emry frowned, leaned against the main counter, and stared at her a moment longer.

"I realize I have a nasty habit of refusing to believe I'm wrong about, well, anything, and I suppose it is possible that the tension between us could be my fault." Emry suddenly reconsidered his words. "Who am I kidding? I'm never wrong. I'm confident I'm right about you and Sheriff Stone. I'm so confident that I'll make you a deal. If you kiss Sheriff Stone, and I mean *really* kiss him, and still feel nothing for him, I'll be willing to seriously discuss altering our "platonic relationship" arrangement."

Jess stared at him with a look of complete surprise. Did that mean what she thought it meant? Was he wagering a bet where he was the prize? She immediately smiled and raised her brows.

"Does "seriously discuss" mean you'll actually let me say those three words you hate to hear together?"

"Don't--"

"You, me--*sex*," Jess teased.

"You should interrogate men professionally."

Jess was suddenly feeling playful. He had just given her hope for the relationship she wanted with him. She smiled lustfully at him.

"Don't give me any ideas, or you may find yourself tied to a bed."

Emry stared at her with little expression to her comment. "Excuse me," he said in an unusually tense tone then hurried from the kitchen.

Jess watched his hasty retreat and grinned deviously. He was easily ruffled some days by her suggestive comments. She always took that as a sign of encouragement to his intentions. Drake entered the kitchen while staring after Emry then looked at Jess with bewilderment on his face.

"Do I want to know?" he asked.

"We were just playing around."

"I won't ask."

"Nothing like that," Jess muttered. "How's Ivy feeling?"

"That sedative Ridley gave her seemed to do the trick."

"We'll use the term *sedative* lightly," Jess muttered with a knowing smile.

She wasn't sure what colorful concoction Emry had actually given Ivy to calm her nerves. There was the very real possibility it was little more than crushed vitamins in cranberry juice with two shots of vodka. His self-proclaimed witch doctor remedies from his stint in New Orleans were usually little more than shots of alcohol mixed with something to give it color.

"Well, after her lengthy nap, she's feeling better now. I'm going to run her back to her apartment in the city. She missed her dance class this afternoon, but they said she could go to the evening class." Drake suspiciously eyed the pot roast then looked back at Jess. "I won't be able to make dinner, but I'll be back for happy hour. We're still on for tonight, right?"

"Yes, we're still on. And don't worry;" Jess said then indicated the pot roast with its layer of seasoning, "you're not missing much of a meal tonight."

"I'll be back in a few hours," Drake said then appeared stern. "And then we're going to discuss what I didn't see this morning."

Jess frowned. Drake dramatically pointed a warning finger at her for added emphasis then left the kitchen. Why was every man suddenly trying to be her father? It was really starting to annoy her.

Chapter Twenty

The tavern was busy for seven that evening. The dance floor, in particular, was crowded with good old country boys and girls in cowboy hats and boots line dancing to the exceptional bluegrass band. The tavern was always crowded on nights when live bands performed. It gave local bands a chance to practice their talents in front of a live audience and have their moment in the spotlight. Jess and Drake played pool in the back of the crowded tavern. While Jess made her shot, Drake performed classic Michael Jackson dance moves to the country music. He was actually quite good. Jess straightened and watched as he grabbed his crotch with a high-pitched yowl. Jess shook her head and laughed at his behavior. She didn't know how she could ever live without him in her life--or why she would ever want to.

"I hope Ivy appreciates you."

"I'm good for a laugh or two. She's not nearly as fond of my "Flashdance"." His look suddenly turned serious. "I can't understand why."

Jess was slightly horrified at the thought and stared at him. "Please, not here. These good old boys think you're weird as it is."

Despite her comment, Jess was trying to picture Drake doing some of those risqué dance moves. She actually wanted to see that.

"You're in a good mood tonight. You and Ridley sneak one in on the kitchen counter?" he teased while cleverly raising his brows.

Jess glared her disapproval. "That's just plain nasty, Drake."

Drake casually leaned on his pool stick and maintained his serious look, although he was rarely serious.

"So what's the deal? I walk out the door and it's wild kingdom with you two?"

"Nothing happened," she insisted and observed the pool table for her next shot. "I was a little drunk and crawled into his bed. He makes me feel safe."

"He'd make the Marine's feel safe," Drake muttered. "I thought you'd gotten over him."

Jess sat on the edge of the pool table, twirled the pool stick between her fingers with style and precision as Emry had on the ship, and sighed softly.

"No, I just kept it to myself. Being Ridley is, well, Ridley--"

"More or less," Drake muttered.

"He's been very strict about the "no sex" thing, but he made me a deal tonight--well, more like a wager. If I kiss Sheriff Stone and don't fall hopelessly in love with him, he'll reconsider our relationship."

"Huh? And it only took six months of begging," Drake teased then grinned lustfully. "Sheriff Stone would have had you bent over the pool table at "would you"."

"That's--graphic," she remarked with a disapproving look. Jess turned serious and appeared deep in thought. "I have to handle Sheriff Stone carefully. I wouldn't want to encourage him. He has enough ideas on his own."

"You could always play pool for it. If you lose, you have to kiss the winner. That way he can't think it means anything more."

"That's pretty ingenious. I guess some of my devious nature has finally rubbed off on you."

"I don't need your help to be devious," Drake gloated with a sly smile.

Victor and Brody entered the tavern and headed toward them. Jess jumped off the table and resumed their game while Drake quickly placed twenty dollars under a glass on the edge of the pool table.

"Just leave the details to me," Drake informed her. "I'll set the whole thing up."

Jess eyed her next shot and leaned over the table. Brody headed for the nearby table while Victor approached Drake and sized up the game.

"Who's winning?"

"It's close," Drake said. "We have an interesting wager going. If she loses, she has to kiss me--on the lips, and I'm taking a picture for bragging rights."

"Seriously?"

Victor appeared unusually silent for a long moment. The lustful images could almost be seen running through his head, evident by his increasing grin.

Drake leaned closer to him with a sly smile and muttered, "I've been slipping vodka into her soda."

Victor looked at Drake with some surprise then grinned. Both chuckled softly. Brody sat at the nearby table while sipping his glass of brandy and watched them play. Jess sank the next two balls and won the game. She claimed the twenty dollars and gave Drake a mocking smile. Drake frowned and shook his head with disgust.

"Someone needs another drink," Drake muttered to Victor then looked at Jess. "You rack 'em. I'll get you another soda."

Victor approached Jess at the pool table and grinned. "I'm a gambling man and fairly decent at pool. I'll play you while Drake gets your drink," he said while placing twenty dollars under the glass.

"Same rules?"

"I'll abide by the wager," Victor replied with a cheap grin.

Jess wasn't sure she liked his enthusiasm. He reminded her of wealthier, less charming Grant. While Jess and Victor played their pool game, good old country boys began to collect mysteriously in the back and watched the game with overwhelming interest. Drake had done a great job of spreading word of the prize to be won. It was unheard of for Jess to make such a wager, and they just wanted to get in on it. All that was missing from the thickening plot was Sheriff Stone. Drake walked past Jess as she was about to make another shot.

"Guess who--" Drake said softly to her.

"Guess I should wrap this up then, huh?" Jess muttered in response.

Jess made several shots, cleaned up all of her remaining balls, and easily won the game. Victor appeared disappointed but not all that surprised by his loss. She collected her money then casually looked around the room and grinned at the collecting country boys.

"Any other takers?"

The young men quickly shouted and raised their money. Sheriff Stone entered the back and appeared unusually annoyed. His expression was almost concerning.

"Now I know there ain't gambling going on back here, because that's against the law," Stone firmly announced and glared at the men standing around.

The crowd of young men quickly scattered. Stone approached Jess and the pool table with his stern look of disapproval. He suddenly slapped a twenty-dollar bill on the table and grinned charmingly.

"Let's go. I ain't got all night."

Jess laughed and appeared relieved. Sheriff Stone wasn't without his charm, even she couldn't deny that. She wondered why she wasn't attracted to him. Jess glanced at him as he selected his pool stick and joked with Drake. She felt a twinge of panic at the thought of having to kiss him, *really kiss him*, as Emry had put it. Jess racked the balls and reclaimed her pool stick. She couldn't understand why she was suddenly so nervous about this. Although, what if Emry was right? What if she kissed Sheriff Stone and fell hopelessly in love with him? She had never known Emry to be wrong. He was annoying that way. A commotion came from the bar. It was undoubtedly the prelude to a fight. Stone became immediately annoyed.

"Jesus," he grumbled then looked at Jess and grinned. "Don't go leaving town."

Stone headed for the bar area. Jess frowned her disappointment. She wanted it over. Brody appeared alongside her, placed twenty dollars on the table, and took one of the pool sticks. Jess appeared surprised and nervously eyed Drake across the room. Drake was at a loss and shrugged. Jess turned back toward the table as Brody made the break. The balls scattered and several went into pockets. Over the next few minutes, Jess watched with amazement and possible horror as Brody dominated the pool table. He called and made shot after shot. As he sank the winning ball, Jess stared with disbelief. Brody reclaimed his money and casually approached her. His look was mostly serious but there was a hint of arrogance on his face.

"Pay up."

Jess's heart nearly leaped out of her chest. She stared at Brody a moment with her mouth hanging open then eyed Drake, who grinned and held up his cell phone. Drake's amusement irritated her more than the thought of actually having to kiss Brody, but she didn't welch on her bets.

Jess looked back at Brody and appeared apprehensive. "It sounded easier in theory."

Without warning, Brody grabbed Jess around the waist, pulled her firmly against him, and kissed her passionately. Jess tensed against him with surprise but knew she was obligated to pay off on the wager. Jess returned the kiss and attempted to relax in his arms, which only seemed to encourage him further. Drake chuckled softly and took the picture with his cell phone. Jess suddenly realized the kiss lasted longer than it should. She made an effort to break it off, but Brody appeared reluctant to end it. Brody finally broke off the kiss and grinned as he released her. She felt slightly dazed by his kiss.

"Let me know if you want a rematch," he said deviously then looked at Drake. "Send me a copy."

"You've got it."

Jess glared at Drake as Brody returned to the table. Victor smiled and proudly slapped Brody on the back. Drake grinned at Jess and mocked her. Drake's grin was infuriating. What she found even more infuriating was the kiss was a little too good.

Chapter Twenty-one

At the same time in the city, a trendy, two-story nightclub was alive with blaring club music, dim lighting, and hundreds of young men and women dressed in their club wear finest. Carla and her two friends, Julie and Shelly, sat at the round booth with colorful martinis before them. Julie and Shelly were both attractive women in their mid-twenties and not beneath Carla's class of friends. All three women wore expensive, stunning dresses that revealed plenty of cleavage and even more leg. They were in full prowling mode, but none was enthused with the evening's offerings.

"I can't believe the limited selection for ladies' night," Shelly said with that all too familiar snobbish appearance Carla had displayed on the cruise ship. "Where are all the good ones?"

"We're too early," Carla said. "I told you we should have waited another hour."

"And then all the good ones are already taken," Shelly said simply.

"No man is truly off the market until he has a ring on his finger," Carla said then reconsidered. "And sometimes not even then."

"Oh, that's disgusting," Shelly said with a look of distaste.

"I don't know about you guys, but I'm getting tired of going home alone," Julie sulked and appeared bored while scanning the room. "I may have to downgrade."

"Don't be ridiculous," Carla said firmly. "I won't allow you to go home with someone who's obviously beneath you. That's what friends do."

"I'm not holding out any hope of a Greek God walking through the door," Julie said plainly.

Shelly suddenly perked up and stared across the crowded room. It was obvious by the look on her face that something or someone caught her attention.

"No? Well, how about a Spanish God?" Shelly grinned. "Zeus just walked in, girls."

Julie and Carla looked in the direction Shelly stared. An incredibly attractive, Hispanic man in his late twenties, Rico, and his five friends made their way through the crowded club with a buzz of attention. Rico was clean-cut with short dark hair, built like a Roman God, and stood an impressive 6'4". His friends, Jacob, Matt, Andy, Trevor, and Lance, were attractive in their own rights, but they didn't stand out like Rico, who was dressed boldly in an expensive, white suit. The six men flirted with the women who flocked around them as they worked the room. They were very popular with the women, but Rico was obviously the main attraction. Carla, Julie, and Shelly stared and marveled at the handsome man.

"Now that's the man I want to take home," Julie said softly.

"Stand in line," Shelly muttered.

Rico and his friends approached them, singling them out, and stopped before their table. Rico looked at Carla and smiled suavely with the most dazzling, radiant smile.

"Pardon me, Mi querida," Rico said with a thick, Spanish accent combined with a deep, manly voice. "Are you not Senorita Carla from the *Andrea Maria*?"

The thickness of his accent was possibly sexier than he was. All three women stared at the tall, muscular man as if unable to speak.

"Wow, that sounded hot," Shelly said softly.

A little while later, Shelly danced with Matt, Jacob, and Lance on the dance floor. The three men competed for her attention, possibly hoping she would choose him over his friends. Shelly danced seductively with all three and appeared to be in her glory. Each man attempted to get closer to her on his turn. Julie sat at the table between Andy and Trevor. She boldly flirted with both men while trying to decide which one she would be going home with. Both men were charming and came on strong, making her decision more difficult. She was giddy with delight at all the attention both were displaying toward her. Andy leaned closer and whispered something in her ear. She appeared mildly surprised and looked at him as if uncertain how to respond.

Carla and Rico sat close together on the other side of the table. Rico held Carla's hand, spoke softly to her, and suavely kissed her hand.   Carla couldn't take her eyes off the handsome man and appeared giddy around him, which was unlike her.   No man had ever been able to sweep her off her feet, but then she had never met a man quite like Rico.   Julie slipped out from the booth and gently cleared her throat to get Carla's attention.   Carla was so captivated by Rico; she didn't even realize Julie was standing over her.   She finally looked up and smiled at her friend.   Rico was now nibbling on her neck.

"I don't suppose you'll mind if I leave early," Julie said with a teasing grin.

Carla glanced at Andy and Trevor, who stood only a few feet away from the table, and then looked back at Julie with a knowing smirk.

"Which one is it?"

Julie just smiled her response.   "If you don't hear from me in a couple of days, don't be too concerned."

Julie turned and approached the two men.   Andy and Trevor placed their arms securely around her and all three headed for the door.   Carla stared after them with some surprise.   Rico spoke softly in Spanish while warmly kissing her neck.   Carla quickly forgot about Julie and looked at Rico.   She didn't know what he said but giggled all the same.

"Was that an offer?"

Rico grinned and chuckled.

✝

It was around nine o'clock that evening.   Carla's home was located on the outskirts of the city in a wealthy neighborhood full of expensive homes.   Her home was no different with an amazing stonewall surrounding the immaculately landscaped property.   The large, wrought iron gate remained closed across the entrance to the driveway.   The exterior was well-lit, but only a few lights were on within the expensive home.   Carla's dimly lit bedroom was decorated only with the finest, name brand furniture, curtains, and bedding. Rico and Carla were mostly hidden beneath the heap of moving covers while moaning loudly.   Their lovemaking was obviously wild and passionate as the loud moans turned to cries of ecstasy and the heavy, solid bed began to thump.   All sounds finally subsided.   Rico moved off Carla and collapsed on the bed while panting heavily with a grin on his handsome face.   Carla attempted to catch her breath as well.   Rico said something in Spanish.

"I don't know what you said," Carla panted while grinning, "but I agree."

114

Rico laughed softly. Carla snuggled against his muscular chest with exhaustion and enthusiasm. He smiled as he held her and said something else in Spanish.

"If that means, "let's do it again", I'm all for it."

"Actually, it translates to "I need a cigarette". You mind, Mi querida?" Rico asked pleasantly while retaining his boyish grin.

"No, not at all."

Rico released her and sat up. He slipped into his pants and searched through several pockets until he finally found his cigarettes. He then removed his cell phone and checked for messages while he lit his cigarette. Carla slipped into his massive shirt and buttoned it. Rico eyed her and appeared offended.

"Where you go, Mi querida?"

"To the kitchen for some drinks. I'll be back." She flashed a lustful smile and kissed him quickly but firmly on the lips. "Don't go anywhere."

Rico's smile returned. "I wait here."

She giggled and left the bedroom. Carla headed down the open stairs in Rico's oversized shirt, walked along the elegant hallway, and entered the dimly lit, modern kitchen. She removed a bottle of wine from the rack without even knowing what it was then rummaged through the drawer for the corkscrew. She suddenly hesitated and looked out the kitchen window with a puzzled look. The wrought iron gate across the driveway was now partially open. She distinctly remembered closing it behind them. Carla lightly tapped the wine bottle with her professionally manicured fingernails and appeared deep in thought.

A few minutes later, a faint scratching sound was heard at the front door. The lock turned. The door slowly opened to reveal a masked intruder dressed in black. He quietly slipped into the house. The first floor was dimly lit and appeared quiet. He turned toward the security system with a small screwdriver in his hand then hesitated with some surprise. The alarm hadn't even been activated. He chuckled softly, replaced the tool, and removed a hunting knife. The intruder quietly headed toward the stairs.

"Mi querida, I still waiting," Rico was heard calling from upstairs.

The intruder suddenly stopped and looked at the stairs. Rico appeared on the second floor landing in just his pants. He walked down several steps in his bare feet with a charming grin on his face.

"Mi querida, Rico get lonely."

Carla didn't respond. Rico was halfway down the stairs when the intruder appeared on the bottom step with the hunting knife clutched in his gloved hand. Rico froze and stared at the masked man. Neither man moved. Carla suddenly appeared from the hallway powder room with a gun in her hand and fired wildly at the intruder. The intruder appeared alarmed and bolted for the front door while dodging the haphazard gunshots. The random shots struck the walls and framed photos but came nowhere near hitting the man. As the intruder ran from the house, something fell from his jacket. Rico sprang into action with a look of rage on his face as he thundered down the remaining stairs, leaped the last four steps, and chased after the man while screaming Spanish profanities. Carla watched Rico run after the intruder and appeared horrified.

"Rico, no!"

Carla ran a couple of steps toward the open door then paused and looked down to the floor at what the intruder had dropped. She stared at a copy of "The Battle for *Andrea Maria*" movie script lying on the floor. Carla stared at the script and appeared bewildered then alarmed.

†

*A*round the same time that evening, Brody and Victor sat at the table in the back of the tavern and sipped their drinks while Jess played pool with Drake. Drake was less interested in the pool game and more interested in tormenting his friend. He followed her around the pool table with a cheap grin on his face and periodically flashed the photo on his cell phone of her and Brody kissing.

"Did he, like, slip you the tongue? Because I'm thinking he slipped you the tongue."

Jess attempted to make another shot, missed the ball completely, and appeared annoyed with him. Drake wasn't about to let it go. He was having too much fun embarrassing Jess over her shared kiss with Brody.

"I bet Sheriff Stone slips you the tongue too," Drake said with a lustful grin.

Jess finally straightened, glared at him with irritation, and snatched the phone from his hand. Drake appeared concerned and tried to retrieve the phone from her. She turned several times to avoid his reach while fiddling with the buttons on the phone.

"Don't you delete that!"

Jess suddenly grabbed him around the neck with one arm, half jumped on him, and kissed him passionately on the mouth. She held the cell phone out and pressed the camera button. Drake attempted to pry her off him. She broke off the kiss and grinned. Drake snatched his phone.

"You know I'm happily dating," Drake pouted.

Drake looked at the picture she had taken of them kissing and hid his proud smile. He obviously didn't mind all that much.

Stone returned to the pool area, looked around, and smiled with a boyish grin. "So, what did I miss?"

Drake smiled and showed him the picture of Jess and Brody kissing. Stone grinned, shook his head, and playfully mocked Jess.

"One of those nights, huh?" Stone looked at the table and became annoyed. "Who took my twenty?"

Jess removed Sheriff Stone's twenty-dollar bill from her pocket and replaced it under the glass. Jess and Stone played their round of pool with Jess purposely missing shots. As the game progressed, Brody approached the table to watch and became increasingly interested. When Jess missed an easy shot, Brody glared at her. Jess caught his look but ignored him. On Stone's next turn, he sank the winning ball and proudly held his hands in the air. Drake and Victor applauded him. Stone approached Jess wearing his best country boy grin.

"I believe you owe me something," Stone said proudly and with amazing charm.

Jess was relieved it was finally over but tried not to act too happy, after all, she did lose.

She smiled warmly and offered a tiny shrug. "Why not? I'm on a roll now."

She was now nervous and didn't know what to expect, especially after that amazing kiss from Brody. Jess uncertainly placed her arms around Stone's neck and kissed him firmly on the mouth while Drake cheered and took a picture with his cell phone. Stone immediately returned the passionate kiss while holding her firmly against him. Jess's thoughts suddenly strayed to the previous night with Emry in her bedroom. She could still feel his body against hers and the way he had aggressively kissed and caressed her. All she could think about while kissing Sheriff Stone was Emry. He had been wrong! Kissing Sheriff Stone changed nothing. She still loved Emry! Jess returned to reality and broke off the kiss despite his attempt to prolong it. Stone held her in his arms and appeared pleased with the payoff.

"How about best two out of three?" Stone teased warmly with a grin.

Jess tried to wriggle out of his arms. "I've played enough pool for one night."

"I wasn't referring to pool."

Stone attempted to kiss her again. Jess wriggled out of his arms and quickly put some distance between them.

Drake quickly moved in and distracted Stone by showing him the photo on his cell phone. Stone looked at the picture and smiled proudly.

"Put me down for an 8x10 and a couple of wallet sizes," he said with a chuckle.

Jess walked away and tried to compose herself. Her thoughts were all over the place, particularly straying to the conversation she and Emry would be soon having. Jess was suddenly aware of Brody standing alongside her on the other side of the pool table. His sudden appearance startled her.

He glared his disapproval. "You *threw* that game."

She refused to look at him. "I don't know what you're talking about."

"What are you up to?"

Jess remained tense and avoided him while replacing her pool stick. She couldn't look at him. He was too good at reading her eyes.

"I'm not up to anything," she said simply and maintained her look of disinterest.

As she turned, Brody moved directly into her path and glared at her, forcing her to meet his gaze.

"Unless you want me to have a nice conversation with some gossip magazines, you'd better start talking."

Jess suddenly tensed and stared into his eyes. He was serious too. She quickly searched for a moderately decent response that he wouldn't see through. Jess finally sighed softly.

"If you must know, I'm trying to make Ridley jealous. As you're probably already aware, I have a thing for older, distinguished men. I thought if I showed an interest in Sheriff Stone it might force Ridley's hand." Jess fidgeted and ran her fingers through her hair. "I'm growing tired of having a one-sided relationship with him."

Ironically, that wasn't far from the truth. Brody studied her but didn't appear to buy it.

"It's like "Water Gate" between you two, but that's not what's going on here," Brody said firmly. His expression suddenly turned more compassionate. "You don't have to play games with Sheriff Stone to solicit his protection services, Jess. I can protect you better than he can. I'm in the protection business, remember? Nothing against good old Sheriff Stone, but he doesn't stand a chance against professional hit men. You'll just end up getting him killed. I know how to handle hired killers."

Jess was astonished by his assessment of the game she was playing. She was actually a little ashamed for not coming up with such a good excuse herself. Then his proposal suddenly dawned on her.

"You want me to *hire* you?"

That could never happen. She couldn't risk having Brody hanging around and chance him possibly discovering Emry's true identity. The irony was she didn't even know Emry's true identity.

"Don't you already have a full-time gig?"

Brody made a face of disgust and waved her off. "That's a baby-sitting job. Everyone knows that. Victor doesn't get up until noon most days. I could work days for him, and evenings and mornings for you. I'll take the bedroom next to yours at night."

Jess couldn't believe he was offering his protection services after all they'd put each other through. She thought he would be the one from whom she would need protecting. Then something suddenly clicked in her head. Could he be one of those good old boys Drake claimed wanted to get into her pants? The way he had kissed her would support Drake's theory. She freely admitted to being dense about men and their sexual intentions. Jess again thought about his offer and became tense.

"I don't know if Ridley would approve," Jess bluntly informed him.

Approve? That was a good one. Emry was liable to throw her out of her own house at the suggestion. She knew him too well.

Brody appeared surprised by her comment. "Why should it matter what Ridley thinks? Who's in charge out there? You or Ridley?"

Jess considered the question only a moment then nodded with conviction. "Hmm? Yeah, I'm pretty sure it's Ridley."

Brody rolled his eyes and groaned.

Sheriff Stone paced near Drake with his cell phone to his ear and a look of concern on his face. His actions caught Jess and Brody's attention.

"Did they catch him?" Stone asked.

Drake had an oddly tense look about him while he watched the sheriff on his phone. Jess noted his interest in Stone's phone call and attempted to eavesdrop.

"Yeah, thanks for calling, Detective," Stone said to the caller. He disconnected the call and approached Jess with Drake on his heels. Stone's look was concerning. "That was the city detective on Conner's case. An armed intruder broke into Carla's house a little while ago."

Jess and Drake suddenly became alarmed.

"Is she okay?" Jess asked with concern.

"Apparently she went psycho on his ass, and unloaded an entire clip into her foyer," Stone said with a hint of satisfaction in his tone. "Unfortunately, she didn't hit him. Her boyfriend chased him for two blocks, but he got away."

Jess removed her cell phone and pressed a single button. The phone rang and Emry's voicemail picked up. She frowned and pressed another button. The home phone answering machine picked up. Jess disconnected the call and looked at Drake with concern.

"Ridley isn't answering his cell phone or the house phone," Jess said nervously. She gave Brody a stern look. "You're hired. Let's go."

Chapter Twenty-two

*D*rake's mustang, Victor's Bentley, and Stone's police blazer pulled up to Jess's unusually dark plantation house around ten o'clock that evening. The outside barn lights were on, but the house was unusually dark. Jess jumped out of Drake's sports car before it even stopped, looked at the house, and appeared alarmed.

"He always leaves a light on for me," Jess said to Drake with a drained look on her face.

Her heart was pounding, and she felt her entire body twitching with anxiety. Jess hurried for the porch. Brody swiftly snagged her around the waist, pulled her back to the car, and gave her a firm look.

"You wait here," Brody said in a stern tone.

Victor placed his arm securely around Jess's shoulder and kept her at a safe distance from the house. She was too preoccupied with concern for Emry to think about Victor holding her. Drake always had the time to think about those things and glared his disapproval of Victor's arm around her. After all, that was *his* job. Brody and Stone removed their weapons and walked onto the porch. Jess, Drake, and Victor watched in silence as the two men entered the house. Stone and Brody entered the foyer and paused just inside the doorway. Stone flicked the light switch. Nothing happened. The two men exchanged looks.

"The barn lights were on," Brody said. "It's possible someone cut the power to the house."

Stone nodded and removed a flashlight from his jacket pocket then gave Brody a serious look.

"I'm allowing you to tag along, so don't do anything stupid like shooting up the place."

Brody glared his annoyance. If they had been comparing gun calibers, it would be an interesting matchup. Brody appeared firearm friendly, particularly being in the protection business. On the other hand, Sheriff Stone was a good old boy. By age ten, every kid in town was a crack shot. They quietly walked along the grand hallway with their guns raised and looked into each dark room as they passed. Stone and Brody entered the dark kitchen. A strange buzzing sound caught their attention. Stone shined his flashlight at the island counter. Emry's cell phone was lit up and vibrated across the countertop. The lights suddenly came on, startling both men. They aimed their guns at Emry, who casually stood next the fuse box in the wall.

Emry didn't appear the least bit fazed by them or the guns aimed at him. He smiled playfully and raised his hands. "Don't shoot. I surrender."

Both men lowered their weapons while groaning. Emry casually picked up his vibrating cell phone with "Jess" displayed on the caller ID. He pressed a button and placed the phone to his ear.

"Hello, Jess," Emry said cheerfully into the phone. "Where are you?"

Her shouting and profanities were distinctly heard through the phone. Emry appeared unaffected by her tone and maintained an innocent look about him.

"Me? I'm in the kitchen. Did you want some tea?"

†

It was a little before eleven o'clock that night. Emry stood behind the bar in the game room and mixed a pitcher of martinis. His jovial mood from early had disappeared. He looked irritated and was unusually silent. Jess quietly sat before the bar and watched him with a concerned expression. She knew his moods well and silence was never good.

"You're mad."

He didn't look at her. "I'm not mad."

"I'm pretty sure you're mad."

Emry suddenly gave her a stern look indicating he was definitely mad. "How could you hire Brody without discussing it with me first? Someone is trying to kill you and you bring a questionable man into our home."

"He's Victor's bodyguard. How is that questionable?" she asked with surprise.

122

"Victor is as crooked as they come, and Brody is the poster child for hired killers. You don't get more questionable than that. Now he's in our house sleeping in the room next to yours. I'm extremely uncomfortable with that."

"Fine, if you want him gone, he's gone. I'll call him at Victor's house and tell him not to bother packing his overnight bag."

Emry frowned, appeared preoccupied, and placed several glasses onto the tray with the pitcher. He seemed less hostile and more defeated.

"No, he'll be back soon. I'll deal with him tomorrow," he said with a frown then gave her a serious look. "But I'm not leaving you alone with him next door to you. I'm afraid that makes us roommates tonight."

Jess tried to hide her grin but failed. "As horrible as that sounds, I'll just have to make the best of it."

He cast a look at her with little emotion and shook his head. "Your enthusiasm is frightening."

Emry picked up the tray of martinis and headed for the game room door. Jess grinned, sprang up from her bar stool, and hurried after him with a lively spring in her step. Bedtime couldn't come soon enough.

†

It was quarter after eleven that night. Sheriff Stone, Jess, Drake, and Emry sat on the porch while drinking martinis. Emry busily worked on his laptop and said little while Jess and Drake talked with Sheriff Stone. Emry paused only once to fiddle with his cell phone, appeared unusually preoccupied by something, and then returned to his laptop. Jess wondered if Brody's overnight visit had him feverishly working on his laptop and avoiding social hour. Emry was usually quite the conversationalist when they received company. He always had something intelligent, or possibly controversial, to add to the conversation. Jess, Drake, and Stone continued to talk in great length about the attack on Carla. Emry added nothing to the conversation and didn't even look up. Stone finally looked at his watch, groaned, and finished his drink.

"I wish I could stay, but I'm on a one-martini limit and the late shift." Stone reluctantly stood and looked at Jess. "Brody should be back soon. As much as I dislike the guy, I'm sure he'll keep you safe. I'll be back to check on you in the morning."

"That's not necessary, Sheriff."

She couldn't easily tell him that Emry was all the protection she would ever need. As far as Stone was concerned, Ridley was just some domesticated butler and not capable of harming a fly. It was a fabricated image, which Emry pulled off brilliantly.

"I agree but the mayor insisted. My hands are tied," Stone told her with a teasing smile. "Walk me out?"

Jess hesitated with some reluctance then walked off the porch with Sheriff Stone. They approached his police blazer in the driveway. Stone paused by the blazer and turned toward her with a smile.

"I was thinking I'd take off tomorrow and spend the day here-- just in case," Stone said.

"I don't think--"

Stone moved into Jess without warning and kissed her passionately. Jess tensed with surprise and braced her hands against his chest. Before she could debate how hard to push him away, Brody's car pulled up behind the police blazer and blinded them with its headlights. Stone broke off the kiss and groaned with annoyance. He looked at the headlights, indicated his blazer, and shooed him away. Brody moved his car, so he no longer blocked the police blazer. Stone turned toward Jess, who had already backed away. He appeared defeated but smiled regardless.

"Night, Jess."

"Good night, Sheriff."

Stone climbed into his blazer and drove away from the house. Jess headed toward the house as Brody mysteriously appeared alongside her and kept pace. His look was suspiciously disapproving. Everyone was looking at her like that tonight. She was starting to think she needed more female friends. Jess avoided looking at him as he followed her toward the porch.

"Sorry if I interrupted the good night kiss," Brody said with little sincerity.

"I doubt that."

"You're right, I'm not sorry," he announced. "I'm going to walk the perimeter."

Brody turned to the left and headed past the house. Jess walked onto the porch and lacked enthusiasm. She paused by the martini pitcher near Emry's chair, refilled her glass, and glanced at his laptop. There were split screens that revealed security cameras mysteriously located around the property. Jess suddenly appeared surprised.

"What's that?"

"Just something I worked on this evening," Emry said with little emotion.

"You did all that tonight? You've been busy." Jess's look suddenly changed to concern as she pointed to one of the screens. "Is that my bedroom?"

Emry didn't respond. That answered that question. Jess was still reveling at how he mounted security cameras and had a system up and running in one evening.

"How much did all this cost?"

"You can't put a price on security," he replied simply without looking at her.

"That much, huh?" Jess muttered.

Drake approached them with his full martini glass, sat on the railing in Jess's usual spot, and already appeared slightly buzzed.

"I can't wait to see how much rent-a-killer costs," Drake said with a humored smile and an added chuckle. "Of course, with the way he's been checking out Jess, he might be willing to take it in trade."

"The guy seriously needs to get laid," Jess muttered.

Emry casually removed his cell phone without looking up from his laptop and placed it on the table to reveal the picture of her and Brody kissing.

"I'm sure he's hoping to," Emry remarked lowly and concentrated on the computer screen.

Jess suddenly felt uncomfortable that Emry saw the picture of her kissing Brody. She couldn't believe Drake sent him that picture. Then it dawned on her. Did that photo spark Emry's sudden mood change? Was he jealous? Although that should have been a good sign, she felt the sudden need to explain the circumstances surrounding the kiss.

"We played pool for it. It wasn't a big deal."

"He slipped her the tongue," Drake teased while playing devil's advocate.

Jess was immediately horrified. Emry glared at Drake. The only time she had ever seen that look on Emry's face was when Brahm reached for the gun down her cleavage. Jess slapped Drake on the chest with a look of annoyance

He cried out and rubbed his chest. "I'm kidding! I'm kidding! Talk about needing to get laid--" Drake again rubbed his chest with discomfort. "Thank God Ivy's coming along on the cruise this weekend. You're usually on your best behavior when she's around. I don't feel like getting beaten up the entire weekend."

"I'm not going on the anniversary cruise. I've sent my regrets."

Drake suddenly appeared offended, stood from where he sat on the railing, and nearly spilled his drink.

"Oh, no! We talked about this! If you don't go, I don't go. I can't disappoint Ivy. She's been looking forward to this for months. Besides, I'd already told Zeke, the publicist, you'd be there."

"What? No, Drake," Jess said hotly. "What's wrong with you? How can you still want to go after what happened to Conner and Carla?"

"Because it's a big deal to the producers and an even bigger deal to Ivy," Drake said defensively. "They want us to do a photo shoot on the ship as a promo to the movie. This will probably be the last time we'll be asked to do anything." Drake's mood was stern and serious. "Carla texted me earlier and said she's still going this weekend. If she's okay with going, so should you."

Jess glanced at Emry, who worked on his laptop and appeared to ignore their conversation. She was surprised he hadn't already added his two cents.

"Are you just going to sit there? Tell Drake that going on the anniversary cruise is a bad idea."

Emry didn't look up from his laptop and appeared almost callous. "I think you should go".

"Hah!" Drake shouted with a mocking grin while pointing his finger at her. Dad sided with him for once.

Jess stared at Emry's profile and appeared surprised by his answer and even more by his tone.

"You're willing to let me out of your sight for an entire weekend after all that's happened?"

Emry still didn't look up. "I'm sure Sheriff Stone will offer his protection services."

Jess was annoyed with the way he kept pushing Sheriff Stone on her and couldn't hide it any longer.

"Or maybe I'll take Brody," she snapped.

Emry glared his disapproval then returned to his laptop without comment. Jess was suddenly uncomfortable. There was a strange tension between them now. Something was wrong. She felt the need to change the subject. She insecurely folded her arms across her chest and looked around.

"What do you suppose Brody's doing out there so long?" she asked softly to no one in particular.

Emry studied the security cameras on his laptop. "A couple of minutes ago, he was pissing on my flowerbed. Now he's by the woods."

Jess and Drake moved behind Emry and watched the security cameras. Brody was seen on the screen near one of the cameras. He moved in closer until his enlarged face was staring at them as he looked at the camera. Jess and Drake instinctively pulled back as Brody's face quickly filled the frame.

"I believe Brody found one of my cameras," Emry said casually. Brody's face moved away from the camera frame. "Five, four, three, two, one--"

Brody appeared around the house, jumped onto the porch, and approached them with a strange look on his face. Emry casually shut his laptop. Brody glared from the laptop to Emry with some surprise.

"You installed security cameras? Why didn't you say something earlier? I should have access to that."

"Get your own toys." Emry glared at Brody then spoke lowly, "and keep your hands off mine."

Brody and Emry exchanged cold stares. There was an uncomfortable silence. Neither man flinched.

"She's not yours, so stop trying to control her," Brody said firmly.

Emry stared at Brody with an all too familiar expression Jess had only seen once on the *Andrea Maria*. Jess and Drake were frozen with alarm.

"Jess, shut him up or I will," Emry growled without taking his eyes off Brody.

Emry's words cut through her. She was genuinely concerned for Brody. Jess quickly moved closer to Brody, took his hand, and pulled him toward the house with her.

"How about a game of pool?"

"I'm not afraid of him, Jess, and you shouldn't be either. I can handle him. I'm ten years younger and three inches taller."

Emry slammed his laptop on the table and suddenly stood. Jess held back her gasp and pulled Brody into the house with her. Drake watched them disappear into the house then looked at Emry, who composed himself and returned to his chair.

"What was that about?" Drake suddenly asked.

"She's trying to make me jealous. She knows there's a camera in the game room and assumes I'll spy on her."

"I actually meant what happened between you and Victor's goon, but I'm up for a little Peeping Tom action." Drake flashed a smile. "So what are we waiting for? Let's spy on them."

He glared at Drake.

"Come on, Ridley, you know you want to."

Emry returned to working on his laptop without looking at him. Drake continued to spy over his shoulder and maintained his semi-drunken enthusiasm.

"Put on the game room channel," Drake teased. "Let's see just how jealous you aren't."

"I hope you realize you're three seconds away from losing a testicle."

Drake's smile suddenly faded. He placed his hand over his crotch and slowly inched away from Emry.

Chapter Twenty-three

$\mathcal{I}$t was nearly eleven thirty that evening. Brody racked the billiard balls on the pool table in the game room. He looked at Jess, who appeared distant as she leaned against the table. She was still trying to understand Emry's wild mood swing. What possibly created the tension between them? Was it just Emry's distaste for Brody or something more?

"You can talk about it, Jess. I'm here to protect you. If Ridley is using your feelings to manipulate you--"

Jess snapped out of her trance, realizing Brody was still in the room. She looked at him and appeared surprised by his assumption of the situation.

"What? No, it's not like that. He's just very protective, that's all. Our relationship is complicated." Jess stopped to consider her comment then muttered, "That's putting it mildly." She straightened, turned to face Brody, and attempted a smile. "My problems with Ridley are my own, and I can end them any time."

"Fine, if you don't want to talk about Ridley, I can respect that. I'd rather not talk about him anyway. Life is too short."

She couldn't believe he thought Emry was somehow abusing her. Other than disapproving stares and firm lectures, Emry was nonthreatening toward her. He never even raised his voice to her that she recalled. If she hadn't witnessed his one-man commando routine onboard the ship, she wouldn't think he was even capable of anything violent.

Brody removed a pool stick and grinned. "What are we playing for?"

"Not much for a friendly game of pool, are you?"

"No, I'm not really big on that winning being its own reward bullshit," Brody teased. "When I win, I want it to mean something."

"How about ten dollars a game?"

"I sort of liked the stakes from earlier tonight," Brody said with a sly grin.

Jess looked at him with some surprise, although she wondered if she really should have been. His agenda was suddenly very clear, and she realized it was going to be a long night.

"You'll have to live with ten dollars a game," she said without hesitation.

"No sense of adventure--"

✝

It was a few minutes past midnight. Emry walked along the second floor hallway with his laptop securely under his arm. He paused before Jess's door and tapped softly on it. The nearby bedroom door opened, and Brody looked into the hall. Brody and Emry exchanged looks. There was no telling what went through either man's head, but their stares were not friendly. Emry glared at him then entered Jess's bedroom without waiting for her permission. Brody watched him disappear into the bedroom and appeared curious. As Emry shut the door behind him, Jess looked briefly at him from her reclined position on the bed while flipping through television channels with the remote control. She had already changed into her usual sleep shorts and tank top. Emry approached and set his laptop down on the nightstand. The tension remained between them. Jess managed a gentle smile despite the mood.

"You should have let the dirty glasses wait until morning. I was about to start the movie without you," Jess said gently in an effort to maintain peace between them.

"Zombies or ghosts?"

"Disaster movie."

Emry removed his jacket and placed it across the bench at the foot end of the bed. Jess watched him closely. His earlier foul mood had put a damper on her enthusiasm toward their first night as roommates. She also knew it meant their "talk" would have to wait until he was in a better mood.

"You seem distracted," Jess said in hopes that he might open up about what was really bothering him and release the tension between them.

"Your stray saw me entering your room."

"Let him think what he wants."

"I'm sure he already does." Emry sat alongside her on the large bed and remained distracted. He finally looked at her with all seriousness. "You know I have very good instincts about people, Jess. There's something about Brody that just doesn't add up. He's hiding something; I know it. I don't trust him and neither should you."

"Funny, he said the same about you."

"I'm sure he did. You must have said some very unflattering things about me to make him think that I'm using you."

"I didn't say any unflattering things," she insisted. "He knew I threw the game with Sheriff Stone. I needed to tell him something, so I told him the truth."

Emry appeared concerned while staring at her. "The truth? Which truth?"

"The one where I'm in love with you, but you don't feel the same way about me," she replied with some bitterness in her tone.

"That's hardly fair, Jess. Our relationship is complicated."

"No, you're complicated." Jess then muttered under her breath, "I'm just the stupid girl wasting her life waiting around for you."

Emry suddenly groaned, allowed his head to fall back against the headboard, and shut his eyes.

"I knew this would never work. I should have left when you threw me out six months ago."

His insensitive comment hit her hard and it was becoming difficult to keep it inside any longer.

"You knew how I felt about you," she snapped. "Did you think those feelings would simply go away?"

"No, but I was sure a dose of reality would kill your romantic fantasies about us."

Jess became enraged and turned on her hip to face him. The hostility and possible hurt showed in her eyes as she glared at him. Her sudden movement caught his attention, but he didn't react to it.

"Fantasies, huh? I didn't imagine that lustful attitude of yours on the ship, and we both know you intended to ask me back to your cabin, so don't you dare pretend you weren't attracted to me. You made me want you then pushed me away."

Emry stared at her and appeared surprised by her hostility and rage toward him. He took a deep breath and attempted to smooth things over.

"What happened onboard was an entirely different situation." Emry was suddenly reluctant to finish his explanation about what happened on the ship. He looked away, ran his fingers through his hair, and frowned. "I'm sorry for everything I've put you through, Jess. I never meant to hurt you."

Jess flopped back into a sitting position and avoided looking at him while she fumed. She wasn't sure what to say, but she was sure she wanted it to be something that would hurt him.

"Well, you've got what you wanted, I'm getting on with my life," she said in a cold tone. "I'm going on the anniversary cruise this weekend, and I'm taking Brody with me whether you like it or not."

"If you're taking Brody just to hurt me--"

"You have no say in it. You've forfeited your right to tell me what to do."

Emry was suddenly silent while staring at her. Although his expression was difficult to read, she knew she had succeeded in hurting him, but it only made her feel worse. He finally looked away and appeared defeated.

"I guess I deserve that," he said softly. "I should probably go back to my room."

"That's probably best," she said but knew she didn't mean it. "We shouldn't be sharing a bed. That just confuses the line between friends and lovers."

Jess couldn't believe she was chasing him out of her bed, but she just couldn't seem to stop her mouth. She knew he had crossed the line with his remarks, but she still wanted him to stay with her. Jess uncertainly looked at his profile. Emry stared at the bed and looked lost. She felt uncomfortable that she had hurt him, but something had to rattle him. She resisted taking back her hurtful comment even though she desperately wanted to. She knew she had to say something to soften the mood.

"You can stay for the movie, if you'd like."

Emry still didn't look at her and retained his defeated expression. "Actually, I never cared for disaster movies. I've lived through too many of them." He moved off the bed and collected his jacket and laptop. "Good night, Jess."

Emry left the room without looking at her. Jess tried to hold back her tears. As the door closed, she allowed her head to fall into her hands and sobbed softly.

†

*D*ana's lavish penthouse suite contained expensive furniture, modern art, and several glass cabinets consisting of every imaginable crystal trinket. The security system alongside the front door was void of its usual lights and hung partially away from the wall. Dana's voice echoed within the hallway just outside the door. A figure in black slipped into the darkened bedroom. He hid just inside the open bedroom doorway and removed a knife while watching the door. The living room door was unlocked and opened. Dana entered her penthouse suite with little enthusiasm. A large, muscular man with a shaved head entered behind her and shut the door. He was her brother, Dale.

"I appreciate you coming to stay with me, Dale," Dana said with a tense smile. "After what happened to Carla--"

Dale had the look of a Marine with his massive build and tough appearance. He glanced around the penthouse living room with a steel cold gaze and no emotion. He was intimidating even without any weapons to back it up.

"Mom said to keep an eye on you," Dale said with some gruffness. He removed a large, semiautomatic from a concealed shoulder holster and cocked it. "Dad said to shoot first and ask questions *never*. I prefer Dad's advice." Dale looked around the penthouse. "Now, you just relax and don't give what happened to Conner and Carla a second thought. I'm going to walk the perimeter. If I'm lucky, I'll find some creep hiding in your closet. I've been itching for an excuse to shoot this bad boy."

"Things a little slow since you got out of the Marines, Dale?" Dana teased.

"A little. I always feel better after I've killed something, but they frown upon that sort of thing here in the civilized world."

"By all means," Dana said with a laugh and shooed him away. "Go find something to kill in the bedroom."

Dale carried his gun against his chest and approached the partially open bedroom door in true Marine fashion. Without warning, he kicked the door open the rest of the way and aimed his weapon inside the dark room. Dale hesitated a moment then entered the bedroom. Dana watched him, shook her head, and then chuckled softly while sorting through her mail. A moment or two passed, but Dale didn't return. Dana set down the mail, looked at the darkened bedroom, and appeared curious. It was too quiet.

"Dale?"

There was no response. Dana uncertainly approached the darkened bedroom doorway and appeared concerned. The attack on Carla had gotten the better of her. She stared at the dark bedroom and tried to keep from trembling.

"Dale?"

Dale suddenly appeared in the doorway with his gun lowered and a frown on his hard face. Dana gasped with surprise and jumped back a step while holding her chest.

"Empty," Dale said with disappointment.

Dana recovered from her surprise and held back her amused laugh even though she still held her chest.

"Did you check under the bed," Dana teased.

"Yeah, and in the closet too," Dale said as he walked past her. "You left your bedroom window open. Not very smart, dumb dumb."

"I did?"

"I thought I heard someone on the fire escape, but sadly, there was no one there."

"Cheer up, Dale, there's always tomorrow to shoot someone," Dana said with a tiny smile on her face.

"You're just saying that. Did you want me to come along on the anniversary cruise this weekend?"

"No offense, but I'm only allowed one guest. I'd rather bring an actual date. I want to take some guy that'll make Carla jealous-- not my horny brother who thinks she's hot. That's the last thing I need."

Dale flopped on the sofa, spread out, and propped his large work boots on the coffee table. He still held his gun, which now rested over the back of the sofa.

"Then you shouldn't have told me she was in *Playboy*." He suddenly appeared curious and stared at her. "Who do you know that could possibly make that little witch jealous?"

Dana frowned, flopped onto the sofa alongside him, and sighed deeply. "I don't, which is why I've been calling every escort service in our area code."

Dale chuckled softly.

†

*I*t was two days later and the weekend of the anniversary cruise. A black limousine sent by the production company pulled up to Jess's house. The super-stretch limousine would comfortably seat fifteen passengers. Drake, Ivy, Jess, and Brody walked onto the porch with their overnight bags and waited for the limousine to stop. The limousine driver got out and opened the back door then approached the porch to collect their bags. Ivy clung to Drake's arm and bounced around with enthusiasm.

"This is so exciting," Ivy said with glee. "I know what happened onboard was a tragedy, but I always wanted to see the ship that made you a hero."

Drake appeared slightly uncomfortable and uncertainly looked at Jess to see her reaction. Jess wasn't even paying attention to them. She was preoccupied with something else. Drake smiled gently at Ivy and warmly caressed her hand on his arm.

"I'm glad you're happy, baby."

The chauffeur took their bags. Drake and Ivy followed him to the limousine. Brody picked up Jess's bag and looked at her. She remained distant and unenthusiastic for more than just the obvious reason. Brody studied her expression and appeared concerned.

"Are you okay, Jess?" There was an odd moment of silence. "You don't have to go if you don't want to. No one's forcing you."

Jess finally snapped out of her distant trance and attempted a smile. "No, if I back out then Drake won't go. I can't do that to him. He'd never forgive me if he had to disappoint Ivy."

"If Ivy's happiness was that important, why wouldn't he just go without you?"

"Because somewhere beneath that love induced cloud he's floating on is the sensible man who's going to need me to push him on that ship," she announced with a sigh. "He's not nearly as brave as he'd like Ivy to believe."

"I guess that's where Drake and I see things differently," Brody said bluntly. "The way I see it, he faced his demons on that ship and came out victorious. There's nothing left for him to fear."

"I guess that's you. I'm still living that nightmare every time I close my eyes. Some days, it's like I never left that ship," she said softly. A chill suddenly swept over her. Jess tensed as the driver returned for their bags. "I just--I should probably tell Ridley that we're leaving."

Brody nodded and handed their bags to the chauffeur. Jess quickly turned and hurried into the house.

Jess uncertainly entered the study and looked at Emry, who sat peacefully behind the desk with his eyes closed. It seemed odd to find him there. He was never in the study this time of morning. She slowly approached the desk, fidgeted, and studied him a moment before speaking.

"I wasn't expecting to find you in here this early," Jess said softly.

Emry kept his eyes closed. "There were too many dirty dishes in the sink. I couldn't face them."

He finally opened his eyes. His expression was solemn as he stared at her. Something about Emry didn't look right. His expression was like none she had ever seen on him before. He looked exhausted.

"The limo is here," she said gently while fidgeting. The tension between them was obvious. "We're going to the city to pick up the others before heading for the dock."

Emry stared at her a moment longer then slowly stood. He hesitated then uncertainly approached her with an unusual awkwardness. The tension between them had turned into something far worse. The closeness they had once shared appeared to vanish. Jess couldn't stand it any longer, so she took the initiative and quickly moved into his arms. Emry appeared relieved, sighed softly, and held her against him as if he would never release her. Jess clung to him, inhaled his familiar scent, and fought her tears.

"I'm so sorry about the other night," Jess said softly. "I didn't mean any of it."

Emry placed his hands on her neck, forced her to meet his gaze, and smiled timidly. "I deserved everything you said. You have no reason to be sorry."

"The last two days have been miserable with you keeping a minimum safe distance from me," she said sadly while clinging to his hands on her neck. "I just want things back the way they were."

Emry gently caressed her face while staring tenderly into her eyes. He allowed his hands to fall to his sides and attempted to distance himself from his emotions.

"You're going to be late."

"I don't care."

Jess subconsciously smoothed his jacket and appeared saddened. There was more on her mind then just leaving for a few days. It was something that worried her every day since he came back into her life.

"Promise me you'll still be here when I get back," she said softly.

Emry offered a tiny, humored smile that almost mocked her. "Have I ever left you?"

Jess stared at him a moment longer and then, without warning, kissed him quickly but passionately on the lips. She broke off the kiss before he could respond, clung to him, and nuzzled her face against his.

"I love you, Emry Hill," she whispered softly with her lips near his ear.

It was the first time she had called him Emry since he moved into her house. Jess pulled away, avoided looking at him, and hurried from the study so he wouldn't see the tears in her eyes.

Chapter Twenty-four

The *Andrea Maria* was docked at the private pier with a cluster of media held back by security. The impressive ship appeared to be in pristine condition and displayed a banner proudly announcing the anniversary cruise and welcoming the survivors. The black limousine pulled up to the red carpet beyond the barricade. As the chauffeur opened the door, Carla was the first to step out of the limousine with Rico just behind her. Carla was wearing an expensive, extravagant dress and looked like a movie star arriving at the Oscars. She latched onto Rico's arm and waved to her adoring fans, who cheered her arrival. Dana, Drake, Ivy, Jess, and Brody followed Carla's grand entrance with less flare for the spotlight. None of them dressed nearly as flashy as Carla had. Drake was unusually cheerful and waved to the fans with the overly enthusiastic Ivy, who proudly clung to his arm. Dana put on a good show but, as usual, couldn't follow Carla's grandeur. She cast envious looks at Rico every chance she got. Jess managed a smile and even a wave but lacked enthusiasm. She subconsciously linked onto Brody's arm to battle her insecurities of being back in the spotlight. Brody played the part and maintained his tough guy act without faltering.

Grant was the last out of the limousine by his own design, since he felt he was the biggest celebrity among the group. According to his wildly cheering fans, that was obviously the case. The lead role in the action movie he was currently filming was sure to elevate his celebrity status and inflate his ego more than it already was. As they walked along the red carpet toward the *Andrea Maria*, Jess stared at the infamous ship with a renewed sense of horror and gripped Brody's arm in response. Brody attempted to loosen her death grip then saw the look on her face and the way she stared at the ship before them. A flood of horrible memories swept over her.

"Oh, my God," Jess gasped softly.

Despite Drake's broad grin, the look in his eyes conveyed something similar to Jess's paranoid state. His enthusiasm was all a show for Ivy. He wanted her to see how brave of a man he was, but it was obvious he didn't want to be there either. As they got closer to the ship, Carla, Dana, and even Grant stared with an overwhelming feeling of dread as their smiles faded. For a moment, all sounds from the crowd seemed to dissipate as the five stared at the *Andrea Maria*. The ship's horn sounded to excite the crowd. All five survivors suddenly jumped in response.

†

*T*he *Andrea Maria* sailed through the calm, peaceful waters with the coast no longer in sight. It was a beautiful, sunny day and perfect for publicity photos on deck. The photographer in his late thirties, Arnold, posed Jess, Drake, Dana, Carla, and Grant at the railing of the bridge deck for the media shots that would promote the upcoming movie. Arnold was full of energy and excitement to what was possibly the biggest break of his career as a media photographer. The film publicist, Zeke, instructed the five about what would be expected from them over the next three days. Zeke, who was also in his thirties, was the passive type, despite his success in a moderately aggressive field. He was a veteran as a publicist and handled the task with professionalism.

Jess appeared distracted during the photo shoot and showed distaste toward Zeke's boasting about all the fun that they were going to have on the three-day cruise. She didn't understand how he could expect them to have fun onboard a ship that was little more than a floating morgue just one year ago. Zeke didn't seem to appreciate what they had gone through the last time they were onboard the infamous ship. Drake placed his arm around Jess, appeared stiff, and uncertainly looked around the bridge deck

"This is *creepy*."

"It seems like yesterday," Jess muttered and subconsciously rubbed her right shoulder.

The sounds of gunfire from that night echoed through Jess's mind, causing her to flinch with each shot. She transported back to the worst night of her life and helplessly watched Emry plummet overboard while taking Brahm with him. Her own screams chilled her. Drake hugged Jess affectionately and brought her back from her nightmare. She clung to him as she trembled in his arms. Arnold snuck a picture of them in their embrace. Many pictures circulated the media in the months following the rescue of Drake holding Jess. In fact, there were few pictures of Jess without Drake by her side.

"I miss him, Drake," Jess whispered.

"It's just three days."

"He won't be there. He didn't say it, but I know he was leaving."

Drake suddenly appeared surprised and possibly horrified at the news. "Jess--I'm so sorry," he said softly then held her more firmly against him. He frowned when she couldn't see it and muttered, "That rotten bastard--"

†

The elegant dining room was beautifully prepared for their first night at sea. The tables proudly displayed fine china, crystal glasses, and large floral arrangements. The captain, a handsome man in his early fifties, stood alongside Zeke and Arnold while wearing his finest uniform and appeared proud to be a part of the anniversary cruise. Jess, Drake, Carla, Grant, and Dana, who were all dressed in casual eveningwear, stood frozen within the entrance to the dining room and shared the same look of doom on their faces. Jess couldn't speak for the others, but all she saw were bodies slumped over tables and lying on the floor. The stench of vomit invaded her senses.

"Tell me they're serving lobster bisque, and I'll puke," Drake muttered to the others.

There was an awkward silence, as the same thought appeared to go through all five of their heads. They exchanged nauseous looks while cringing then turned and left without saying a word to the others. Zeke, Arnold, Brody, Rico, and the captain watched them leave then looked at one another in silent question.

†

The nightclub had been painstakingly restored to its original condition. It was nearly impossible to tell that nearly fifty men and women were slaughtered within the massive room just one year ago. Jess, Drake, Carla, Grant, and Dana sat at the bar with a bottle of whiskey before them. They solemnly did shots while toasting those whom had died onboard the ship and for their fallen comrade, Conner. Aside from their toasts, there were few words spoken. Zeke entered the nightclub and looked around. He saw the five sitting at the bar and appeared relieved finally to have found them.

He returned to the nightclub door and poked his head into the corridor.

"Found them. They're in here," Zeke announced to the others.

✝

*L*ater that evening, Jess slowly entered the lounge with Brody following her. The lounge was the only place on the ship she actually wanted to see again. It seemed like a lifetime since she had been there, but she remembered it like yesterday. She paused by the pool table with billiard balls scattered along the top as if a game had been interrupted. An empty scotch glass remained on the edge of the pool table and still contained some ice. She wondered if Zeke and Arnold had been entertaining themselves prior to their arrival. Although, that didn't explain the ice that remained in the glass. Perhaps it had been the captain or one of his crew.

Jess stared at the pool table and drifted back to one year earlier. She stood motionless and watched the entire evening with Emry in the lounge play out before her. The sounds and images were vivid. Jess insecurely rubbed her chilled arms. She suddenly realized those couple of hours spent in the lounge with Emry were the happiest moments of her life. She fell in love with him there. If the massacre hadn't happened, she knew Emry would have asked her back to his cabin, and she knew she would have said yes. Brody watched her in silence. Tears suddenly filled her eyes over the thought of Emry not being there when she returned. Brody, who naturally assumed she was mourning her dead Romeo, moved closer to her and pulled her into his arms. She allowed him to hold her briefly but then pulled away and held back her sorrow.

"I need a moment alone. It's personal."

Brody nodded and left the lounge without hesitation, shutting the door behind him. Jess quickly wiped her tears, removed her cell phone, and pressed a button. She listened to the endless ringing of Emry's cell phone. Jess disconnected the call, ran her fingers through her hair, and sobbed softly. She suddenly hesitated and uncertainly peeled something from her neck. She stared at the tiny, thin disk in her hand. Her look suddenly hardened. It was an electronic bug stuck to her neck behind her ear!

"You son-of-a-bitch!" she shouted into the bug. "You bugged me!" Jess replaced the disk behind her ear and looked around the lounge with hostility. "I know you can hear me. You have three seconds to call, or I'll do more than kick your sensitive area."

Jess's cell phone rang almost on cue to reveal "Ridley" on the caller ID. She pressed a button, put the phone to her ear, and sneered.

"You bastard--"

"Let me explain," Emry said over the phone.

"Explain what? That you're a sociopath?"

"Someone murdered Conner and tried to do the same to you and Carla," Emry said over the phone. "Did you really think I'd let you go on that ship unprotected?"

Jess considered his words then appeared horrified as she quickly looked around. Her eyes then fell upon the empty scotch glass on the pool table.

"Oh, my God--you're on the ship!"

There was a long silence.

"I'm not going to respond in fear of losing my testicles," Emry said from the other end.

Jess groaned loudly with hostility and frustration into the cell phone then disconnected the call. Her cell phone immediately rang. She angrily answered it without looking at the caller ID.

"What?" she demanded.

There was a moment of silence.

"Uh--what's with the non-party like attitude?" Drake said from the other end.

"I'm sorry. I was just talking to that little prick, Jeeves."

"Uh, oh, someone needs a drink," Drake said from the other end. "Get your hot ass back to this nightclub and party with us, baby!"

"I'm on my way. I'm getting drunk and then I'm getting laid. Brody won't know what hit him."

She was sure Emry overheard that. She wanted him to hear that. She wanted to hurt him for all the things he had done to her-- for not loving her.

✝

Loud club music blared from the jukebox within the nightclub. Drake, Ivy, Carla, and Rico danced seductively on the dance floor. Dana and Grant sat at the bar and watched with disgust while Carla and Rico were obscenely bumping and grinding as they danced.

"I don't get it," Dana said flatly. "She and I had the same bit part in this cruise ship horror story, but she gets all the attention."

"Probably because she made two, wise initial investments," Grant informed Dana with a serious look. "I believe they're called "D" cups."

Dana looked at Grant with some surprise to his comment. Both suddenly smiled and laughed. It was obvious they were drunk.

"You know, I was always surprised that you and Carla never got together while we were touring."

Grant chuckled softly. "I considered it for two seconds, but then I got a look at the tall pedestal she put herself on and didn't think she was worth the climb."

Dana smiled and laughed.

"There was a time I went for her type," Grant said with a sigh. "But a lot has changed since we stopped touring. I'm envious of Drake." He looked at Drake and Ivy on the dance floor. "He somehow made it all work. He's in a committed relationship, and he's still best friends with Jess. I wish I had that. Fame and fortune is nice, but at the end of the day, I'm still alone."

Dana appeared surprised. "Wow. That sounded nothing like the Grant I remember. I thought your new movie star status would have changed you for the worse." She offered a pleasant smile and leaned closer to him on the bar. "I'm really impressed."

"Why didn't things work out with you and Drake? I mean, the two of you hooked up before, you know--" He offered a charming smile and poured another round of drinks for each. "I just don't understand why you two didn't get together after the rescue."

"There was an ugly backstory to our time alone in my cabin after, you know--" Dana appeared tense and took a large swallow of her drink. "Drake was obsessed with finding Jess, but I wouldn't let him leave the cabin. He tried to forcibly remove me from the door and unintentionally hurt me. I played on his guilt, and he stayed with me. After Jess was shot, he wouldn't talk to me."

"He barely talked to any of us the two days that followed the bridge battle," Grant said simply. "I'm sure it wasn't personal."

"That's where you're wrong," Dana replied. "I stopped him in the hallway just before he left for the bridge. I tried to make him stay with us. If he had gotten to the bridge just two seconds sooner, he could have stopped that man from shooting Jess. He never forgave me for that. I saw his detest for me in his eyes."

"Huh?" Grant appeared deep in thought. "I wonder if that's the look he's been giving me."

Dana smiled and raised her glass. "To those who despise us."

Grant laughed, clinked his glass to hers, and both drained the entire contents of their glasses in one swallow. Grant cheerfully poured more drinks for them. Arnold and Zeke joined Dana and Grant at the bar and appeared drunk themselves. Zeke eyed the two couples on the dance floor, nudged Arnold, and pointed out the risqué dancing. Carla was always good for a scandalous sex story, which there had been plenty in the last year.

"Get some shots of that," Zeke said with a grin. "That should sell some magazines."

Arnold eagerly grabbed his camera and headed for the dance floor. Jess and Brody entered the club. Jess's mood hadn't improved any. Drake and Ivy drunkenly cheered to them from the dance floor.

"Do you dance, Brody?" Jess asked him as she forced a smile and linked onto his arm.

"Like that? Not sober."

"Then we should probably get you a few drinks first," Jess teased.

Brody eyed her and hid his surprise. Her cell phone rang as they approached the bar. Zeke was now playing bartender for Dana and Grant.

"That's the fifth time Ridley's called in the last ten minutes. Don't you think you should answer?"

"If he wants me, he knows where to find me."

Brody appeared bewildered as they sat at the bar. Zeke handed them each a glass of scotch, which they accepted. Jess clinked her glass to Brody's glass and drank the entire contents in one swallow. Brody eyed her with some surprise then drank his down as well. Brody nearly gagged. Jess indicated for Zeke to refill her glass. Zeke laughed and refilled both their glasses.

It was an hour or two later and the small party continued on a less sober note within the nightclub. Carla sat on Rico's lap at a corner table near the back. They kissed passionately and pawed at each another like young lovers. On the other side of the nightclub, Dana sat on Grant's lap as well. They too kissed passionately in their drunken condition. It was the first time they had interacted on a more intimate level. Dana never cared for Grant and his womanizing ways. There was the distinct possibility that she would regret her actions in the morning. Drake and Ivy were noticeably absent. Brody and Jess slow danced to the romantic song. Jess rested her head on his shoulder and appeared preoccupied while Brody firmly ran his hands along her back. Both were clearly drunk, but despite her drunken state, Jess couldn't get Emry out of her head. She wondered what she was doing dancing so close to Brody and allowing him to caress her as if it meant something. Even if Emry didn't want a sexual relationship with her, she wasn't ready to give up on him just yet. She loved him too much. Jess became tense, stopped dancing, and pulled away from Brody. Brody seemed puzzled by the mixed signals she was sending.

"Are you okay?"

"I thought I could drink away the memories, but it's making them worse," she said timidly and looked into his eyes. "I can't do this."

"Do what? Dance with me?" Brody teased with a charming, drunken smile.

When did Brody suddenly become so charming? She wondered how that rivalry between them faded so quickly and what brought them here to this point in time. Had she changed? She suddenly realized Brody had changed. He spontaneously transformed into a caring person. If Emry never existed, perhaps she would be happy with Brody, but that wasn't the case. She loved Emry, and she knew she had to fight for what she wanted. Even if it was Emry she had to fight.

"I don't want you to think I invited you along on this cruise for something more," Jess said drunkenly then considered the statement. "I mean, maybe I did, but it was out of spite toward Ridley." Jess groaned softly and held her head. "I've had too much to drink. I don't even know what I'm saying anymore."

Brody offered her a tiny, drunken smile and gently caressed her shoulders. "Relax, Jess. When you asked me to accompany you on this cruise for protection, I didn't interpret that to mean you wanted a wild fling at sea. I know you have unresolved feelings for Ridley, and I respect that." He maintained his warm smile and secured his arm around her waist. "Would you like me to take you back to your cabin?"

In her condition, she wasn't sure allowing Brody to walk her back to her cabin was a good idea. Part of her still wanted to seduce him to get even with Emry. Another part of her wanted to seek out Emry and sexually hit him with everything she had. Then there was that very small part of her that was feeling nostalgic for lobster bisque.

"I think it would probably be best if Drake walked me back to my cabin."

"I realize I'm drunk and horny, but I wouldn't dream of taking advantage of you if the answer is no," Brody said. "I'm here to protect you, remember?"

He was right. She was being foolish. Jess smiled gently, nodded in agreement, and walked with him toward the nightclub doors. Drake miraculously appeared alongside them as if summoned by some divine, psychic power to come to her aide. Drake placed his arm around her shoulder, leaned heavily on her while holding her close to his side, and smiled drunkenly at Brody.

"Take the night off, Brody," Drake said. "I'll walk Jess to her cabin."

Jess was suddenly curious from where he appeared. He and Ivy had been missing for at least half an hour. She thought they had returned to their cabin for a fun filled evening of sex between the sheets.

"I don't know if--" Brody began.

"I got a blow job in the ladies room five minutes ago," Drake casually informed him. "I'm safe."

The look on Brody's face was next to priceless, and Jess was nearly floored by Drake's candor and possible boasting about his drunken, sexual antics with Ivy in the restroom. At least that explained where they had been so long. Drake flashed a lustful smile, raised his brows suggestively, and led Jess from the nightclub. Brody stopped dead in his tracks and stared after them with a stunned look.

Chapter Twenty-five

*D*rake and Jess leaned heavily on each other for support as they staggered along the upper deck corridor while singing a dirty song. Both laughed at their behavior. It had been a long time since they acted so poorly together. Drake was always trying to impress Ivy, and Jess didn't want Emry to see her as a silly, impulsive little girl. She sometimes thought that's how he actually saw her. Maybe she did seem that way to him. Maybe she was too young for someone of his maturity. She didn't want to think about him anymore tonight. She just wanted to go back to her room and pass out.

"Are you sure you can make it back to the nightclub without falling overboard?" Jess asked while clinging to him as they stumbled along the corridor.

"All the corridors between here and the club are inside, so it's unlikely I'll fall overboard. Haven't you been on this ship before?"

Jess glared at him then appeared humored. "I'd love to say I hadn't."

"I know the feeling," Drake muttered and frowned drunkenly. "Do you know why I wanted to come this weekend?"

"Hmm? I don't know? Hero worship sex from Ivy?"

Drake glared at Jess. She grinned and giggled drunkenly. He gave her a playful shove but held onto her so she wouldn't fall.

"No, you silly girl." Drake turned serious and looked down the corridor. "I intended to propose."

Jess suddenly stopped Drake and turned to face him. Both struggled to maintain their balance from the sudden stop. Jess's look was serious.

"Really?" She attempted a smile despite a flood of thoughts racing through her mind. Jess smiled with delight. "I mean, I'm very happy for you, don't get me wrong. I just don't understand why you'd want to propose *here.*"

"Because this is where I became a hero in her mind," Drake said. "And I thought if I took the place that held the worst memory in my life and replaced it with the best one; I would no longer fear the memory of this ship."

Jess stared at Drake a long moment with a strange look. She suddenly smiled, laughed, and hugged him. Both nearly fell over.

"Do it, Drake!"

Drake uncertainly pulled away from her and frowned. "I'm having second thoughts. It's a lie, Jess. The reason she fell in love with me is because she thinks I'm a hero, but I'm not."

Jess smoothed his jacket and smiled warmly. "You are a hero. You killed the man who shot me, remember? He was about to kill Emry and me. You shut down the ship's engines." Jess gently touched his face. "You kept me from going insane after we were rescued. In what world are you not a hero?"

Drake smiled almost down to tears and hugged her. "Thank you, Jess. You've never let me down." Drake pulled away and wiped the tears from his eyes then smiled. "Let's get you to your cabin before I forget where it is."

Drake placed his arm around Jess's shoulder, leaned heavily on her, and guided her along the corridor. Both stumbled drunkenly.

"Must be some rough waters out there," Drake teased.

Jess laughed knowingly. Drake pointed to the nearby door and almost didn't make the stop. He struck the door and laughed at himself.

"I'm pretty sure this is where you belong," Drake announced while wearing a strange grin on his face.

Jess collapsed against the wall while laughing at him and removed her card key from the cleavage of her revealing dress. Drake eyed the card key then her cleavage with surprise as he straightened and tried to keep his balance.

"No wonder you made Brody carry your cell phone. What all do you have in there?" Drake asked drunkenly.

"Just a pair of "C" breasts."

Drake eyed her chest, placed his finger in her neckline, and pulled the dress away from her chest while peering down her cleavage. Jess laughed with surprise then embarrassment and playfully smacked his hand. Even in her drunken condition, she knew Drake was just joking around. He enjoyed getting her going. The cabin door suddenly opened, causing both to look at the door. Emry casually stood in the doorway of the presidential suite, which clearly wasn't her cabin. Drake grinned at Emry and handed him the card key.

"She's all yours, Jeeves."

Jess appeared stunned. Did Emry instruct Drake to bring her to him? She didn't know with whom she was more angry. Drake quickly kissed Jess on the cheek and darted down the hall to avoid whatever wrath she was about to unleash on either or both of them. Jess glared at Emry as he gently guided her into the room.

"You called him, didn't you?"

"Yes, I called him."

Jess drunkenly stumbled into the presidential suite with Emry. The suite living room was more elegant than most rooms at luxury hotels. It had expensive furniture, a big screen television, kitchenette, full bar, and glass doors leading onto its own private balcony.

"He put me on hold while he and Ivy performed unspeakable acts in the bathroom," Emry said with distaste as he shut and locked the door behind them. "If he'd actually hit the "hold" button, I would have been grateful." He turned toward her, gave her a disapproving look, and appeared offended. "I can't believe you didn't answer my calls."

Jess pulled away from Emry and stumbled several steps. She was furious with both men. She angrily turned to face him and nearly lost her balance in her drunken state. Emry caught her around the waist and held her against him to keep her from falling to the floor. She immediately pushed against his chest in protest.

"You bugged me, you bastard!" she cried out in anger. "You bugged me, so you could spy on me!"

Emry stared into her eyes with little emotion to her drunken outburst. "If you were so mad about it, why didn't you destroy the bug?"

Jess stopped pushing against him and now clung to his shoulders to maintain her balance. Emry patiently waited for a response. Jess stared at him and searched for one. He was far too clever to begin with and her drunken state just left her with less ammunition to fight him. She usually resorted to name-calling and idle threats in such cases, but she wouldn't dream of talking to Emry that way.

"You're a prick," she said lowly. "And when I'm sober, I'm going to kick your ass."

But then again, she was drunk.

"If you must."

Emry held her against him while gently caressing her back. Jess glared at him with irritation then ran her hand along his chest while avoiding looking into his eyes. She loved the feel of his expensive clothes.

"I hate you," she remarked lowly.

"I know. I hate me too."

Emry watched her hands on his chest. Her mood softened as she caressed him, despite her attempt to remain hostile. It wasn't fair, he just smelled so good! She realized she would have to work harder to remain angry with him. After all, this was his fault.

"I considered sleeping with Brody, you know," she said in an attempt to irritate him.

"Yes, I know. I was on deck waiting to throw him overboard," he replied.

Jess appeared surprised then became upset. "You're not allowed to be jealous--no matter how good you smell. You gave up that right when you gave up me."

Emry's hands firmly caressed her back as he brushed his lips past her cheek and spoke softly near her ear. "I know. I'm an idiot."

Jess was bewildered by his words and actions but didn't attempt to move from his arms. As his hands caressed her, she suddenly tensed and appeared bewildered.

"Is your hand on my ass?"

Emry continued to run his lips along her cheek without pulling away. "I believe it is."

"Oh--"

Jess had to think about it for a minute. Why would his hand be there? Emry gently backed her against the bedroom doorframe and warmly kissed her neck. That answered her question. His hand traveled down her buttocks to her thigh, caressed her leg below her dress, and then maneuvered her leg up to his hip. He gently pressed against her while kissing her throat. Who was this man? Then it suddenly dawned on her. This was the man she met and fell in love with onboard the *Andrea Maria*. She didn't know where he had been the past year, but she was glad he was back. Emry then kissed her warmly but passionately on the mouth as he firmly caressed her body and pressed himself against her. Jess immediately returned the kiss with a soft groan while clinging to him. He broke off the kiss and resumed kissing her neck with more aggression.

"I want you to know I'm still pissed at you," Jess said softly between gasps.

"You can be pissed all you want, but tonight I'm having my way with you. It has to be that way."

Jess smiled drunkenly, having understood every word. She ran her hands along his shoulders and chest.

"I'm in no condition to stop you," she replied softly with delight.

Emry kissed her passionately and aggressively on the mouth. She immediately returned the kiss. In one, swift motion, he swept her off her feet, carried her into the bedroom, and kicked the door closed behind them.

It was a little while later. The exterior lights beyond the partially open curtains dimly lit the presidential suite bedroom. Emry was on top of Jess beneath the covers and gently moved against her. Jess clung to him and feared if she let go, he would cease to exist. Their kiss turned more passionate and aggressive as they continued to grope each another beneath the covers.

"Oh, Emry--"

"Oh, Consuela--"

They hesitated a moment to look into each other's eyes, grinned, and laughed softly.

†

Later that night, Arnold walked along the bridge deck with his camera around his neck. It was a beautiful, clear night with a bold, nearly full moon, which gave the vast calm waters before the ship an almost glassy appearance. The *Andrea Maria* sailed slower tonight then she had during the day. It was obvious, as Arnold stumbled toward the bridge, that he was intoxicated from the wild party still going strong in the nightclub. Arnold aimed his camera at the bridge above and took several pictures. The flash lit up the sky and the bridge exterior. Arnold hesitated and stared at the bridge a moment longer with a concerned look. A streak of fresh blood along the window dripped down. Someone moved past the bridge window for the door. Arnold became alarmed then turned and hurried away. Someone ran down the metal steps from the bridge and chased after him. Arnold had no intention on looking back and, despite his drunken state, ran along the deck with amazing speed. The person from the bridge ran behind him but appeared to be losing ground.

†

The nightclub was still in full swing with loud dance music playing as the remaining passengers had a good time in their mostly drunken condition. Arnold suddenly appeared in the open doorway while panting out of breath. He was about to enter the club, when someone grabbed him from behind and pulled him out of view into the corridor. Brody glanced at the doorway with a puzzled look as if he had seen something. He uncertainly approached the club doors. Brody stepped into the corridor and looked around. The corridor appeared vacant and quiet, despite the noise from the nightclub behind him. Just out of view around the corner, someone held Arnold immobile with a gloved hand covering his mouth. Arnold struggled against the gloved hand. Brody continued to scan the empty corridor then took a few steps in Arnold's direction.

"Brody!" Drake called from the loud nightclub.

Brody hesitated, stared down the corridor a moment with a curious look, and then returned to the nightclub. Arnold fought against the hand over his mouth and tried to scream. A hunting knife suddenly appeared and slashed his throat from behind, leaving a large, gaping slit with blood spilling down his neck and along his chest. Arnold muffled a gasp and slowly stopped thrashing. As his eyes rolled back, his attacker pulled him into the nearby storage closet.

Chapter Twenty-six

$\mathcal{I}$t was one o'clock in the morning. Light shining through the part in the curtains dimly lighted the bedroom of the presidential suite. Jess lay in Emry's arms beneath the covers as he breathed heavily while affectionately holding her naked body to his. She gently caressed his chest, inhaled his wonderful scent, and attempted to contain her pleased smile. She was definitely sober now.

"Not half bad for an old man," Jess teased while she nuzzled her face against his bare chest.

Emry attempted to glare at her where she lay in his arms and hid his smile. "That was good for any man."

Jess giggled softly and enjoyed the secure way he held her to him. As she lay in his arms, she suddenly appeared deep in thought and became more serious.

"What changed your mind about us? I was positive you were going to leave before I returned."

Emry gently caressed her shoulder and hesitated only for a moment.

"I'd considered it. Considering all the tension between us, I thought it would be in your best interest if I left. I felt it was my fault you couldn't move on." Emry sighed softly. "Then I read the articles about the rescue on the study walls. I'd read them before, but I never really *read* them. That's when I realized you had been right all along. Ours was a love story, but I was the one with the romantic illusions."

Jess was surprised to hear him admit that.

"I was the one who couldn't stay away from you. I'd pursued you ever since the rescue. There were times I was so close; I could have touched you. As long as we're being honest, I did touch you once."

Jess suddenly looked at him with surprise and a strange realization. "You were the reporter with the Russian accent, weren't you?"

Emry appeared surprised then slightly embarrassed. He hid his smile while clinging to her. "Yes, that was me," he reluctantly replied. "How did you know?"

"I was convinced you were there, but I thought it was a dream. I was in a fog for the first five months. Most of it, I don't even remember."

"I thought I was protecting you from me--from the person I'd been trying to forget I was all these years. Becoming romantically involved would only cause you that much more pain when you eventually found out about my past. Then it occurred to me that you'd already seen my darker side the night we'd met." Emry hesitated then appeared almost humored. "You knew I had a tainted past yet you gave me access to your home, carte blanche with your bank accounts, and the freedom to invade every aspect of your life at my discretion."

"Your past doesn't change the man I fell in love with that night," Jess said gently. "As for my home and money, I only have that because of you. You're the reason I survived that night, and you were the story I had to tell. What I have is just as much yours as mine."

"You may regret that," Emry teased. "I've been pricing wine cellars."

Jess laughed softly.

"Seriously though, I just couldn't understand how or why you'd want someone like me. You deserved someone better, someone like Sheriff Stone. All the things I've done--" he said gently then appeared to sink into his past. He returned to reality. "Sure, I had a reason for everything I'd done, and I had the best of intentions, but sometimes I question the severity of my actions. I'm my own worst enemy. I give *myself* nightmares."

Emry hesitated and clung to her. Jess remained silent and stared at him. She always told him his past didn't matter to her, but she still wanted him to confide it to her. She was dying to know who Emry Hill really was.

"Yes, you were right. I wanted you that night, and I would have asked you back to my cabin. If you said yes, it would have been an amazing night, and I would have disappeared before you learned the truth about me. Of course, that was before all hell broke loose."

Emry drifted out and into his own thoughts. Jess stared at him for a long moment and appeared curious. He frowned and appeared ashamed.

"When I went overboard, I heard you screaming. You don't know how badly I wanted to call back to you, how much I wanted to be with you, but I thought I was doing you a favor by letting you think I'd died. Even after all that, I still couldn't let you go. I just couldn't stay away."

Jess gently nuzzled her head against his chest. "So why didn't you take advantage of me when you showed up at my house six months later? You had the opportunity. If you intended to just disappear anyway--"

"I couldn't do that to you. From the moment you kissed me in the hallway, I knew I'd never be able to walk out that door. You don't walk out on the woman you love."

Jess lifted her head from his chest and met his gaze through the dim lighting of the bedroom. She appeared pleased and smiled timidly.

"You love me?"

"You know I do."

"I knew you loved me like a daughter--"

Emry groaned softly, smiled warmly, and kissed her quickly on the lips. "You know that wasn't true. I wanted you from the moment I saw you and Drake dancing in the nightclub. It had been a while since I'd entertained such lusty thoughts, but I was easily turned off when I saw you together with Carla. Then you said something I'll never forget. You said, "I've got my bitch on"." Emry laughed softly then sighed. "I didn't know who you were, but you had me after that."

Jess smiled and laughed softly. She rested her chin on his chest and stared into his eyes. "Is that why you didn't leave when I told you to get out six months ago?"

"I didn't leave because I couldn't. I hadn't left you since the day we'd met. Where would I go? I was living in your barn for nearly seven weeks."

"You told me you were in the loft a couple of days," Jess said with surprise.

"I certainly wasn't going to tell you the truth. You would have thought I was deranged."

"I already did." Jess thought about what he said and shook her head with astonishment while studying him. "Seven weeks? Really?"

"There's electric in the loft, which allowed for a hotplate and a space heater. The bathroom in the lower level was convenient."

"I can't imagine you without a shower for two days let alone seven weeks."

"Oh, I just used the one in the spare bedroom when you'd go to town or out riding."

Jess appeared stunned.

"Since Drake stayed over a lot, I didn't think you'd notice subtle signs of use. I also used your washing machine, kitchen, and did some lite cleaning while I was there."

Jess just stared at him with her mouth hanging open. She suddenly smiled, shook her head, and laughed. "I wouldn't doubt you could have lived in the house without my knowledge."

"Well--"

"Forget it, I don't want to know."

Emry laughed softly. "It just seemed easier to live in your house as a guest. All that sneaking around was fun for a little while, but the mess in your kitchen was getting on my nerves. And your dirty clothes on *top* of the hamper--"

"Yeah, I get the point." Jess wondered why she was even surprised by anything he said. "It's almost hard to believe I was the one chasing you. It sounds almost as if you were chasing me. I'm surprised you were able to resist all that temptation."

"It wasn't easy living a monk's life with you. There were times I was only one word or a single gesture away from jumping you. Believe me, there were a lot of cold showers." He then appeared to entertain another thought and grinned. "And many long, hot sudsy ones too."

Jess hid her smile and tried to keep from reacting. "Does this mean I get to keep you?"

"As long as my past doesn't catch up with me, and I can continue to play Ridley, I'm not going anywhere."

Jess grinned.

"But," Emry remarked causing Jess to frown, "if my past threatens to harm you, I won't hesitate to disappear from your life forever. If anything happened to you, I wouldn't be able to live with the guilt. I won't go through that pain again. I have no intentions of surviving you."

Jess appeared slightly concerned by his words. She wanted to believe he was too much of a fighter to end it that way, but she knew exactly how he felt. She wasn't sure she wanted to ever live without him again either. If that was the case, they really would become the *Romeo and Juliet* of the *Andrea Maria*.

"Then we'll just have to make sure no one ever knows you're not Ridley, won't we?" Jess said with a gentle smile.

†

*I*t was early the next morning. Brody, who was freshly showered and changed, wearily walked onto deck looking worse for wear and leaned against the railing. The sun was shining brilliantly, almost as if mocking his hung-over state. He stared at the calm, still waters surrounding the motionless ship. Brody stared a moment longer then suddenly appeared alarmed. Why had the ship stopped? He realized something was terribly wrong.

†

*D*rake and Ivy snuggled against each another while they slept peacefully beneath the covers. Both appeared pleasantly mussed from whatever extracurricular activities their drunken night had brought them. An urgent pounding on the door startled both. They jumped up and apart, immediately feeling the effects of their sudden movement and excessive amounts of alcohol. Drake held his pounding head, groaned softly, and climbed wearily over Ivy and out of the bed wearing just his boxer shorts. He tumbled to the floor with a loud thud. Ivy collapsed onto her pillow with a groan. The pounding on the door continued.

"Yeah, yeah--" Drake moaned from his awkward position on the floor.

He picked himself up off the floor and shuffled toward the cabin door. He unlocked and opened the door to reveal an enraged Brody. Brody suddenly grabbed him and slammed him against the wall just inside the doorway to the cabin. Ivy jumped up in bed with a startled gasp and held the sheet to her naked body.

"Where the hell is she?"

"What? Who?" Drake asked with surprise while fighting the disorientation from his hangover.

"Jess! Her bed hasn't been slept in! You were supposed to walk her to her room last night!"

Drake groaned and attempted to relax. "She's fine." He tried to loosen Brody's arm against his chest holding him to the wall. "Take it easy, Brody."

"The ship is adrift and the crew is missing. I will not take it easy!"

Drake suddenly appeared horrified.

✝

*M*oments later, Drake, who was now dressed, hurried along the corridor while pulling Ivy behind him, his hand firmly clutching hers. She was barely able to keep up with his long strides as they followed Brody to the presidential suite. Ivy appeared genuinely alarmed. Brody stopped before the door and immediately pounded on it.

"Why the hell did you bring her here?" Brody demanded while continuing to pound on the door.

"It's okay. She's with Ridley."

"Ridley?"

"He was concerned for her safety. He gets a little crazy like that. It's complicated."

Brody again pounded on the door, this time with more urgency and possible irritation. There was no response. Without further consideration, he kicked in the door. Drake and Ivy jumped with surprise. Ivy held back her startled scream and stared with alarm. The door flew open with a bang as the frame splintered. Jess stood within the living room halfway to the door as she held a robe closed against her wet body. Jess gasped as Brody stormed into the room with his gun drawn. She wasn't sure if she was more surprised or enraged at his "shock and awe" on her door.

"What the hell!" Jess cried out with a look that conveyed both emotions.

"Where is he?"

"Who?"

Brody stormed across the living room and entered the bedroom. He returned only a moment later and glared at Jess with a demanding look.

"Ridley."

Jess suddenly frowned with the realization that Drake had sold her out. She folded her arms across her chest and showed less hostility.

"He went to my cabin to get my things. What the hell is wrong with you, Brody? You're acting like a lunatic. Just because--"

158

"The ship's floundering, the bridge is strewn with blood, and the crew is missing," Brody said lowly with a serious look in his eyes. "Sound familiar?"

Jess appeared alarmed and stared back at him. She suddenly fidgeted and tried to piece everything together, but his attitude still puzzled her.

"A little too familiar, but what does that have to do with Ridley?"

What made him think Emry was suddenly the bad guy in what had happened to the ship's crew? And who the hell was Brody to judge anyone? He just wasn't making any sense. His attitude went way beyond simple jealousy.

"Drop the "girl next door" act, Jess," Brody said with irritation and startled her with his sudden hostility. "Ridley; AKA Emry; AKA Dalton; AKA Renshaw. The list goes on. He's been so many people; I doubt he even remembers his real name anymore."

Jess tried to hide the concern she felt to his discovery and quickly covered the best she could.

"I don't know who you think he is or what you think he did, but you're wrong."

"Is that why he snuck onboard without anyone's knowledge?" Brody demanded to know in an accusing tone. "I suppose it had nothing to do with the others being able to identify him as Emry, your dead Romeo?"

Jess stared at him without comment. She knew her look was revealing far too much already, but she couldn't think of anything to say. How had he figured that out? Her urge to dislike him was quickly returning.

"That's what I thought," Brody snapped with annoyance. "Get dressed."

Jess glared at him and wondered who the hell he was to give her orders. Unfortunately, for Emry's sake, she couldn't afford to test him right now. She turned, stormed into the bedroom, and slammed the door behind her. Brody glared at Drake, who nervously chewed his fingernails and appeared alarmed by the look he had received.

"Don't look at me," Drake said defensively. "I never met her Romeo."

Chapter Twenty-seven

*J*ess had little choice but to wear her dress from the night before. She walked beside Brody in silence along the main deck of the motionless ship. The ship floundering on the calm waters was an eerie remembrance of their last voyage the two days prior to their rescue by the U.S. Navy. Jess could practically smell the faint scent of decaying bodies wafting through the hot, stagnant air from the corridors. She would never forget that vile smell. Drake and Ivy followed without a word. Ivy clung to Drake's arm to the point of causing him physical pain. Brody looked at Jess's profile several times. She was annoyed with him, which was obvious by her refusal to look at him. It seemed her opinion of him plainly mattered to him. He searched for the right thing to say to her.

"I'm sorry I was so hard on you back there," Brody said gently and with an unusual tenderness. "Men like Ridley come off very charming, and it's natural to want to protect them. It's how they operate."

Jess's mood remained cold toward him, and her sudden glare offered little warmth. "Men like Ridley?" she scoffed. "You know nothing about Ridley."

Jess was feeling particularly vengeful toward Brody. Because of him, Emry would probably leave and never come back. She again wondered why he was acting so superior for a hired goon and became curious.

"Who are you *really*?" Jess demanded to know with a slight hiss in her voice as she contemplated hitting him.

"FBI," Brody replied gently while glancing at her as they walked.

Jess was slightly surprised by his admission, but his status as a federal agent didn't soften her mood any. She actually wished she had hit him before learning who he was. Now it would be a federal offense. He obviously realized she wasn't impressed with his FBI status and again attempted to win her respect by explaining himself.

"I was undercover gathering evidence on Victor Raymour for a whole laundry list of illegal activity when I made Ridley a couple of months back."

They headed toward the stairs to the bridge deck. Jess continued to walk alongside Brody while Drake and Ivy listened to their conversation with great interest.

"There had been speculation that a former CIA assassin turned fugitive, Kaplan Bogart, had stowed away onboard the *Andrea Maria* last year in Costa Rica," Brody said as they walked up the steps to the bridge. "Kaplan was the best operative in his field and a certified genius. Combine the two and you have one hell of an agent or one extremely dangerous man. He managed to hack into the CIA computer and completely erased himself from existence. All that remained of him was a vague description and a grainy photo. No fingerprints, no DNA, nothing."

They entered the bridge. Jess, Drake, and Ivy suddenly stopped and stared at the blood strewn along the bridge floor, walls, and windows. The crewmember's bodies were missing. It was an eerie remembrance of the last time she had been on the bridge--minus the bodies. Brody had already seen the bridge earlier and appeared unaffected by all the blood. Even though Jess and Drake had seen worse, it was still a chilling sight. Ivy just stared at the blood and clung to Drake as if her life depended on it.

"At first it seemed impossible that Ridley could be Kaplan," Brody said. "A former CIA assassin couldn't be that domesticated. But Kaplan was known for being very patient and methodical, so I continued my observation."

Brody played with several switches on the control panel. Nothing happened.

"She's been disabled all right." Brody looked back at Jess. "Once Victor moved into your circle, everything started coming together. If Kaplan had been your Romeo, it would explain why he stuck around. He had unfinished business with you."

"Yeah, he wanted to get in her pants," Drake muttered beneath his breath.

Jess and Brody glared at Drake. He wasn't helping to defuse the situation. Drake suddenly tensed then became defensive.

"Even if Ridley is her dead Romeo," Drake said to Brody with some irritation, "there's no way he could be this Kaplan guy. He won't even kill the spiders in Jess's house. The only thing Ridley is guilty of is being in love with a girl half his age. And I say kudos to him." Drake's look became cold and irritated. "Admit it, Brody, you're just pissed because he got into her bed and you didn't."

"Nice try, Drake. Even if neither of you will admit that Ridley is Emry, one fact still remains; if Kaplan was onboard the *Andrea Maria* last year, there's no telling what part he played in that tragedy," Brody remarked firmly.

"Emry gave his life for mine," Jess said hotly and tried to hold her composure. "Does that sound anything like the man you're describing?"

Brody shrugged. "That depends on who you ask. There are agents out there today who still defend Kaplan and believe he was framed. Others claim he's a psychopath with a lust for killing and a flair for the macabre."

"Where do you stand?" Drake asked with a curious look and increasing agitation.

"Agents turn, but that doesn't mean our government wouldn't frame one to protect their own ass. Kaplan was the only survivor in a botched mission eight years ago. His superior blamed him for the deaths of the agents working with him. A week later, his wife was found dead in their New Orleans home, and the men sent to capture him were found hanged, gutted, and half eaten by alligators."

Ivy appeared horrified and gasped, "Like the scarecrow--"

Drake frowned and suddenly gave Ivy a firm squeeze to silence her, but it was too late.

Brody looked at Ivy and nodded in agreement. "Those were my thoughts exactly."

"Ridley was with me all night," Jess said firmly. "I told you that."

"Forgive me if I don't take your word on it. You've already lied about his identity once in an attempt to protect him. You have no credibility. You have to accept that Ridley could be the mastermind behind everything that's happened then and now."

"I accept nothing of the kind. If you knew him, you'd know that's impossible."

Her look appeared to spark his interest. "What really happened on this ship one year ago? You already admitted you were on deck that night. Obviously, that's when you were shot in the shoulder, not in the lounge as you originally reported."

Brody studied her a long moment, considered something he hadn't before, and then looked at Drake with surprise as if suddenly putting it all together.

"But she wasn't on deck with you, was she?" Brody looked at Jess with amazement. "You were on deck with *Emry*. You and Emry won the battle for *Andrea Maria* and covered up his death so he wouldn't be identified. I can't believe I didn't put that together before."

Ivy appeared surprised and looked at Drake as if suddenly realizing he had lied about his role that night. Drake wasn't even thinking about what must have been going through Ivy's head. His anger with Brody was already boiling over. Drake pointed an angry finger at Brody.

"Emry saved our lives! He wasn't thinking about himself or saving his own ass. When he went overboard, it nearly killed Jess. She didn't lie about his death. She really thought he was dead. I know, I was there and stopped her from jumping into the water after him."

Drake's entire body was twitching with excess adrenaline, and his arms were wildly flapping. Jess was beginning to worry about Drake's explosive state of mind. He looked as if he was about to strike Brody to prove his point. Ivy was now staring at him as well. It was a side of him she had obviously never seen before.

"He and Jess were the real heroes that night--not me and certainly not Grant! You know nothing about Emry or Ridley! And if Emry is actually this Kaplan guy, then you obviously know nothing about Kaplan either. You're just another asshole with a badge trying to make a name for himself no matter who you hurt in the process!"

Jess's entire body suddenly tensed, and she gently cleared her throat. "Drake--"

Drake didn't look away from Brody and retained his rage. "No, I'm not going to stand here and let him accuse Emry of being some crazed killer! If it wasn't for him, we'd all be dead!"

Jess became more demanding and irritated. "Drake!" she lashed out.

"What?"

Drake and Brody looked at Jess. Emry casually stood alongside Jess with a gun aimed at Brody and showed little emotion. Drake suddenly tensed with surprise and became motionless. It was the fastest he had ever come down from an adrenaline rush.

"Oh--"

"Jess, kindly relieve Brody of his weapon," Emry said simply.

Brody glared at Emry as he removed his gun and handed it to Jess. He cast a look at her and frowned.

"I hope you're right about him, Jess," Brody said while shaking his head, "or you just killed me."

Jess frowned and took Brody's gun. She had more faith in Emry than that. Emry glared at Brody with the gun still aimed at him. There was a tense moment suggesting Emry might possibly shoot Brody. No one breathed. Emry casually lowered his gun. Ivy clung to Drake's arm and breathed a sigh of relief.

"I appreciate the warm sentiments, Drake," Emry said with little emotion and cast a glance at him. "It was touching. I really appreciate what you said. Pity you have such a big, fucking mouth."

Emry slammed his gun against Drake's chest, indicating he should take it. Drake gasped painfully, took the gun, and placed it down his pants.

"Yeah, you're welcome--and I'm sorry."

Ivy was still staring at Drake. Drake avoided looking at her and appeared ashamed that he had led her to believe he was a hero. Emry glared at Brody then paced before the controls and looked over them.

"Yes, I stowed away on the *Andrea Maria* last year. My real name is Emry Hill." Emry turned to face Brody. "I had a run-in with the Costa Rican police and jumped on the first available ship, but my being a stowaway then and now should be the least of your worries."

"How am I supposed to trust you?" Brody asked in a demanding tone. "How I am supposed to know you didn't plan this and intend to kill all of us?"

"Trust me, if this blood bath was my party, you'd already be dead--and I think you know why," Emry remarked simply while glaring at Brody.

There was a long, silent moment as the two men stared at each other. Brody glanced at Jess with some reluctance, appeared to understand, and then looked back at Emry and frowned.

"Okay, I believe you," Brody said with a sigh. "Can I assume you have a plan?"

"I'm never without one. They've cut off communication and disabled the bridge, but we can start the engines from the engine room. We need to reach land. According to the ship's last coordinates, time of hijacking, and speed, that would place New Orleans roughly four hundred miles," Emry pointed beyond the ship's railing, "that way."

"How can you possibly know New Orleans is that way?" Brody demanded to know.

Emry sharply eyed Brody and appeared insulted. "Because that's north, Brody. I know you feds are a little slow, but please don't make me explain everything to you."

"How did you know I was a federal agent?"

"I have a keen sense of smell, and you have fed stench all over you," Emry retorted.

Jess had to turn her head to hide her smile while subconsciously running her finger over the bug behind her ear. Emry glanced at Jess. She met his gaze with a tiny, knowing smirk. Emry winked at her. She almost felt bad for Brody. Emry had been listening to their entire conversation since Brody broke into the suite, giving him superior intelligence over Brody. Brody appeared mystified and speechless by Emry's response.

Chapter Twenty-eight

Grant and Dana finished dressing as they hurried after Drake and Ivy along the corridor toward the captain's cabin. Both looked worse for wear from their unintended, drunken one-night stand. Despite that they had been rudely awaken and caught in bed together by Drake, they were genuinely concerned by what he had told them.

"Please tell me this is some practical joke and in very poor taste," Grant said.

"I wish it was, but I saw the bridge," Drake replied without looking back at them.

"Just how screwed are we?" Dana asked as she tried to keep from panicking, although the look on Ivy's face told her she had every reason to panic.

Grant and Dana followed Drake and Ivy into the captain's cabin. As they entered, they saw Emry standing across the living room while he casually loaded an assault rifle. A duffel bag with assorted weapons lay open on the table before him. It was obvious Emry had prepared for just this sort of emergency prior to sneaking onboard. Grant and Dana stopped and stared at Emry, a ghost from their past, with identical looks of horror. It was an overpowering feeling of déjà vu and not in the good way.

"Oh, we are so screwed," Grant suddenly muttered under his breath.

Emry eyed them from across the room and smiled cheerfully. "Grant, welcome to the sequel." He cocked the assault rifle, causing Grant to flinch.

Jess appeared from the captain's bedroom wearing one of his white uniforms. She didn't want to remain in her dress from last night, and there was no chance to go back to her room for a change of clothing. She wanted to be prepared for whatever plan Emry had been conspiring in his devious mind. Jess approached the table, rummaged through Emry's bag of weapons, and found a small derringer pistol. It was cute and fit nicely in her pocket. Brody entered the cabin just behind Grant and Dana, startling both. He looked disgusted while returning his gun to his shoulder holster. Ivy looked at him with surprise and appeared concerned.

"Where are the others?" Ivy asked while nervously wringing her hands together.

Ivy wasn't handling the situation well at all. She appeared moments away from slipping into hysteria. Drake tried his best to keep her calm, although he wasn't faring much better. This time was different. He not only had his best friend to worry about, but the woman he loved now had her head on the chopping block as well. Jess was also worried about how well Drake would handle the situation now that Ivy was involved. He didn't look nearly as calm as he had been during their first encounter on the infamous ship.

"They weren't in their rooms and their beds were still made," Brody said lowly, "but I did find Arnold's body stuffed in a closet near the nightclub."

Ivy nervously clung to Drake. Jess handed guns to Drake, Ivy, and Dana. Dana held onto her gun like a security blanket. Ivy just stared at her gun as if unable to comprehend what it was. Jess extended a weapon to Grant. Grant, being the big hero he was, refused the gun. Clearly, he wasn't going to be much help this time around. Not that he was much help last time either. Grant poked through the drawers in the captain's desk and removed a bottle of bourbon. Drake eyed the drawer, approached without hesitation, and removed one of many master card keys. He handed it to Ivy and offered her a reassuring smile.

"This is a master key. Keep it on you, just in case."

Ivy uncertainly nodded and accepted the card. Emry tossed an assault rifle to Brody, who easily caught it.

"Brody and I are going to look around. Drake will stay here and protect--" he cast a disapproving glare at Grant, "--*the girls*."

Grant wasn't the least bit amused but seemed reluctant to challenge Emry. After a year of prancing around pretending to be the illustrious hero, he apparently felt small in Emry's presence. Jess, on the other hand, had no issues challenging Emry's authority.

"Now wait just one damned minute," Jess protested to Emry with a hostile look.

There was no way he was excluding her. What made him think she would stay behind while he and Brody went off to battle? Didn't he know her at all?

Emry looked at Jess and smiled charmingly. "Relax, my dear. I know you have my back."

His words immediately silenced her and a smile crossed her face. She liked hearing that. They were a team. Jess realized that he would never deny that part of their relationship, and she loved him for it.

†

The elegant spa was filled with half burned candles, giving off a romantic glow. Romantic relaxation music played softly throughout the room. Carla slept peacefully and was obviously naked beneath a pile of satin sheets on the floor. Rico, who was also naked beneath the pile of satin sheets, gathered Carla into his arms from behind and affectionately kissed the back of her neck. They clearly had a thrilling night of passion in the most sensual possible manner. Carla moaned wearily and immediately smiled at Rico with a look of complete satisfaction. Rico was obviously the suave, capable lover, and her disheveled look verified the fact.

"You taste like vanilla, Mi querida," Rico said with his usual charming smile.

Carla giggled. "I should. We were both drenched in vanilla scented oil last night."

Rico rolled Carla onto her back, moved on top of her, and passionately kissed her throat and neck. She was extremely receptive to his sexual advances. He spoke softly in Spanish while nibbling on her neck and shoulders. Carla giggled while enjoying his traveling kisses and his hands firmly running along her body. She was quickly leaving her state of tranquil bliss and into one of ecstasy.

"Translation?"

Rico smiled slyly and pulled her leg up to his hip while pressing firmly against her body. She let out a surprised but welcomed gasp.

"You figure it out." Rico then returned his mouth to hers and kissed her passionately.

A little while later, Rico collapsed alongside Carla while both panted heavily now out of breath. Carla clutched the sheet to her naked body, leaned over him with a lustful smile, and gently caressed his muscular, bronzed chest.

"Care to join me in a shower?"

Rico met her gaze with his own lustful smile. He was obviously pleased with the idea. "I catch my breath and join you--yes?"

"Don't be long."

Carla kissed him, slipped out of the sheets, and headed for the spa shower behind a set of frosted doors. Rico took a moment to watch her naked backside as she walked away. He grinned lustfully then looked at the sheets and began poking around them with a more serious expression.

"Cigarettes? Where you go?" he asked while searching for the pack of cigarettes.

The spa door slowly opened. A shadow loomed over Rico from behind as he searched the pile of sheets for his cigarettes. Rico hesitated to the presence of someone standing over him and slowly looked behind him.

✝

The fitness steam room was thick with steam allowing for limited visibility. The outline of a motionless and naked man lying on the wooden bench could barely be made out. His condition appeared uncertain. Zeke slowly woke with a moan, looked around the steam room, and then at his naked body. He appeared disoriented then managed a soft, humored laugh while closing his eyes.

"This would be a great story to tell if there had been a woman involved."

Zeke sat up with a hung-over groan and clutched his head. A shadow moved past the steam room window. Zeke looked at the door through the thick steam and appeared bewildered. The small, frosted window was barely visible.

"Hello?"

✝

Carla wearily stood beneath the hot spray of water in the large, spa shower for two. A thump came from the spa beyond the shower. Carla glanced at the frosted door with a concerned look on her face.

"Rico?"

There was no response. Carla hesitated only a moment before deciding she should check on Rico, who should have joined her by now. Carla stepped out of the shower, grabbed one of the official, plush spa robes from a nearby shelf, and slipped into it. She opened the door, uncertainly entered the spa, and nervously looked around. The candles throughout the room were still flickering with their romantic glow as the music continued to play. The pile of satin sheets were now thoroughly scattered along the floor. Rico was gone! Carla immediately appeared tense and stared across the empty spa room.

"Oh, why does this feel familiar?" Carla muttered to herself.

Carla hurried to a nearby candle and blew out the flame. She removed the candle from the brass candlestick, clutched it in a deadly fashion, and slowly crossed the room. She paused before the pile of sheets. There were droplets of blood on some of the sheets. Carla appeared concerned and hurried toward the main door. As she approached, she saw fresh blood streaked across the floor leading out the closed door. Carla held back her gasp, stared at the blood a moment longer, and then slowly reached for the doorknob. The doorknob turned before she touched it. Carla jumped back as the door opened to reveal someone who was clearly not Rico. Carla swung the candlestick and nearly struck Zeke, who suddenly cried out and ducked the swinging candlestick. Carla screamed having almost struck him. Zeke stared at Carla with wide eyes from his crouched, cowering position near the floor with one hand to his chest and the other defensively over his head.

"Damn it, you scared me!" Zeke cried out. "What's wrong with you?" He appeared reluctant to stand or remove his hand that shielded his head.

"What's wrong with me?"

Carla relaxed her grip on the candlestick then pointed impatiently at the blood on the floor. Zeke looked at the streak of blood near him and his footprint left behind within it.

"Oh, shit!"

Zeke quickly straightened and sidestepped away from the blood. He stared at the blood and appeared almost paralyzed for a moment. Carla continued to scan the room with a look of concern for Rico's welfare.

"Rico was here a minute ago, and now he's gone. I'm afraid something terrible has happened to him," Carla said while fidgeting. "We need to find the others. Jess will know what to do."

Zeke finally looked away from the blood then at Carla with the fear evident on his face. "Yeah, I'm all for that. I know I'll feel better standing behind Grant."

Carla frowned and rolled her eyes with disgust at the suggestion. "Personally, I'm feeling nostalgic for a shorter, more nerdy sort of guy."

Zeke looked at her and appeared bewildered. Carla ignored his confused look and immediately began dressing into her clothing that lay scattered along the floor. She showed little concern for Zeke's presence. Zeke strained to watch while pretending not to. He had seen enough of her naked profile to cause him to blush and look away. Carla carelessly tossed the robe and candlestick aside. They turned toward the door and nearly collided with Rico as he entered. Rico eyed Zeke then looked at Carla with obvious jealousy.

"Mi querida trade-in Rico?"

Rico again eyed Zeke with disapproval. Carla appeared relieved, threw her arms around Rico's neck, and clung to him. He returned the embrace.

"I was so worried about you." Carla quickly pulled away and indicated the blood on the floor not far from Rico's feet. "You were gone and there was all that blood--"

Rico didn't even look at the blood on the floor. "No, that not Rico's blood."

"Whose blood is it?" Zeke asked.

Rico looked at Zeke and suddenly thrust a hunting knife into his abdomen. Zeke gasped to the pain of the knife rammed into his midsection. Carla jumped back with a look of horror and screamed. Rico looked into Zeke's eyes with a devious, twisted smile while holding the knife in him as blood seeped out around the wound.

"Some cowardly deckhand who'd been hiding," Rico said without his charming accent.

Rico pulled the blood-covered knife from Zeke's body. Zeke clutched his bleeding abdomen and sank to the floor onto the plush, white robe while gasping. Carla stared at Rico with horror, held back her scream, and tried to bolt for the door. Rico cut off her path, pulled her harshly against him, and placed the knife to her throat while holding her seductively in his arm.

"Poor, spoiled Carla," Rico said with a humored look while preserving his lustful grin.

Carla braced her hands against his chest, tensed from the bloodied knife against her throat, and held back her sobs. His sexual display toward her after having stabbed Zeke and holding a knife to her throat made the situation even more disturbing. It was as if the physical violence gave him some perverse pleasure. He appeared almost aroused by it.

"After you prevented my man from killing you that night at your house, I decided you might still be useful."

Carla stared at him with complete horror and was almost down to tears while shaking her head with disbelief. Rico practically held her up from her frightened, weakened state. He was enjoying her fear.

"Why are you doing this?" Carla sobbed. "I thought you loved me."

"You really don't know?" Rico chuckled softly as if she should already have figured that out. "Last year you and your friends cost me millions in confiscated drugs."

Carla stared into his eyes with horror and appeared unable to move. Rico smiled with his bright, charming smile and added a throaty chuckle.

"Now she understands," Rico said mockingly as he ran his hand along her buttocks. "She was being fucked by a drug lord--*and she liked it.*" He once again turned serious. "But I'm not completely without compassion. If you tell me where my diamonds are, I'll consider letting you go."

Carla appeared surprised. There had never been mention of diamonds. She quickly hid her look of surprise, glanced behind him, and then met his gaze. She carefully considered her answer while painfully aware of the knife to her throat.

"I don't have them, but I know who does," she said softly while trembling.

Rico removed the knife from her throat without releasing her. He smiled while seductively running the tip of the knife blade along her neckline, leaving traces of Zeke's blood on her chest.

"I'm listening--"

"Zeke." Carla trembled while watching the knife as it caressed her chest.

Rico suddenly appeared bewildered and uncertainly released her. "Zeke?"

He looked behind him to where Zeke had fallen. Zeke now stood before Rico, despite his severe injury, and struck him on the head with Carla's discarded candlestick. Rico was thrown sideways from the blow. Zeke cried out and, with all his strength, attempted another swing at Rico's head with the heavy candlestick. Rico suddenly thrust his hunting knife into Zeke's side. Zeke gasped and half collapsed while still clutching the candlestick.

"Run, Carla!" Zeke cried out with his last ounce of strength as the blood seeped from his mouth.

Carla appeared uncertain what to do. She couldn't just leave him at Rico's mercy even though he was pretty much dead already. Rico straightened and violently slashed Zeke's throat. Zeke collapsed to the floor while attempting another gurgled plea for Carla to run. Blood ran from the slit in his throat and down his neck in a waterfall of blood. Carla screamed and ran from the spa. Rico slashed at her with the knife but missed. He clutched his bleeding head, looked at the blood on his hand, and then attempted to run after Carla.

Chapter Twenty-nine

The casino door flew open. Carla ran into the ship's casino and darted behind a bank of slot machines. The ship's casino was grand and extravagant with hundreds of slot machines of every variety. Slot machines lined the walls and were also in rows on either side of the main aisle like bookshelves in a library. Toward the far right of the casino was the massive bar. Dozens of table games filled the large area beyond the bar and near the back entrance. The casino doors could be heard opening. Carla quietly scurried along the row of machines toward the far end closest to the wall. She positioned herself on the end, so someone walking along the center aisle wouldn't see her. Rico walked along the aisle and peered down each row while attempting to locate her. From her position on the far end, Carla could see Rico pass through the main aisle.

Once he passed, Carla hurried in the opposite direction and again hid along the end. She remained safely hidden, held her breath, and looked at the casino doors not far from her. She gathered her courage and was about ready to bolt for the doors, when they opened to reveal Jacob. Carla recognized him as one of Rico's five friends from the club where she had first met him. Jacob's presence surprised her at first, but then it all made sense. His friends were in on it from the beginning. Undoubtedly, one of them had been the man who broke into her home in an attempt to kill her, and Rico ran after him only for show. Jacob carried a gun and looked ready to kill the first person he saw.

Carla stared at Rico's friend with concern as he patrolled the casino not far from her. Rico motioned for him to take the end aisle. Jacob headed in Carla's direction. Carla hurried down the next row toward the main aisle and the bar. She looked down the aisle to check Rico's position. Rico headed for the poker tables beyond a bank of slot machines near the second set of casino doors. Carla darted across the main aisle and behind the bar. She crouched down behind the bar and again peered out. Jacob was in the aisle she had occupied and now approached the bar. Carla remained silent and suddenly tensed. He hadn't seen her, but he would be on her in just a few seconds, leaving her pinned.

The casino doors again opened. Jacob darted behind a bank of slot machines not far from her and the bar. Carla moved to the other end of the bar and looked toward the entrance to see what had startled Jacob. Jess and Brody entered and casually looked around the silent casino. Carla tensed and looked from Jess and Brody to Jacob, who waited to ambush them not far from her. The unsuspecting couple would reach him shortly, and he would easily get the drop on them. Carla considered her options. She could easily wait for Jacob to attack Jess and Brody and make her run to safety while he was busy killing them. She gave it only a moment of thought and knew what she had to do. Carla suddenly darted out from behind the bar and ran for Jess and Brody.

"Run, Jess!"

Jacob stepped out from behind his bank of slot machines with his gun aimed at Carla's back as she ran for Jess. Carla had to know her selfless act was a one-way trip, but Jess had done the same for her not so long ago. It was as if the world was suddenly running in slow motion. Jess and Brody looked at Carla as she ran for them. Jacob's gun suddenly fired. Carla looked into Jess's eyes to the distinct sound of the gun firing and knew what was coming. The image from one year ago of Jess sacrificing herself for her in the bathroom flashed through Carla's mind. As Carla ran for Jess, she heard nothing but the sound of her own heartbeat while awaiting the sting of the bullet in her back.

Time seemed to speed back up. Emry suddenly appeared out of nowhere and tackled Carla across the main aisle and out of the bullet's path. Both rolled several feet together and behind a bank of slot machines. Jess and Brody dove to machines on either side of the aisle and removed their weapons. Emry sprang up while drawing his weapon and moved into a crouched position behind the machines. He immediately fired at Jacob down the main aisle. Carla scrambled to her hands and knees with some disorientation and stared at Emry with disbelief and possible horror at the man who she had known to be dead.

"My God, it's you!"

Emry barely looked at her while keeping his eyes and his gun on the target just down the main aisle. He showed no emotion.

"Are you really surprised?"

Carla considered his comment then shook her head. "Actually, no."

Emry turned toward her while keeping low to the floor, removed a large, semiautomatic handgun from a belt holster beneath his jacket, and handed it to her.

"Can you shoot?"

Carla took the gun without hesitation and appeared almost offended. "Of course I can shoot," she replied. She then hesitated, considered her comment, and frowned. "I just can't hit much."

"Exhale then squeeze the trigger. The bullet will take care of the rest." Emry nodded down the far aisle along the back wall. "I'm going for a rear assault. If that bastard sticks his head out, I want you to put a bullet in it."

Carla appeared horrified at his order. Emry hurried down the aisle toward the wall. Jess watched him approach the back aisle from her bank of slot machines not far from the main entrance. He stopped at the end of the row and looked at Jess as if giving her some secret signal. Jess boldly stepped into the aisle from the safety of her fortress of slot machines and rapidly fired at Jacob. Jacob dove behind his machine. Several bullets struck the machine and lit it up. The jackpot alarm sounded and coins began dropping into the tray. Emry bolted down the aisle unnoticed. Once he was safely on his way, Jess leaped behind her machine and looked across the aisle at Brody, who stared at her with a dumbfounded expression.

"And you hired *me* to protect *you?*" Brody shook his head with disbelief.

The casino door partially opened behind them. Brody looked back. A small disk suddenly rolled into the aisle between them, sending horror through him.

"Move!" Brody cried out to Jess.

Jess ran past the bank of slot machines toward the back aisle. Carla darted behind her slot machines, and Brody ran in the opposite direction toward the bar. The disk flashed and erupted into a thick cloud of smoke but there was no explosion. The smoke began to clear. Brody and Carla looked around from their respective hiding places for signs of Jess. Rico stood before the bank of slot machines they had once occupied with Jess in front of him and a gun to her head.

"Time to surrender, amigos," Rico called out.

175

As the smoke rolled through the center aisle and dissipated, Emry stood at the other end of the aisle holding his gun to Jacob's head. Rico stared at Emry with surprise and bewilderment. Emry had not been with them when they boarded the ship, he clearly wasn't one of the crew, and he certainly wasn't one of Rico's men.

"Who the fuck are you?" Rico demanded to know of the man he had never seen before.

Emry's look was cold and emotionless as he stared at Rico without twitching. "You can call me Kaplan," he remarked lowly.

There was something oddly unfamiliar about Emry at that moment. Jess suddenly didn't recognize him, and his words sent a chill through her. Kaplan butchered the men who had killed his wife and was the bearer of death and destruction. That Emry referred to himself as Kaplan was possibly an indicator of his intent to kill mercilessly. She was suddenly afraid of what he might do. Rico remained unaffected and overly confident. He didn't perceive Emry to be a threat. Emry was non-impressive and often underestimated, which was undoubtedly the secret behind his success as a CIA assassin.

"Put down your gun, Kaplan. My hostage is more valuable than yours."

It was clear Rico held little regard for his man's life. He was confident and arrogant, which would ultimately be his undoing. Emry showed no emotion to Rico's comment and continued to stare with the frozen look of a cold-blooded killer in his eyes. Jess carefully removed the derringer from her pocket and clutched it in her hand. Emry's eyes briefly strayed to the little gun she clutched and his look turned less psychotic. He appeared to be reading her mind and immediately anticipated her next move.

"I don't know that she's more valuable," Emry said with a slight tilt of his head and a tiny, twisted smile, "but she's definitely more dangerous."

Jess slowly aimed the little gun behind her body toward Rico's leg while clinging to his arm around her neck with her free hand. She stared at Emry and awaited some secret signal from him.

"A little to the south, my dear," Emry said casually.

Rico suddenly appeared baffled by Emry's words. As Rico moved slightly to see what Jess was up to, his gun moved away from her temple. Jess moved the little gun south. Emry subtly raised his brow to her. Jess pulled the trigger. The small derringer fired into Rico's thigh. He cried out with pain and surprise. Jess quickly turned and kneed him in the groin. He clutched himself without dropping the gun and sank to his knees. Carla appeared from her aisle with a look of relief on her face and quickly approached them.

Rico raised his gun despite his agony and shot Carla. The bullet struck her and forcibly tossed her to the floor.

Emry saw Carla drop and became immediately enraged. He swiftly broke Jacob's neck with little effort and aimed his gun at Rico as Jacob fell lifelessly to the floor. Jess shared his rage and spun into a roundhouse kick, striking Rico in the head while he was hunched over, and dropped him to the floor. She kicked the gun away from him and rushed to Carla's fallen side. Carla clutched her bleeding shoulder in agony as she pulled herself into a sitting position on the floor. Emry approached Rico with little emotion, stood over him where he knelt, and aimed the gun at his head. Emry sneered and said something not particularly pleasant in Spanish. What he said didn't matter, because his intentions were made clear as his finger tightened against the trigger. Rico maintained his humored grin despite the gun aimed at his head. He obviously didn't believe Emry would pull the trigger. Brody suddenly stood alongside them and aimed his gun at Emry.

"Don't even think it," Brody growled with hostility. "I'm in charge, and we do things my way."

Emry sneered, pulled his gun back with disgust, and hurried for Jess to check on Carla's injuries. Emry knelt before Carla, removed her hand from her wound, and examined her bleeding shoulder.

"Are you okay?" he asked with concern.

"Never been better," Carla gasped while writhing in agony and allowed her head to fall against the slot machine behind her. "Please tell me he's dead."

"I'm afraid not," Emry said with the disgust evident in his voice.

"You disappoint me," Carla scoffed softly.

"Your injury doesn't look too bad," Emry informed her. "Let's get you to the infirmary and patch you up."

Carla slowly nodded while cringing in agony. Emry attempted to help her to her feet. The intercom suddenly crackled.

"They're here!" Ivy screamed over the intercom.

The sounds of gunfire immediately followed and the intercom went dead. Emry, Jess, Carla, and Brody looked at the ceiling with surprise and horror. Ivy tried to shout a warning from the captain's cabin but had gotten it out too late. Rico slowly and painfully moved to his knees while holding his bleeding thigh and panting.

"Seems my men found your friends," Rico said with an evil, twisted smile then looked at Jess. "Your wardrobe choice betrayed them."

Jess uncertainly looked at the captain's uniform she wore. Rico must have seen what she was wearing and told his friends to check the captain's cabin for the others before he captured her. Jess appeared concerned and looked at Emry with the horror evident in her eyes.

"Drake--"

"We'll help them," Emry said to her.

Rico suddenly swept Brody's legs out from under him, punched him in the groin as he hit the ground, and ran for the casino doors despite his injured leg. Emry quickly turned and fired a shot at Rico but missed him by a fraction of a second, hitting the doorframe instead. Emry quickly approached Brody, who writhed in agony while clutching himself, and glared his disapproval.

"Lesson number one," Emry snapped lowly while lacking sympathy for Brody's pain. "The only good bad guy is a dead bad guy. Lesson number two. Fucking learn lesson number one." Emry roughly pulled Brody to his feet and returned his gun to him by slamming it into his chest. "Now we do things my way. I'm in charge. You help Drake and the others. I'll take care of the pretty boy."

Jess jumped to her feet near where Carla sat on the floor and stared at Emry. She was more worried about Drake than simply needing to feel included.

"I'm going with you."

He turned toward Jess from several feet away and firmly glared his response. "No, you're going to stay here and keep Carla from bleeding to death."

Emry didn't even give her a chance to protest as he stormed out the casino door. He was waging a war, and it was best to stay out of his way. Brody slowly and painfully followed Emry. Jess lowered herself to the floor before Carla, who still sat against the slot machine, and applied pressure to her wound.

"The bleeding seems to be slowing. You're going to be okay," Jess said softly but remained distracted with her concern for Drake and Ivy. "We should get you to the infirmary. I can give you a shot of morphine--"

Carla stared at Jess with a strange look in her eyes and suddenly appeared enraged.

"I don't need you baby-sitting me!" Carla lashed out with hostility and for no apparent reason. "Go do something useful, damn it!"

Jess stared at Carla with surprise to her sudden hostile outburst. She had never seen her like this before. Carla then smiled gently, indicated her discarded, semiautomatic handgun, and appeared more timid.

"Just leave that with me, okay?"

Jess smiled gently and handed Carla the gun. Carla clutched the gun and looked into Jess's eyes. At that moment, Jess realized the enormous amount of respect Carla had for her. They may have altered the original battle for *Andrea Maria* story for the press, but she still remembered what Jess did for her and how they managed to survive that night. Carla wanted her to save the others and knew she could do it. Though neither would admit it, they actually liked each other.

Chapter Thirty

Brody cautiously entered the captain's cabin through the broken door. The cabin was in complete disarray with overturned furniture and broken objects. Blood spatters and bullet holes covered the room. It was impossible to tell who was shot, how bad their injuries were, or even if they had gotten away. The open balcony door had a bloody handprint on the glass. Brody hurried for the balcony door, eyed the blood, and then looked outside. There was movement across the captain's cabin. Brody quickly turned with his gun aimed and saw Jess standing in the cabin doorway. She slowly entered the cabin and looked at the destruction and blood. She was even more concerned for Drake and Ivy after seeing the condition of the cabin. She couldn't stand the thought of losing her best friend, and even less for him losing the woman he loved. Brody relaxed with a groan and slowly lowered his gun.

"Weren't you supposed to stay with Carla?"

"Yeah, but I never do what I'm told--or so I'm told," Jess replied. "I can't just sit by not knowing if Drake and Ivy are okay."

"Well, there's not enough blood to suggest anyone was fatally shot, so there's still hope that they're alive," he said while looking around the cabin with a frown. "We only missed them by a few minutes, but they could be anywhere on the ship by now."

"Not just anywhere. You forget who you're dealing with, Brody. The five of us lived through this nightmare before. If they escaped, I think I have a pretty good idea of where we should start looking for them."

Jess hurried to the captain's desk and rifled through one of the drawers. She removed a master card key. "Let's go."

†

$\mathcal{T}$he electronic door lock hummed. The door to cabin #302, Dana's old cabin, slowly opened to reveal Jess and Brody with their guns aimed. They slowly entered. The old, familiar cabin appeared empty and quiet. Jess pushed open the bathroom door and peered inside. It was empty. Brody opened the closet door and suddenly aimed his gun at Grant, who was crammed into the corner of the closet. Grant appeared alarmed and held his hands up defensively.

"Don't shoot! It's me!" Grant cried out.

Brody lowered his gun with a groan. Grant appeared relieved to see them and stepped out of the closet with a grateful sigh. Brody looked around the cabin and appeared concerned.

"Where are the others?"

"I don't know," Grant said with a shake of his head as he collapsed onto the bed. "When those guys broke in and started shooting up the place, we scattered."

"Was anyone injured?" Jess asked.

"I really don't know. It happened so fast. One minute everything was quiet, the next, the door was broken down, and they were firing on us. It was like they knew exactly where to find us."

Jess frowned and looked at the captain's uniform she wore. She looked away with disgust and shook her head. Brody looked at Jess.

"It's not your fault, Jess."

"No? It sure feels like it is." Jess turned to Grant on the bed. "Let's go. We'll look for the others in the infirmary."

Grant appeared horrified. "Are you kidding? If they're not dead, they're probably hiding. It's what smart people do."

Jess glared at Grant with annoyance. She had forgotten how much she wanted to punch him in the face. There was a good chance she might just do it this time.

"Oh, yeah, I forgot. You only played a hero in the fictitious version of this story." Jess turned to Brody. "Let's go."

Grant appeared annoyed, sprang off the bed, and approached Jess with hostility. "And you seem to forget that your John Wayne attitude nearly cost you your life last time. I was there. I remember how poorly you handled Emry's death. You were reduced to a basket case, so don't play the tough girl act with me."

Jess punched Grant in the mouth, knocking him backwards and onto the bed. He clutched his bleeding mouth, attempted to sit up,

181

and appeared surprised while staring at her. Jess glared at him through narrow eyes.

"I'm not playing."

Jess turned and left the room. Brody eyed Grant, chuckled softly, and followed Jess.

†

The Andrea Maria sailed through the clear waters at cruising speed in the early afternoon sunshine. Despite the ship's infamous legacy, she was truly majestic.

†

The empty nightclub was littered with bottles of alcohol, glasses, and snacks. It was a grim reminder of a fun filled evening preceding what would be life-and-death for the ship's passengers. The intercom suddenly crackled breaking the silence.

"Good afternoon, *Andrea Maria*," Drake's voice was heard loud and clear over the intercom. "This is your cruise director, Drake."

†

The empty dining room was clean of all dishes from the prior evening. The crisp, white linens remained on the tables with the elegant floral arrangements proudly displayed on the center of each.

"We're sailing at cruising speed toward some seriously rough terrain," Drake's voice continued over the intercom. His voice suddenly went from jovial to hostile. "So if you bastards want to live to see tomorrow, you'd better bring my girlfriend to the engine room in twenty minutes, or I'm going to sink this mother fucker and everyone on it."

†

The empty lounge appeared untouched from one year ago. The pool table was ready for a game to be played. The empty scotch glass remained on the edge of the pool table.

"I'd like to dedicate this next song to Emry," Drake's voice continued over the intercom. "Remember what you promised me one year ago, you son-of-a-bitch? Well, the time is now."

An eerily dismal song began to play over the intercom.

†

Jess and Brody stood in the infirmary near a pile of bloody rags on the exam table. Several tools had blood on them and bandage wrappings were tossed carelessly on the floor along with an empty syringe. Jess stared at the ceiling and listened to the dismal music playing. Brody held a dish with a bloody bullet in it.

"Drake was shot," Brody said.

Jess suddenly looked at him with alarm. That was the last thing she wanted to hear. The news went through her like a shockwave.

"How do you know it was him? It could have been one of *them*," Jess said with noted concern in her voice.

She had just heard his voice over the intercom. He sounded strange, almost cold and unfeeling, but there was something else in his voice--that of pain. She didn't want to admit that he could be running around the ship while bleeding to death.

"This bullet doesn't belong to any of the weapons in Ridley's arsenal. It had to be fired from one of their guns. There's a pair of bloody surgical gloves on the table. They're too small for Drake to have worn." Brody set down the dish with the bloody bullet. "If they have Ivy, it must have been Dana who removed the bullet from Drake. We don't know how badly he was injured or how well she patched him up. Judging by the empty syringe and the bottle of morphine, I'd say she gave him a healthy dose of painkillers."

"He'll be fine, I know he will," Jess told Brody, although she wasn't so sure she could convince herself of that. "Drake is holding the ship's engines hostage in exchange for Ivy. You need to help him save her. It's what you're trained to do, right? You're his best hope of getting her back alive. Our bad guys will need to shut down the ship's engines or steer her off course to avoid a collision. They have little choice but to bring Ivy to him."

"Why do I get the feeling you're up to something?"

"I need to help Emry with part two of Drake's plan," Jess informed him while checking the clip in one of her guns.

She frowned and tossed the gun aside with disgust then removed a second gun and checked its clip as well. There were two bullets left in the clip. She wasn't exactly happy with her ammo supply.

"Did I miss something?"

"Last year in the cargo hold, Emry told Drake he could storm the bridge next time." Jess slammed the clip back into her gun and cocked it. She met Brody's stare and appeared emotionless. "Well, it's next time. He wants Emry on the bridge."

"Does he really think Emry will remember that?"

"Emry remembers everything," Jess said bluntly. "It's one of his many amazing and sometimes annoying qualities. Drake must believe they intend to fix the controls and alter the ship's course. We don't have much time."

Chapter Thirty-one

 $\mathcal{T}$ he cramped engine room appeared oddly deserted. The roar of the ship's engines was loud throughout the narrow corridors of endless walkways between the machinery. Lance, one of Rico's friends from the nightclub, appeared in a walkway with Ivy in front of him and a gun pointed to her head. Her hands were tied before her. She appeared unharmed, but she was obviously frightened. Lance forcibly pushed her along the aisle ahead of him. Drake stepped into the aisle several feet in front of them with his gun aimed and a look of mayhem on his nearly psychotic, pale face. Blood saturated the shoulder of his shirt. He was obviously hurting but managed the pain rather well. The morphine injection probably contributed to his pain management. Ivy saw Drake, appeared alarmed by his condition, and held back her sobs. Drake's eyes softened for a brief moment as he stared at her frightened face.

"Are you okay, baby?" Drake asked gently while quickly scanning her for any evidence of injury or mistreatment from her captors.

Ivy sniffed and slowly nodded. She appeared reluctant or unable to speak. She was concerned about more than the man holding the gun at her head. Drake offered her a surprisingly reassuring smile.

"It's okay, Ivy. I know it's a trap."

Ivy's expression suddenly dropped, and she appeared to stop breathing while staring at him. For a brief moment, she was possibly convinced he was crazy. Drake's expression once again turned cold and hostile as he glared at Lance holding the gun to Ivy's head.

"I'd like to make you a deal to release my girlfriend," Drake said to Lance.

"Move!" Dana's gruff voice shouted from nearby.

Another one of Rico's friends from the nightclub, Matt, walked toward them from a different location with his hands behind his neck and a look of concern on his once tough face. Dana stood behind him with her gun aimed at his head. Dana's expression no longer contained any of its usual warmth and compassion. Perhaps it had to do with the blood staining the once elegant dress she still wore from last night. Since she showed no signs of injuries, the blood was probably Drake's. Drake maintained his glare at Lance and appeared cold and emotionless.

"You kill her, she kills him, I kill you," Drake informed Lance casually. "The way I see it, there's no scenario where you walk out of here alive except for a hostage exchange. I don't give a shit who you are or what you want with this ship. I just want my girlfriend, and I'm crazy enough to kill us all if I don't get my way." Drake indicated Dana with a casual nod and a slightly devious smile. "And Dana there just recently discovered she has a violent streak that's more than a little disturbing."

"She's crazy, Lance," Matt said in a concerned tone. "She grabbed my balls and nearly ripped them off."

"I kind of enjoyed that," Dana said with an enthusiastic grin.

Dana was definitely walking on the dark side after whatever happened in the captain's cabin or possibly in the infirmary while performing meatball surgery on Drake.

"I'd like to make an alternate deal," Lance said casually while studying both Drake and Dana.

"I don't see any alternative," Drake said with little emotion.

Victor approached Drake from the left side with a gun aimed at him and stopped several feet away. Drake glanced briefly at Victor with a look of surprise but kept his gun trained on Lance.

"Victor?"

"Surprised?" Victor asked with a smirk.

Drake's expression once again turned cold. "I suppose I should be, but I can't say that I am." Drake kept his focus on Lance holding Ivy. "What brings you to this little reunion from hell?"

"Money, naturally. I'll admit things didn't exactly go according to my plan. I intended to charm my way into Jess's life to gain access onto this ship, so I was a little put off when Brody horned in on her, but it worked out in the end. Security on the ship was tight, but his invite helped me find my own way onboard."

Drake shook his head with annoyance. "What is so damned important about this ship? Personally, I'd love to see it on the bottom of the ocean."

"They weren't just smuggling drugs that night, they were also smuggling millions in diamonds," Victor said. "After the drugs were confiscated, the feds sealed off the ship to conduct their six month long investigation of the attack. When they didn't find the stones in the first two months, we naturally assumed one of you must have found them and taken them. We searched your homes but didn't find any evidence of them. That had to mean they were still on the ship somewhere."

"It was you who broke into our homes?"

"Well, not me personally--colleagues of mine," Victor replied with a smug smile on his face.

"Why kill Conner and attempt to kill Jess and Carla?" Drake demanded. "What was with the drama of leaving the movie scripts?"

"That was Rico's macabre sense of humor," Victor said. "That man's idea of a friendly breakup is strangling his girlfriends during sex. Incidentally, he was breaking up with Carla this morning, so I wouldn't hold my breath on seeing her again, if I were you."

Dana cast a concerned look at Drake. "Carla--"

Despite all their fights, it was obvious she didn't want to see any harm come to Carla. Drake didn't flinch at the comment or take his eyes off Lance.

"Rico thought if we eliminated some of the original survivors with that whole movie premiere notion, it would cancel the anniversary cruise, lessen security around the ship, and make her more accessible to us. Naturally, it backfired. Rico's style is too dramatic. Simplicity is the key. I figured the anniversary cruise was our best shot of getting onboard to search for the diamonds. All we had to do was hijack the ship and deal with a couple of crewmembers and a few passengers. After that beautifully orchestrated hijacking last year, this was nothing."

Drake frowned with disgust. "Yes, big brave men shooting unarmed people. It may be me, but I don't recall that beautifully orchestrated hijacking exactly working out for you. In fact, I remember those pussy ass, terrorist wannabes dropping like flies."

"We had a few unexpected surprises," Victor said then appeared almost humored with the entire situation. "Killing off you and your friends on the anniversary cruise is actually quite poetic. There are still some hard feelings about what you and your shipmates did to our people, but more importantly, for all the money we'd lost when the authorities confiscated our shipment."

"Then you're going to be even less pleased about your diamonds," Drake said in a casual tone. "I'm afraid they went overboard with that guy, what's his name, Brahm. Sorry." Drake flashed a devious smile to his fabricated story. Obviously, he knew nothing about the diamonds, but he wanted to watch Victor squirm. "But you're welcome to keep the ship as a consolation prize." Drake then sneered. "That is until we run aground in New Orleans."

"Brahm had them?" Victor suddenly asked with surprise then shook his head with disgust. "You don't know how disappointed I am to hear that, but I'm afraid we won't be running aground, and we're certainly not heading for New Orleans. Rico's on the bridge fixing the controls as we speak. He'll be setting an alternate course-- one of our choosing. Not that you'll ever see land again."

"Huh?" Drake lacked interest with the conversation. "Who would have guessed you'd have a man fixing the controls on the bridge? Honestly, I never would have seen that one coming." His tone was callus. "You're too smart for me, Victor."

Drake's casual reaction concerned Victor. It gave the impression that Drake knew what he was up to and had already planned a counter attack. Victor wasn't convinced Drake was that smart.

"You seem awfully relaxed considering your situation, Drake."

"Aside from being loaded up on morphine, there's nothing wrong with my situation." Drake upheld his superior attitude and was definitely up to something. "Tell me something, Victor. Did Brody mention that he was an undercover federal agent when he came to work for you? Or was that little fun fact, like, a secret?"

Victor's expression suddenly dropped as he stared at Drake. It was obvious Victor was trying to read Drake's expression for signs of bluffing.

Drake grinned and chuckled softly. "Oh, it was a secret? Sorry for blowing your cover, Brody."

"That's okay," Brody responded from the shadows.

Brody appeared in the aisle and had his gun aimed at Lance with the look of a sniper waiting for a clean shot. The alarmed look on Lance's face indicated he knew he was in trouble. Lance quickly moved the gun from Ivy's head and aimed it at Brody. The moment the gun moved away from Ivy, Brody pulled the trigger and shot Lance in the head just over her shoulder. Ivy screamed as Lance's head snapped back from the bullet striking him dead center in the forehead. She crouched down and shielded her face as Lance dropped to the floor. At the same moment, Victor aimed his gun at Brody. Drake turned toward Victor and, without hesitation, fired two shots into his chest. In all the excitement and commotion, Dana's gun suddenly fired and Matt dropped to the floor before her. She let out a startled scream and jumped. Drake and Brody looked at her with horror.

187

"What the hell was that?" Brody cried out.

Dana appeared terrified and looked at Brody while frantically waving her gun around. "It just went off! I swear I didn't mean--"

Both men ducked and shielded themselves from the waving gun in her hand. Brody lunged for Dana and grabbed the gun from her. Dana appeared embarrassed and avoided looking at Brody's disapproving glare. Drake hurried to Ivy, who remained huddled on the floor in a state of panic, and knelt before her. Despite her tied wrists, Ivy threw her arms around his neck and clung to him while sobbing. Drake held her in his arms from their position on the floor and gently rocked her.

"It's okay," Drake whispered softly in her ear. "I've got you, Ivy."

Chapter Thirty-two

Rico hurried along the bridge deck with a severe limp from the gunshot wound on his left leg. He was obviously hurting despite it having been a small caliber bullet. He had tied a cloth around his thigh to stop the bleeding but blood still soaked through. Rico turned toward the bridge steps and suddenly stopped to see a gun aimed at his face. He stared at the gun then looked at the man holding it. Emry stared back at him with a steel cold gaze.

"Apparently you didn't get my message," Emry said in a low, unsettling tone.

"What message?" Rico studied Emry and appeared confused. "Do I know you?"

"You were warned to stay away from her."

Emry's look was far more sinister than it had ever been. In his current state, there was no telling what he was capable of doing.

Rico's eyes suddenly widened as he stared at Emry with realization. "It was you? You gutted my man!"

Emry didn't react and remained unnaturally calm to the accusation, which was all the response Rico needed. Emry stared at Rico with an icy glare.

"When you're trained to kill men for a living, you learn to remove all emotion," Emry said callously. "It's just another job. It's never personal. I don't care about much, but when someone threatens what I do care about, I take it very personally." Emry's eyes narrowed sharply and his voice lowered considerably. The look on his face was almost psychotic. "And when I take things personally, I tend to leave behind one hell of a mess."

Rico stared at Emry a moment and appeared uncertain what to make of this man calling himself Kaplan. He was used to being feared by all men, but Emry showed no fear. There was a slight glimmer of anxiety in Rico's eyes, but his ego got the better of him. He suddenly chuckled and mocked Emry with his playful grin.

"So you like that one, huh?" Rico leaned a little closer and smiled lustfully. "Then I'll be sure to take extra special care of her before I kill her."

Without warning or emotion, Emry redirected the gun to Rico's crotch and pulled the trigger. Rico gasped as the gun fired and dove out of the way. The bullet grazed his hip but missed its intended target. One of Rico's other friends from the nightclub, Andy, emerged from the bridge and was suddenly behind Emry. He cocked his gun, which was now aimed at Emry's head. Emry hesitated at the distinctive sound of a gun to the back of his head and remained motionless. While keeping his gun trained on Rico, Emry assessed Andy's position on the steps behind him out of the corner of his eye. Emry was in a bad position where he stood on the stairs and had no recourse. Had Andy been smart, he would have shot him immediately.

"Drop it," Andy ordered.

Andy wasn't that smart. Emry frowned and tossed his gun over the railing to the deck below. Rico straightened, eyed the bleeding bullet graze to his hip, and appeared almost humored. He moved closer to Emry, who was just a few steps up from him, smiled charmingly, and then punched him in the groin. Emry immediately clutched himself and doubled over on the steps. Rico struck him on the back of the head. Emry fell to the deck alongside him and was barely conscious. Rico grinned and appeared pleased with himself. He looked at Andy and indicated Emry.

"Take him to the bridge and tie him up. I want him to see what we're going to do to his little girlfriend before we kill them both."

Andy hurried the rest of the way down the steps, kicked Emry in his side where he lay, and then roughly pulled him to his feet. Emry didn't resist or attempt to fight back. Andy appeared overly confident as he shoved Emry toward the steps. Emry obediently walked up the steps but continued to watch Andy out of the corner of his eye.

†

Several minutes later, Rico replaced the panel beneath the controls on the bridge and began hastily adjusting the ship's current course. Emry stood on the bridge several feet behind him with his hands tied in front of him around a pole. He showed no emotion to his predicament while closely watching Rico at the controls. It seemed odd that he wasn't searching for some way to escape his imprisonment. His overly calm demeanor was eerily unsettling. Andy stood near the bridge door while keeping an eye on Emry and watched for any approaching intruders. Rico finished adjusting the controls to alter the ship's course then casually turned and smirked at Emry. Emry stared back at him with the appearance of a cobra preparing to strike. For a brief moment, Rico appeared chilled by the look, but his charming smile and arrogance quickly returned.

"Now to find the rest of your friends--and your little playmate." Rico grinned and eyed Andy. "Feel free to tenderize him a little, Andy, but not too much. I want him to be conscious when I castrate him."

Emry's expression remained unchanged, and he barely flinched to his possible fate. Rico chuckled, appeared pleased with himself, and left the bridge by the port door. Andy returned his gun to his shoulder holster and smirked as he approached Emry.

"He really doesn't like you," Andy said with a humored laugh. "He usually reserves live castrations for only a select few."

"He wouldn't be the first man to try to castrate me." Emry wore a twisted, evil smile and appeared almost humored. "You should see what happened to them."

Andy removed a switchblade knife and skillfully flipped it open. He grinned at Emry.

"Yeah? Well, wait until you see what he does to that pretty girlfriend of yours. He's going to make her suffer for what you did to our friend in that cornfield. You'll be begging him to kill her just to stop her screaming."

Emry stared at Andy and showed no emotion, but the flicker in his eyes told a different, more chilling story.

"And to think, I was going to be nice and not kill you," Emry said then sighed softly as he shook his head. "I'm such a disappointment to me."

Andy laughed since it was obvious the threat was an empty one. "You're the one tied up, remember?"

"Yes, it would appear that way. But sometimes to get our way, we must sacrifice a little freedom and an ounce or two of dignity," Emry said casually. "If I thought I could fix the ship's controls myself, I would have. I seriously doubt your boss would have fixed them simply because I asked nicely, and I've never been one to resort to torture. So what choice did I have?"

Andy appeared puzzled by the comment. His prisoner didn't appear to be making any sense, unless he was playing mind games.

Emry suddenly offered an unsettling smile. "Tell me something, *Andy--*"

Andy twitched slightly to the disturbing way Emry said his name and appeared reluctant to move any closer to the restrained man.

"Does your boss have some sort of calling card when it comes to his kills?"

Andy appeared humored, relaxed slightly as he regained his confidence, and played along. "You want to know his calling card? When he's sending a message, he usually stabs the poor bastard in the heart and through both eyes."

Emry frowned with a look of distaste. "That sounds terribly messy." He appeared to consider his comment. "Of course, so is gutting a man." Emry laughed then said in Spanish, "A cada uno su propia."

Andy chuckled softly having understood him. "Yes, to each his own."

✝

*R*ico walked down the bridge steps with a pronounced limp and his gun in his hand. He reached the bottom of the steps and turned for the nearby doorway. Rico was suddenly kicked in the gunshot wound on his leg. He cried out, stumbled backwards while clutching his thigh, and raised his gun in response. Jess kicked the gun from his hand, and it flew across the deck. She stood in a defensive stance and glared at Rico with a hard, cold expression.

"You know, there's no love lost between me and Carla, but she didn't deserve to be shot."

Rico slowly straightened and released his bleeding leg while grinning at Jess. It must have pleased him that he didn't have to travel far to find her.

"I disagree," Rico said simply. "Carla was a bitch and was only useful while lying on her back. She served her purpose, but the relationship needed to be terminated." He again studied Jess. "I do, however, have some use for you." Rico smiled charmingly and said something in Spanish while lustfully gazing over her body.

"I don't speak Spanish," Jess said lowly and raised her brows, "but I understood enough to know you have a foul mouth and an inflated ego."

Rico maintained his grin and paced with a limp before Jess. He lustfully looked her over and appeared almost turned on by her lack of fear for him.

"Normally, for a beautiful, young woman such as yourself, I'd consider killing you quickly and with little pain. But since you shot me," he said seductively, "I'm going to take my time, kill you slowly, and enjoy every minute of it."

"Yeah? One problem with that--"

"What's that, Mi querida?" Rico remarked with a look of humor on his handsome face.

Jess's eyes suddenly narrowed. "I'm just the opening act."

Rico appeared humored, casually looked around the empty deck, and held his arms out. "Opening act for what? We already have your boyfriend." He grinned lustfully. "I'm afraid he won't be of much use to you when we're finished with him, not that it matters, because *I'm* your boyfriend now." He waited for her reaction, but she didn't give him the satisfaction. It obviously irritated him. "Of course, if you'd like to beg for mercy, I may be willing to listen."

Jess stared at him with little emotion, remained unimpressed, and slowly shook her head. "Wow, Kaplan is going to tear you apart."

Rico chuckled in his throat. "You're in for a rude awakening, Mi querida. He can't help you. I'm afraid you're all alone."

"I'm never alone."

The last of Rico's men, Trevor, suddenly appeared behind Jess with his gun drawn. Rico grinned with pleasure. Without looking, Jess spun into a roundhouse kick and knocked the gun from Trevor's hand. Rico's smile suddenly faded. Trevor threw a punch, but she was already kicking in the opposite direction and blocked the punch. Since last year, it was obvious she had been trained to defend herself, and there was little doubt who had been her teacher. Rico's smile faded, and he appeared slightly alarmed by how easily she handled his man. He turned and hurried for the bridge steps.

"Andy!"

Rico attempted to run up the steps on his injured leg. Andy suddenly fell on top of Rico, knocking him down the steps and to the bridge deck below. Rico landed roughly on his back and appeared momentarily stunned from the impact. Andy lay motionless on top of him. Rico heaved Andy off him then stared at his mutilated, blood soaked body lying on the deck. Andy had been stabbed through both eyes and his switchblade was embedded deep in his chest. Rico jumped up, appeared alarmed by *his* signature kill, and looked up the steps. Emry casually walked down the bridge steps with Andy's blood covering his hands and shirt. His eyes were locked on Rico. Clearly, this was very personal. Jess kicked Trevor in the face and glared back at Emry on the steps. She wasn't particularly fazed by the blood covering him.

"What took you so long? Where the hell were you?"

Emry kept his eyes locked on Rico and showed no emotion to her questions. "I was a little tied up, darling," he replied as he reached the last step.

Rico was now enraged and lunged for Emry. Emry kicked him forcibly in the chest and barely moved the large man. Emry again attempted to kick him. Rico blocked his kick with his arm and body slammed him to the deck. Emry landed on his back with a loud crack. He slowly recovered with some discomfort then looked up. Rico was about to stomp on his head. Emry quickly rolled out of Rico's path, caught his foot on the way through, and knocked him over. Rico roughly struck the deck but quickly jumped to his feet. Emry painfully pulled himself up, immediately spun into a kick, and struck Rico in the chest. Rico was barely even fazed. Emry went for the return kick. Rico caught his foot, held it, and smiled deviously while towering over Emry by over six inches. Emry kicked out with the leg he stood on, flipping his entire body, and kicked Rico in the face. Rico was thrown backwards a few steps but didn't fall and appeared only moderately dazed. He had a deep cut on his cheek from the impact of the kick. Rico wiped the blood from his cheek and maintained his grin.

Emry struck the deck harshly and immediately rolled back into a crouched position. He assessed the situation then leaped forcefully through the air and into a kick. Rico easily caught his leg. As if anticipating the catch, Emry flipped his entire body in mid-air, caught Rico around the neck with his leg, and threw him to the deck by his neck. As they struck the deck, Emry clenched Rico's neck with both legs. Rico thrashed wildly for a moment. There was a cracking sound, and Rico suddenly became still. Emry rolled off Rico with exhaustion and jumped back to his feet. Jess kicked Trevor in the groin then punched him across the face and dropped him to the deck. She grabbed one of the discarded guns and eyed Emry, who clung to the railing while panting.

"You okay?" Jess asked now concerned.

"I'm fine," Emry replied with a tiny smile, "but you may want to lower your expectations for tonight."

Jess hid her smile then looked at Rico who lay motionless on the deck. She looked back at Emry. "Is he dead?"

Emry casually approached her, held out his hand, and indicated the gun. Jess handed him the pistol. He cocked the gun while turning toward Rico. To their surprise, Rico was already on his knees with the other discarded gun and fired at them. Emry suddenly stepped in front of Jess, took the shot to his chest, and propelled backward into her, knocking her to the deck with him. For a brief moment, Jess was stunned from the impact and paralyzed with fear as Emry lay motionless on top of her. Rico slowly pulled himself to his feet as Jess attempted to move out from under Emry's motionless body. Rico panted while glaring at her. He was obviously in bad shape but still determined to finish the job. Jess slowly moved to her knees alongside Emry, stared at him with a look of horror, and appeared unable to move or breathe. She only heard the sound of her own heartbeat.

Without even looking, she knew Rico was standing over her. Jess slowly and uncertainly took Emry's hand in hers then looked at Rico with no emotion. Rico smiled his charming, suave smile and aimed the gun at her. Jess just stared at the barrel of the gun pointed at her face. She wasn't thinking about revenge, she was only thinking about Emry lying dead alongside her. She looked back at Emry and welcomed the end to a life without him and fulfilling their prophecy as the *Romeo and Juliet* of the *Andrea Maria*. A gunshot echoed through the silence. Jess gasped and waited for the all too familiar sting of the bullet piercing her body, but it didn't come. She looked at Rico. He clutched his bleeding abdomen and stared past her with a surprised look on his face. Jess quickly looked behind her. Carla stood a few feet behind Jess with her gun aimed at Rico and a cold, harsh look on her face.

"*¿fue bueno para ti?*" Carla said lowly.

Rico appeared stunned, his eyes wide with horror, and stared at her. Carla exhaled slowly and squeezed the trigger, shooting Rico three times in the chest without even flinching. He maintained his stunned look as he fell to the deck.

"Translation?" Carla smirked and cleverly raised her brows. "Was it good for you?"

Jess stared at her a moment with shock then quickly turned to Emry where he lay on the deck. She frantically opened his shirt to check his wound then appeared dumbfounded as she stared at the bulletproof vest beneath his shirt. Jess uncertainly looked at Emry's face.

Emry slowly opened one eye and stared back at her. "Is he dead?"

Jess exhaled with relief and hid her smile. "Yes, very much."

Emry groaned lowly and attempted to sit up. Jess helped him into a sitting position and happily hugged him. He made an effort to return the hug, but it was obviously painful for him to do.

"I thought you were dead too," she said gently and held back her sobs.

"Oh, darling, I've been dead so many times, I've lost count," Emry said simply with a soft groan.

Jess laughed softly and wiped the tears from her eyes. Carla clutched her bleeding shoulder and glared impatiently at them.

"I don't mean to interrupt this little episode of "Love Boat"," Carla snapped, "but could I maybe get a little sympathy here?"

Trevor groaned from where he lay nearby and slowly moved. Without even looking, Carla raised the gun and shot Trevor in the head. His head snapped back, and he fell lifelessly to the deck. Jess and Emry jumped with surprise and stared at her with shared looks of horror.

"I hate this fucking ship," Carla muttered and carelessly tossed the gun aside.

Chapter Thirty-three

*D*rake, Ivy, Carla, and Dana sat at the lounge bar with colorful drinks before them. The four clearly had too much to drink, but none cared. Carla and Drake were a little worse for wear with their matching shoulder wounds, mended carefully by Emry's backstreet surgery.

"Should someone tell Grant it's safe to come out now?" Dana teased while sipping her drink.

"After he pushed me aside to save his own ass?" Ivy scoffed. "Let him rot."

"I could kill him on that score alone," Drake muttered softly. "I'd rather not see him in my current condition. The term "friendly fire" comes to mind."

"I'll tell you one thing," Carla said bluntly, "he's not coming out looking like a hero this time."

"Not if I have anything to say about it, and I will," Ivy said firmly.

"God, I can't believe I slept with him," Dana said with a sickened look on her face.

Carla suddenly looked at Dana and appeared horrified. "You slept with Grant?" She hesitated then considered her comment and made a face. "Ah, hell, who am I to judge? My wonderful boyfriend turned out to be a psychotic, mass murdering drug lord who tried to kill me."

"Yeah, I was a little jealous of your relationship at the beginning of the cruise," Dana said simply. "Not so much now."

Dana looked at Ivy then Drake, who warmly caressed her hand. A diamond engagement ring was proudly displayed on Ivy's left ring finger.

"You don't know how lucky you are, Ivy. You not only found a man who loves you, but one who's willing to die for you." Dana then hesitated and reconsidered. "And *kill* for you--"

"Yes, you have a good man, Ivy," Carla said gently.

Drake was surprised by Carla's comment. Carla and Drake exchanged tiny, knowing smiles. There was a time not so long ago when Carla was convinced Drake was beneath her. The anniversary cruise obviously changed her perspective. Ivy smiled at Carla's comment and placed her head on Drake's injured shoulder while clinging to his arm. Drake cringed from the discomfort but made no effort to move her. He was willing to live with the pain.

"He's my hero," Ivy said proudly.

"I could use one of those myself," Dana said softly with a defeated sigh.

"You know what you need, Dana? You need a good old boy," Drake said in his buzzed condition.

"Tell me something I don't know."

"No, I mean that literally," Drake said plainly. "The sheriff of our little town is about to have his heart broken when he hears the news about Jess. You'd like him. He's a good man--with just enough rough edges to make him interesting. I think you'd be good for each other."

"I wouldn't mind meeting him," Dana replied with a slightly drunken smile.

"What's going to happen to Emry?" Carla asked softly and appeared concerned. "Do you think Brody is going to arrest him?"

"He better not," Drake drunkenly muttered. "I'm not beneath throwing him overboard and making up some story for the press."

"I saw the whole thing," Dana announced with a grin. "Rico did it."

Drake and Dana laughed softly.

"We need to protect Emry," Carla firmly insisted. "Brody can't arrest him. I won't allow it."

†

*T*he *Andrea Maria* majestically sailed through the calm, evening waters toward the distant port in New Orleans. The bright, city lights could just barely be seen ahead. Jess sat on Emry's lap on a lounge chair below the bridge. They held each another and stared at the distant city lights. A million thoughts raced through Jess's head. Emry's fate seemed uncertain now.

"So what happens now?" she asked while nuzzling his neck.

"I guess that depends on Agent Kroft."

"Haven't heard much out of him," Jess said.

"He's been busy skippering the *Andrea Maria* in a desperate attempt to forget that you threw him over for me," Emry said with a teasing smile.

A shadow loomed over them.

"Okay, you can stop talking about me," Brody said while standing over them with a harsh look on his face.

Jess and Emry looked at Brody as he took a seat on the lounge chair alongside theirs. Jess uncertainly moved off Emry's lap and to the foot end of the lounger. Brody looked at Jess with all seriousness.

"During our attack, a man identifying himself as Emry Hill, your supposedly dead Romeo, was shot and killed while saving our lives. His body went overboard and wasn't recovered."

Brody shifted uncomfortably in his chair and maintained his stare at Jess. She listened closely with anticipation.

"I'm convinced that man was former CIA operative, Kaplan Bogart. We'll probably never know why he stowed away on the anniversary cruise, but we suspect he returned to be with his beloved Juliet."

Jess stared at Brody with some surprise, smiled, and appeared pleased. She couldn't believe he was willing to lie to protect Emry.

"So the world will finally know Emry Hill died a hero?" she asked gently.

"I'm only telling you what happened from my perspective," Brody said. "I guess this will finally put an end to the manhunt for Kaplan Bogart too."

Jess smiled and cast a glance at Emry. He hid his smile but didn't comment.

"I'm going to discuss what happened this weekend with the others, so we can keep our stories straight for my superiors and the press," Brody said.

"I can see the others going along with that story, but what about Grant?" Jess asked. "He might be unwilling to back that story. He doesn't exactly care for either of us."

"You let me worry about Grant," Brody said simply. "I've read his file and it's not pretty. He'll go along with whatever story I give him."

Jess smiled warmly, took Brody's hand in hers, and squeezed it affectionately. "Thank you, Brody."

Brody returned the smile and reluctantly nodded. "Yeah, I'm a real prince." He stood then gave Emry a serious look. "Consider this your only warning, Ridley. Mistreat her, and I'll find a way to hurt you."

"If I ever do, you have permission to feed me to the alligators," Emry teased.

Brody glared at him, groaned softly, and shook his head as he walked away. Jess returned to Emry's lap with renewed enthusiasm, clung lovingly to him, and breathed a sigh of relief.

"Looks like I got my wish. Emry Hill will be remembered for the hero he was, and you're finally free from Kaplan's past."

"You know what this means, don't you?"

Jess eyed him with a serious look and hid her devious smile. "That I'm stuck with Ridley and his feather duster for a very long time?"

"No, that's a given. As his beloved Juliet, you're obligated to give Emry a proper burial. It's only fitting."

Jess stared at him with some surprise. "Proper burial? What do you mean by a proper burial?"

Emry smiled charmingly and appeared delighted with the whole "proper burial" idea. "Nothing fancy," he said then became enthusiastic. "How about an Irish wake? I've always wanted an Irish wake--with Uilleann bagpipes. I could make Emerald Isle martinis, and we'll sing Irish songs. Oh, that would be fun."

"You're a bit morbid, you know that?" Jess then appeared humored and played along. "Are you sure you wouldn't want an old-fashioned New Orleans style wake? We'll be in the vicinity."

"No, I already had one of those. It was pretty wild. The police had to break it up. Would you like to see my tomb? It's quite jazzy."

Jess gave him a bewildered look, hid her smile, and shook her head. "What I wouldn't give for a small glimpse into that head of yours."

"Even I don't want to know what's in my head," he muttered with a teasing smile.

Jess sank into thought. "What really happened to Kaplan Bogart?"

Emry hesitated only a moment then sighed softly. "His commander botched a mission and several agents died because of it, leaving Kaplan the sole survivor and the perfect scapegoat. In order to pin blame on him, he needed to eliminate Kaplan. He sent several assassins to silence him, but they ended up killing his wife instead."

There was a long silence. It was obvious he was still deeply disturbed by her death. Jess didn't want to press him on what happened to her.

"They were severely punished for what they did to her," Emry said simply and with little emotion.

Jess tensed and considered the condition in which Brody described the bodies found within the swamp. She wanted to ask, but decided against it. She wasn't sure she wanted to know.

"He then spent the next six years eliminating assassins sent to kill him, and the last two enjoying the peace and quiet."

Jess tensed slightly and studied him a moment. "And the man in the cornfield?"

Emry suddenly eyed her. "You knew, didn't you? That's why you were so quick to give me an alibi."

"I know you're a bit of a clean freak, but it's unusual even for you to be shower fresh at three in the morning," she explained. "Sheriff Stone confided that the man in the cornfield died from a broken neck before being gutted. That's when I knew I'd been right." She stared at him a moment. "You found him in my bedroom, didn't you?"

His look hardened. "He was standing over your bed with a knife in his hand," Emry remarked. "His intentions were obvious. It would only have been a matter of time before he went into Drake's room thinking you were the woman with him. He wouldn't have hesitated to kill them both."

There was an awkward silence. Jess considered his words and suddenly felt chilled. If she hadn't gone down to his room that night, that man may have killed her. If Emry hadn't heard the man enter the house, Drake and Ivy could have been the ones dead.

"I know a professional hit when I see one. Others would have been sent if he had failed. They got the message to stay away from you." Emry caressed her and shifted with discomfort to whatever thoughts were racing through his head. "Kaplan was a necessary evil and did what needed to be done while working for his government-- and while running from them." He stared at her a long moment and appeared tense. "I know it's a lot to ask, but can you get past the man I used to be and the horrors that I'd done?"

There was a brief silence between them. Jess moved against Emry. She met his gaze with a serious look, and gently touched his face.

"I accept you for who you are--and for all the men you ever had to be," she said gently then hesitated. "But for the record, I'd appreciate it if you'd go easy on the neck breaking thing. It sort of creeps me out. Just use a gun like any normal home owner."

Emry tried not to laugh, pulled her back down against him, and nuzzled her. "I'll try my best, darling."

Chapter Thirty-four

*I*t was the day after the *Andrea Maria* docked at the port in New Orleans. Despite the media frenzy surrounding the ship's return, Jess and Emry had managed to slip away with limited press exposure. Jess's well-lit plantation house appeared quiet in the late evening setting. The sound of crickets was almost deafening. Sheriff Stone's blazer was parked in front of the house. Stone and Jess sat on the porch in an odd silence while drinking martinis. Stone wore a strange grin on his face while he studied Jess, who sat quietly and sipped her martini. She was aware of the way he was staring at her but refused to question the look. He seemed unable to contain his silence any longer.

"Okay, now that we're finally alone," Stone said, "tell me what really happened on the anniversary cruise."

Jess appeared offended by his insistence to her story's inaccuracies. She looked at him and managed a tiny, knowing smile.

"It happened just like we said." Jess studied him a moment then swiftly changed the subject with enthusiasm. "I hear you have a date with Dana next weekend."

"Yeah, we're going paintballing with Drake and Ivy."

Jess appeared horrified and nearly choked on her drink. "You're not serious! You can't take her paintballing on a first date!"

"It was her idea, and I happen to think it was a great suggestion," Stone said then immediately frowned. "And don't go changing the subject. You can't seriously expect me to believe that Grant hid in a closet while Carla killed a drug lord and his men."

"That's how it happened," Jess said simply. She appeared lost in thought. "I can't imagine Ivy paintballing. She's not nearly ruthless enough to survive."

Stone stared at her with a look of disbelief. "You're doing it again." He shook his head. "We were discussing what happened on the anniversary cruise."

"You were discussing the cruise," Jess informed him. "I'm discussing your date with Dana."

"You're hiding something."

"I'm not hiding anything," Jess insisted simply. "Although you should be warned, there's a good chance Dana will kick your ass at paintballing. I heard she recently came out of her shell."

"There are laws against lying to a police officer," Stone snapped.

"I somehow doubt those laws apply in this case," Jess informed him. "I don't think you have jurisdiction over paintballing."

"Enough with that." Stone groaned and appeared frustrated. "What about Ridley?"

"I think Ridley would enjoy paintballing," Jess said casually.

"You know what I mean. What about those rumors I'd heard about Ridley on the cruise?"

"What rumors about Ridley?" Emry asked from the open doorway while holding a full pitcher of martinis.

Stone looked at Emry, who glared at him with some annoyance. Stone appeared slightly tense then smirked as his arrogance returned. "We're supposed to believe that you nearly died saving Jess's life?"

"I don't know about nearly--"

"He's being modest, Sheriff," Jess said with enthusiasm. "You have my permission to engrave his name on the plague in town square."

Stone groaned lowly while shaking his head and finally stood. "Well, if he did save your life, it would certainly explain whatever this is going on between you two since you're back."

Stone headed for the porch steps. Jess and Emry exchanged bewildered looks. What was it between them since they got back? And how could he possibly know what they did behind closed doors last night? Stone looked back at them. Both maintained their innocent looks.

"So no book tours or talk shows?" Stone asked.

"The spotlight is on Carla," Jess said proudly. "I hope it makes her happy. Ridley and I pass."

"I'm going to be too busy with the new wine cellar to be bothered with such nonsense," Emry said simply.

Stone rolled his eyes as he left the porch and headed for his police blazer. Jess and Emry watched him drive away. Emry appeared slightly bewildered and eyed Jess.

"I barely said two words to you while he was here," he said firmly. "How could he possibly think there's something between us?"

"Do you think he's smarter than we give him credit?"

Emry eyed Jess and raised his brows. She hid her smile and looked away with embarrassment. Emry shook his head and groaned softly.

"I don't know why I thought he'd make a fine suitor for you," Emry scoffed lowly. "I suppose even I have momentary lapses in judgment."

"You're not completely infallible, Ridley."

"Let's not get carried away, Jess." Emry sighed softly. "I suppose I did Sheriff Stone a favor by taking you off the market."

"Oh? How do you figure?"

"You're a bit of a handful," Emry said simply. "In and out of the bedroom--"

Jess eyed him and hid her smile. "That incident in the kitchen was all you."

"Not exactly what I was referencing, but thanks for pointing that out."

"Incidentally, how would you feel about crashing Sheriff Stone's date with Dana? They're going paintballing with Drake and Ivy next weekend."

Emry stared at Jess a moment with an intrigued look in his eyes. He suddenly smiled. "Can I count on you to have my back?"

"Always."

Emry chuckled softly and appeared delighted. "Naturally, I'll need to scope out the lay of the land prior to the coup d'état and then come up with a battle plan." Emry grinned deviously. "It's going to be a massacre."

"I'll leave this military skirmish in your hands," Jess said then turned toward the house. "Have fun with that. I'll see you in the morning."

Emry grabbed her from behind and spun her into his arms. "Don't you dare pretend to play hard to get with me. We're way beyond that now."

Jess playfully smiled while lovingly caressing his chest. "Want to finish those martinis in the garden tub by candlelight?"

"Now that's more like it," Emry replied with a lustful smile.

Jess eyed the dirty glasses on the porch then looked at Emry. "You're actually going to leave the dirty glasses?"

Emry appeared offended. "I'm not as domesticated as you seem to think. They can wait until morning," Emry said firmly then quickly kissed her. "You start the bath, and I'll be up with the martinis."

Jess appeared pleased then smiled, kissed him, and entered the house. Emry watched her enter the house, hesitated only a moment until he was sure she was gone, and then hurriedly placed the dirty glasses onto the serving tray. He glanced at his watch then hurried into the house, kicking the door closed with his foot.

✝

*J*ess sat on the edge of the large garden tub in the master bathroom wearing her short, satin robe. The tub was nearly filled with hot water and bubbles. She felt she waited a long time for Emry to join her, but she knew it took time for him to properly wash and dry the martini glasses. Emry didn't fool her. She knew he would have to wash them before he would ever consider going to bed. Emry finally entered the bathroom. He carried a bottle of champagne, two glasses, and the *Andrea Maria* life ring. He set the bottle of champagne and glasses down but retained the life ring. Jess eyed him and appeared humored. She wasn't sure what he was up to this time, but she always found him to be cute in his own strange, little way.

"You don't need to worry about drowning. What's with the preserver?"

"Do you remember the incident with Brahm on the bridge deck last year?"

Emry casually leaned against the doorframe with the life ring in his arms. Jess eyed him and raised her brows. Was he serious?

"I recall it vaguely," she replied sarcastically.

"Remember how he clung to this thing for dear life?"

"As I recall, it didn't do him much good. I fished it out of the ocean when I was looking for you. Why?"

"Rico and Victor were searching the survivor's homes and the ship for their missing diamonds, but they didn't know where Brahm had hid them."

Jess stared at Emry with a strange look. What was he getting at? Emry pulled a leather pouch from the seam of the life ring while grinning deviously. He tossed the preserver aside, held out Jess's hand, and poured a pile of large diamonds into her palm. Jess stared at the diamonds with complete shock. Emry sat on the edge of the tub alongside her and maintained his smile to her shocked expression.

"I had them the entire time?" she asked while staring at the mound of diamonds in her hand. She quickly looked back at Emry. "What should we do?"

Emry removed one of the diamonds from her hand and studied it with great interest. "I'm thinking Rio, baby," he said with a lustful grin and suggestively raised his brows.

"You're actually considering keeping them?"

"Naturally we'd share them with the others." He studied the one in his hand. "Except this one."

Jess eyed the moderately sized diamond he held between his fingers.

"This one would look very nice on your finger," he said with a warm smile then looked into her eyes.

Jess stared at the diamond he held then met his gaze. She hid her smile. "Then I guess we're going to Rio."

There was no doubt. She loved this man--whoever he was.

The End

Insanely Deadly
Coming Soon!

Preview Excerpt

A moderately expensive home was nestled in the middle of nowhere and surrounded by mostly farmland and woods. The nearest neighboring house was barely visible beyond the field. Dennis's sedan pulled up to the well-lit house. Dennis got out of the car, grinned at the meteor he held, and then looked at the gash on his hand. It was now red and swollen. His rare find was overshadowed by the reality that he would need to visit the doctor for a course of antibiotics. Dennis headed into the house, shut the door behind him, and paused within the foyer.

"Pam! Pam, wait until you see what I found," he called out while studying the meteor more closely in the light. "You won't believe it."

"I'm upstairs, dear," Pam called back. Her tone turned seductive. "And wait until you see what I have for you!"

Dennis grinned with a lustful realization, placed the meteor on the hall table, and hurried up the stairs. As he reached the top of the stairs, a masked intruder suddenly appeared and struck him on the head with a tire iron. Dennis fell backwards down the stairs and roughly hit the bottom. The intruder descended the stairs and leaned over Dennis's lifeless body. A young, attractive woman in a sexy, white satin nightgown, Pam Albright, appeared at the top of the stairs. The intruder removed his mask to reveal a handsome man in his mid-thirties, Brian Fitch. Brian looked up at her and appeared pleased.

"He's dead," Brian informed her while grinning.

Pam appeared relieved and slowly walked down the stairs. "What do we do now?"

Brian hurried up the stairs, met her halfway, and kissed her quickly on the lips. "Just like we planned it. Give me fifteen minutes to get back to the tavern and establish my alibi before you report an intruder," he said with enthusiasm. "When Sheriff Palmer and his lackeys arrive, you'll tell them you heard a scuffle, and they'll think Dennis surprised an intruder."

Pam nodded with apprehension.

He smiled reassuringly and caressed her face. "Relax, baby. It'll all work out, I promise. I'll leave the door open."

Brian kissed her again with more passion. She uncertainly returned the kiss. He glanced over her in the sexy nightgown, groaned lustfully, and then hurried down the stairs and out the door. He left the door open as promised. Pam wrenched her fingers together and stared at Dennis's lifeless body at the bottom of the stairs. It didn't seem as easy as it sounded during the planning stages. She composed herself and hurried back up the steps.

†

𝑃am paced the bedroom and nervously looked at the clock and then her watch. It had only been ten minutes, but it seemed an eternity. She heard movement from downstairs. Had Brian forgotten something and returned? Pam fidgeted with concern and hurried from the bedroom. She cautiously walked along the upstairs hallway and paused at the top of the stairs. She didn't want to look at her dead husband again, but she forced herself to look to the foyer below. Dennis's body was gone! All that remained was a small pool of blood where his body once lie. Alarm swept through her, and, for a moment, she was frozen with fear. She gathered her courage and uncertainly scanned the lower level from her position at the top of the stairs. The front door was now closed. Concern that Dennis may have left the house to get the sheriff suddenly swept over her. She had to be certain.

"Dennis?" she called out with a soft quiver in her voice.

There was no response. Pam slowly walked down the stairs in her bare feet and stopped to stare at the blood soaking into the light colored carpet. It was going to leave a nasty stain. She didn't know why she was worrying about that right now. She carefully stepped over the pool of blood and again looked around.

"Dennis--*baby*?

She heard what sounded like someone rummaging through one of the kitchen cupboards. She uncertainly walked along the hall and approached the kitchen. Pam paused in the archway and stared at the glaring, bloody handprint on the once white island counter. The kitchen appeared empty. Where could he have gone? Her eyes strayed to the partially closed laundry room door near the back entrance. He could be in the laundry room tending to his head injury. She nervously walked across the kitchen toward the laundry room and appeared frightened at what she might find. He was supposed to be dead. How had he survived?

"Dennis?"

She slowly approached the partially open door and uncertainly reached to push it open. She suddenly felt the presence of someone behind her. Pam hesitated then quickly turned to see Dennis standing behind her with blood streaking his face from the gash on his forehead just above his eye. He had a glazed over look in his eyes. His condition and the fact that he was alive surprised her. She twitched with fear.

"Oh, my God, Dennis!" He couldn't have known she was involved. If he saw anything, he saw an intruder in a mask. She was safe. Now she had to act the part of the concerned wife. Actually, she was almost relieved he wasn't dead. "What happened?"

He reached for her with his bloody hand. She now felt sorry for him and for what she'd been an accomplice to. She hurried for the nearby telephone on the wall.

"We need to call Doc right away."

Dennis placed his hand on her shoulder. She glanced back at him. He suddenly bared his teeth with a snarl, lunged for her neck, and tore into her flesh with his teeth. Pam screamed with terror and agony as she forcibly pushed him away, tearing her flesh. He had a large chunk of her flesh between his teeth. Pam screamed while clutching her bleeding neck and stared at her flesh in his mouth. As he attempted to grab her again, she stumbled along the kitchen in an attempt to escape, but she was bleeding profusely. Dennis casually followed her while chewing on her flesh as blood ran down his chin. Pam fell to the floor and weakly tried to pull herself to the laundry room door. She heard him snarl behind her. As she looked back, Dennis dove on top of her. She screamed as his bloodstained teeth came at her face.

Available Spring/Summer 2015

ABOUT THE AUTHOR

Holly Copella has been writing since the age of twelve when her frustration at a book's poor plot drove her to author her own story. Over the last decade, she's written a number of screenplays, some of which she's now adapting into novels. Her fascination with zombies and other darker material lends an edge to her writing, which tends to lean toward horror. As a fan of Agatha Christie, she appreciates the craft of a good plot and the importance of creating significant characters.

Hailing from Pennsylvania, Copella lives in the Endless Mountains on a farm with her rescue horses and other animals. In addition to writing and reading fiction, she enjoys riding horses and traveling to Las Vegas and Disney World.

18152926R00123

Made in the USA
Middletown, DE
24 February 2015